Jane and the Barque of Frailty

~ Being A Jane Austen Mystery ~

by Stephanie Barron

BANTAM BOOKS
NEW YORK • TORONTO • LONDON • SYDNEY • AUCKLAND

JANE AND THE BARQUE OF FRAILTY
A Bantam Book / December 2006

Published by
Bantam Dell
A Division of Random House, Inc.
New York, New York

Book design by Laurie Jewell

Bantam Books is a registered trademark of Random House, Inc.,
and the colophon is a trademark of Random House, Inc.

Library of Congress Cataloging-in-Publication Data

Barron, Stephanie.
Jane and the barque of frailty / by Stephanie Barron.
p. cm. — (Being a Jane Austen mystery)
ISBN-13: 978-0-553-80226-9
ISBN-10: 0-553-80226-7
1. Austen, Jane, 1775–1817—Fiction. 2. Women novelists—Fiction. 3. England—
Fiction. I. Title. II. Series: Barron, Stephanie. Jane Austen mystery.

PS3563.A8357J328 2006
813'.54—dc22
2006042765

Printed in the United States of America
Published simultaneously in Canada

www.bantamdell.com

10 9 8 7 6 5 4 3 2 1
BVG

This book is dedicated to the memory of Georgette Heyer,
in thanks for all the hours of pleasure
her books have given me.

Chapter 1

A Night Among the Ton

No. 64 Sloane Street, London
Monday, 22 April 1811

~

CONCEIVE, IF YOU WILL, OF THE THEATRE ROYAL, COVENT Garden, on an evening such as this: the celebrated Mrs. Siddons being rumoured to appear, after too many months' absence from the stage; the play *Macbeth,* with all the hideous power of Shakespeare's verse and Sarah Siddons's art; and the Polite World of London brawling in the midst of Bow Street, in an effort to reach its place in the box before the curtain should rise.

Such a welter of chairmen, link boys, fashionable carriages, street sweeps, porters, and coachmen! Such oaths, blasted into the ears of delicately-nurtured females, carried hurriedly to the paving lest their satin slippers should be soiled in the horses' dung! Such an array of silks and muslins, turbans and feathers, embroidered shawls and jewelled flounces! The scent of a thousand flowers on the air, the odour of tobacco and ripe oranges and fish from the markets in Covent Garden, the great theatre's windows thrown open against the warmth of the spring night and the heat of too many bodies filling the vast hall! The flickering of wax candles, a fortune's worth thrown up into the gleaming chandeliers; the rising pitch of conversation, the high screech of a woman's laughter, the impropriety of a chance remark, the hand of a gentleman resting where it should not, on the person of his lady—all this, like a prodigal feast spread out for my delectation.

The vague shadow, too, of a Bow Street Runner lounging in the doorway of the magistrate's offices opposite—which I chanced to glimpse as brother Henry swept me to the theatre door; lounging like an accusation as he surveyed the Fashionable Great, whose sins and peccadilloes only he may be privileged to know.

It is a scene hardly out of the ordinary way for the majority of the *ton,* that select company of wealthy and wellborn who rule what is commonly called Society; but for a lady in the midst of her thirty-fifth year, denied a proper come-out or a breathless schoolgirl's first Season, a shabby-genteel lady long since on the shelf and at her last prayers—it must be deemed a high treat. Add that I am a hardened enthusiast of the great Sarah Siddons, and have been disappointed before in my hopes of seeing her tread the boards—and you will apprehend with what pleasurable anticipation I met the curtain's rise.[1]

---

[1] In a letter to her sister, Cassandra, dated April 25, 1811, Jane states that Henry gave up their tickets for this performance, and that she was unable to see Mrs. Siddons—a curious prevarication, in light of this text. —*Editor's note.*

"Jane," Eliza murmured behind her fan as the Theatre Royal fell silent, "there is Lord Moira, Henry's particular friend and an intimate of the Prince Regent. Next his box you will recognise Lord Castlereagh, I am sure—was there ever anything so elegant as his lady's dress? It is as nothing, however, to the costume of the creature seated to our left— the extraordinarily handsome woman with the flashing dark eyes and the black curls. *That* is the great Harriette Wilson, my dear—the most celebrated Impure in London, with her sisters and intimate friends; do not observe her openly, I beg! Such gentlemen as have had her in keeping! I am sure our Harriette might bring down the Government, were she merely to speak too freely among her intimates. They do say that even *Wellington*—"

The pressure of Henry's hand upon his wife's arm silenced Eliza, and I was allowed to disregard the men of government equally with the demimondaine in her rubies and paint, and sit in breathless apprehension as a cabal of witches plotted their ageless doom.

I am come to London in the spring of this year 1811— the year of Regency and the poor old King's decline into madness, the year of Buonaparte's expected rout in the Peninsula, of straitened circumstances and immense want among the poor—to watch like an anxious parent over the printing of my first novel. Yes, my *novel;* or say rather the child of my heart, which is to be sent into the Great World without even the acknowledgement of its mother, being to be published by Mr. Thomas Egerton only as *By a Lady.*

And what is the title and purport of this improving work, so ideally suited to the fancy of ladies both young and old?

I have been used to call it *Elinor & Marianne,* after the fashion of the great Madame d'Arblay, whose exemplary

tales *Camilla, Evelina, Cecilia,* etc., have set the fashion in literature for ladies. Mr. Egerton, however, is of the opinion
that such a title is no longer the mode, the style being for
qualities akin to Mrs. Brunton's *Self-Controul.* I have debated
the merits of *Worthiness and Self-Worth,* or *An Excellent Understanding.* Eliza, on the other hand, would hew to the sensa-
tional.

"How do you like *The Bodice Rip'd from Side to Side,* Jane?
Or perhaps—I think now only of Marianne—*The Maid For-
sworn and All Forlorn?*"

"But what of Willoughby?" brother Henry objected.
"Should he not be given pride of place? Call it then *The Se-
ducer,* and have done."

"It shall be *Sense and Sensibility,*" I replied firmly, "for I am
partial to sibilants; and besides, Cassandra approves the division: Elinor a creature of Reason, and Marianne entirely of
Feeling. You must know I am in the habit of being guided by
my sister. —Insofar as my inclination allies with *hers,* of
course."

Henry and his wife cried out against this, abusing
Cassandra for the excessive starch of her notions, and the
quiet propriety which must always characterise my sister's
views. I ought possibly to have paid more heed to their
opinions—it is Henry, after all, who has franked me in the
publishing world, having paid Mr. Egerton to print my little
book—but I am tired of toying with titles. All my anxiety is
for the pace of the printing, which is excessively slow. I am
resident in London a full month, and yet we have arrived
only at Chapter Nine, and Willoughby's first appearance. At
this rate, the year will have turned before the novel is bound,
tho' it was faithfully promised for May—a set of three volumes in blue boards, with gilt letters.

"Jane," Eliza prompted as the curtain fell on Act I of *Macbeth,* "you are hardly attending. Here is the Comtesse d'Entraigues come to pay us a call. How delightful!"

I roused myself quick enough to observe that lady's entrance into our box, with a headdress of feathers nearly sweeping the ceiling—a quizzing-glass held to her eye—an expanse of bony shoulder and excess of décolleté—and schooled my countenance to amiability. There are many words I might chuse to apostrophise the French Countess—one of Eliza's acquaintances from her previous marriage to a nobleman of Louis's reign—but *delightful* is not one of them. The Comtesse d'Entraigues was used to be known as Anne de St.-Huberti, when she set up as an opera singer in the days of the Revolution; but by either name she is repugnant to me, being full of acid and spite. Eliza hints that her friend was the Comte's mistress before he was constrained to marry her—and at full five-and-fifty, Anne de St.-Huberti must be grateful for the protection of d'Entraigues's name. She paints her pitted cheeks in the mode of thirty years since; is given to the excessive use of scent; affects a blond wig; and should undoubtedly be termed a *Fright* by the ruthless bucks of Town.

"Eliza, *mignon,*" she crooned as she presented one powdered cheek in all the appearance of affection; "how hagged you look this evening, to be sure! The years, they have never sat lightly upon you, *bien sûr!* You have been fatigued, *sans doute,* by your visit to Surrey last evening—it was a great deal too good of you to solace my exile!"

We had indeed ventured into Surrey last night, despite all my doubts regarding Sunday travel, to enjoy an evening of music at the d'Entraigues abode. The old Count spoke nothing but French, and I understood but a fraction of the communication, tho' Henry admirably held up his end, and declared the gentleman to be a man of parts and considerable information. The son, young Count Julien, who appears everything an Exquisite of the *Ton* should be, with his excellent tailoring, his disordered locks, his shining boots, and his quantity of fobs and seals, delighted us with his superior performance upon the pianoforte.

The Comtesse had deigned to sing.

Taken all together, I should rather endure a full two hours of her ladyship's airs in the Italian than a few moments of her conversation; and as she and Eliza put their heads together, I considered instead how the Theatre Royal might serve in a novel: the comings and goings of great personages, a lady's chance encounter with an Unknown; or the appearance of a Rogue, for example, who might interpret the slight nothings and subtle displays of the *ton* with an understanding far more penetrating than my own ...

It was impossible to be in London at the height of the Season without reverting in thought to Lord Harold Trowbridge. That late denizen of Brooks's Club, that consummate sportsman and intimate of princes, should certainly have graced one of these lofty boxes, and been in close converse even now with Lord Castlereagh, perhaps, however little he liked that Tory gentleman's conduct of war. He should have profited by the play's interval in dallying with a lady, or shown himself one of Harriette Wilson's favourites, his sleek frame displayed to advantage against the marble columns of the tier. But would he, in truth, have noticed *Jane?*

The question arose with a pang. At five-and-thirty I cannot pretend to any beauty now. My evening dress of blue, the beaded band encircling my forehead, the flower tucked into my hair—arranged with all the genius Eliza's French maid could command—is yet nothing to draw the eye. One must be possessed of extraordinary looks or a great deal of money to figure in London. Had his lordship lived, he might have *called* at No. 64 Sloane Street, as he condescended to do in Bath and Southampton—and left his card as my Willoughby does for Marianne—but in the Greater World Lord Harold's notice may have been denied to me.

I like to think, however, that he would have approved of my book. It was always an object with Lord Harold that I should write.

"Blue-deviled, Jane?" my brother Henry enquired gently as he reappeared in the box. "We have been leading you quite the dance these past few weeks. I daresay you're wishing yourself back in Hampshire!"

"Not at all," I replied, banishing my ghost with effort. "You know me too well for a frivolous character, Henry, to imagine me ungrateful when such divine absurdities are laid at my feet! What writer worthy of the name should prefer the confined and unvarying circle of the country to this? Only observe Eliza's French count, old d'Entraigues, paying court before Mr. George Canning—and he no longer Foreign Minister, with favours to bestow. Observe Lady Castlereagh endeavouring to ignore the fact that Beau Brummell and the Ponsonbys prefer Harriette Wilson's box to hers! But tell me—who is that woman with the aquiline nose and jewelled tiara, quite alone in the seat opposite? She cannot tear her regard from Lord Castlereagh. I should consider her excessively rude, did I not imagine her to be a princess of the blood royal, and thus beyond all censure."

"A princess indeed," my brother replied with a careless

gesture of his quizzing-glass, "but not of the Hanoverian line. You have detected a Russian noblewoman, my dear—the Princess Evgenia Tscholikova. She is resident in London nearly a year, and may be claimed as one of our neighbours—for she has taken a house in Hans Place, hard by Sloane Street."

"A princess, rusticating in the oblivion of Hans Place!" I declared. "I should rather have expected Berkeley Square, or Brook Street at the very least."

"Her means, no doubt, are unequal to her station."

"But why does she gaze at Lord Castlereagh so earnestly? His lady certainly does not notice the Princess; and the gentleman is deep in conversation with another."

"That is like Evgenia," broke in the Comtesse d'Entraigues, with a disparaging glance at me over her bare shoulder. "The Princess will always be playing the tragic actress, *non*? A man has only to spurn her, to become the most ardent object of her soul."

Eliza rapped her friend's knuckles with a furled fan. "You will *shock* my sister, Anne. Do not be letting your tongue run away with you, I beg."

"But surely you have seen the papers, Eliza?" The Comtesse's voice was immoderately loud; several heads turned. "It is everywhere in the *Morning Post,* if one has eyes to see and the mind to understand. The Princess's letters to Castlereagh—most importunate and disgusting, the very abasement of a woman in the throes of love—were sold to the *Post* but a few days ago. The editors would disguise the principals in the affair, of course—as 'Lord C——,' and 'the Princess T——,' but the truth is known among the *ton.* Evgenia has disgraced herself *and* his lordship. Lord

Castlereagh has only to conduct himself as usual, to silence the impertinent; but I wonder that *she* dares to show her face."

The malice behind the words was sharp and pitiless; a worse enemy than the Comtesse d'Entraigues I should not like to encounter, and of a sudden my sympathy went out to the Russian noblewoman, who alone among the Great at the Theatre Royal was lapped in a chilly solitude, no friend to support her. I, too, had read the salacious excerpts in the *Morning Post*, but lacking all familiarity with the *ton*, had no ability to put a name or face to the initials. My cheeks flushed with consciousness as I recalled a part of the correspondence. *My limbs burn with the desire to lie once more entangled in your own . . . There is nothing I would not sacrifice, would not risk, for the touch of your lips on my bare skin . . . I can hardly write for anguish, I tremble at the slightest glimpse of you in publick, my dear one, desperate to have you alone . . .* However abandoned the prose, it was vile to consider of it strewn before the publick eye.

"What I desire to learn," I said indignantly, "is *who* should undertake to traffick in a lady's intimate correspondence?"

"Her maid, perhaps—if the girl was turned off without a character," suggested Eliza.

"But Castlereagh was the recipient of the letters," Henry objected, "which must point to a culprit in his lordship's household."

"Unless he returned the Princess's correspondence," I offered.

"I will lay odds on it that she sold them herself," the Comtesse d'Entraigues pronounced viciously. "She would enjoy the fame, however black."

"You are acquainted with the lady, I apprehend."

"Twenty years, at least. She has the habit of inserting herself in my affairs; I will not deny that I abhor the very sight of her." The Comtesse rose abruptly, smoothed out her silk gown, and said, "Eliza, I will wait upon you in Sloane Street tomorrow. Do not fail me."

Eliza bowed her head in acknowledgement, and the Comtesse swept away—the curtain being about to rise on the second act, and all further conversation being impossible in the presence of Sarah Siddons, and the blood that stained her hands.

BY THE MORNING I HAD ENTIRELY FORGOT RUSSIAN PRINcesses and French countesses, their affairs of the heart or their implacable hatreds—for it was *Tuesday,* the twenty-third of April, and thus the very date determined by Eliza nearly two weeks before, for an evening of musical entertainment, the professional performers to include a player upon the harp, one upon the pianoforte, and a succession of glees, to be sung by Miss Davis and her accompanists. The evening was intended as a sort of tribute to Mr. Henry Egerton—no relation to the publisher of my book, but the son of one of Henry and Eliza's friends—and Henry Walter, a young gentleman who is a cousin in some degree to all of us. I like to refer to the party as "the evening of the three Henrys," and have served my hostess best by staying out of the way. There is a great deal to be done—the final orders to the cook, the shifting of a quantity of furniture from the passage and drawing-rooms, the disposition of chimney lights—but at ten o'clock in the morning Eliza and I paused to draw breath, and to drink a cup of tea. Eliza has suffered the slight indisposition of a cold, resulting no doubt from the necessity of quitting the coach briefly on our journey into Surrey Sunday evening—it being a chilly night, and the horses jibbing at some rough paving on the hill prior to the descent into the village, and all of us forced to stand about in the cold air while the coachman went to the leaders' heads and led them over the broken ground. Eliza's nose is streaming, and she will not be in looks this evening for her party—a vexation she is happily able to disregard, in all the bustle of preparing for her guests.

"Here is Henry," she said impatiently as my brother stepped into the breakfast room, the morning paper under his arm, "come to eat up all the toast! I dare swear you smelled the bread baking halfway down Sloane Street, and hurried your feet to be in time."

I held out my plate, but Henry was not attending to Eliza's teazing words. His face was very white, and his countenance unwontedly sober.

"What is it?" his wife demanded with sudden perspicacity. "You look entirely overset, my dearest. Surely it is not—not one of the family?"

Henry shook his head, and set the newspaper on the table. "Nothing so near, thank God. But terrible, for all that. I suppose it is because we saw her only last evening. I cannot get over how *alive* she was, at the Theatre Royal ..."

As one, Eliza and I bent over the *Morning Post*. And read, in implacable print, the news: the Princess Tscholikova was dead—her throat slit and her body thrown carelessly on the marble steps of Lord Castlereagh's house.

Chapter 2

Blood and Ministers

Tuesday, 23 April 1811

~

"How very dreadful," Eliza breathed. She set down her plate of toast and pressed her hand to her heart. "And to think she lodged but a few steps from our door! How thankful I am that she was not killed at home!"

"*Was* it murder, Henry?" I enquired.

"The editors would intimate suicide. The Princess is believed to have done herself a violence after being refused admittance to his lordship's household."

"But at what hour?" I reached for my brother's *Post.* "Only consider—she cannot have importuned Castlereagh on the very steps of his home, even at the close of Mrs. Siddons's play, and not been remarked by all the world! London does not go to bed so early as one o'clock!"

"Neither would she have sought an interview with his

lordship at dawn, Jane." Henry frowned. "Yet her body was found by a charley in Berkeley Square at a few minutes past five o'clock in the morning."[1]

"She might have lain there some time, I suppose. Does a London watchman make *regular* rounds?"

Eliza sniffed. "*Never* if he may avoid it. The charleys, as you will observe, are elderly louts. I cannot recollect ever meeting with one in the lawful conduct of his duties—even when we resided in Upper Berkeley Street, which you must know, Jane, is most select. We must account it the merest mischance that the Grosvenor Square man stumbled upon the body at all."

The *Post* had furnished its readers with a small line drawing of the Princess, in full evening dress, her looks ghastly and her torn throat dark with inky blood. The editors were amply recompensed for their part in the poor creature's ruin; her violent end should sell numerous copies.

"And was this revenge?" I mused. "Her character destroyed by the publication of her correspondence, did the Princess think to shatter Lord Castlereagh's peace? Prick his conscience? Shame his wife? Or was she simply mad with grief?"

"All Russians are mad," Eliza observed.

"She did not appear to be out of her senses last evening, however. Recollect her earnest gaze! Princess Tscholikova greatly desired to be private with his lordship—but could

---

[1] A charley, as London's night watchmen were termed, was supposed to make the rounds of his neighborhood every half hour during a set period of work—usually twelve hours at a stretch—and could rest in his wooden booth when not so employed. In point of fact, however, many such watchmen never bothered to make the rounds but drew their minimal pay for huddling in their boxes and periodically announcing the time and weather. They were frequently bribed by prostitutes and petty thieves to ignore minor acts of crime; they were also subject to being overturned in their booths by drunken young gentlemen. At this time there was no regular police force in London.—*Editor's note.*

have no opportunity. It must be impossible to command Castlereagh's notice in so publick a venue as the Theatre Royal. Did she seek him, then, on his very doorstep? And to what purpose?"

"It cannot look well, her having been found at his lordship's," Eliza said doubtfully. "If the world fails to credit the notion of suicide, Lord Castlereagh *must* be suspect."

"Fiddlestick," I retorted. "Why should a gentleman of high estate—heir to an earldom, and known to be powerful among government circles—chuse to discard the body of his mistress in his own entryway? It will not do, Eliza, and you know it. Throw the lady into the Thames, by all means, but do not leave her lying about for the charley to find. Besides, Lord Castlereagh has no need of murder. He is the sort of man so complaisant in his own regard, as to consider the denial of his society as punishment enough."

"What is this?" Henry cried. "Is *Jane* to ridicule a Tory minister? And she such a staunch opponent of the Regent and his Whiggish friends!"

"I cannot admire Lord Castlereagh," I admitted, "Tory tho' he is; and he has not been in government these many years, for which we are taught to be thankful. The little fact of his having a mistress is as nothing to his want of brilliance in oratory; and you well know, Henry, that his conduct of the Walcheren campaign was everywhere deplored.[2] The Great

---

[2] In June 1809, the Portland Cabinet authorized a military campaign to take the Island of Walcheren, in the Dutch river Scheldt, held by Napoleon. The object was to destroy the arsenals and dockyards at Antwerp and Flushing. Some 40,000 troops and 250 vessels were dispatched in a well-publicized raid, conducted with poor intelligence and worse weather. By August, the Cabinet ordered a withdrawal. The Walcheren campaign has gone down in history as a fiasco.—*Editor's note.*

World did not mourn when he resigned the post of Minister of War."

"—Because he afforded the Great World such sport, in throwing over his political career!" my brother countered. "Consider, Jane, his treatment of Mr. Canning! Surely the violence he showed on *that* occasion is a great deal more to the present point, than all your talk of oratory?"

"You would refer to the celebrated duel, I suppose." It has been nearly two years since Lord Castlereagh, incensed at the poor opinion of his fellow minister, George Canning, called out the latter to defend his honour on a ground of his lordship's chusing. Pistols at dawn might seem a dubious method of debating Cabinet policy, but both gentlemen are Irish, and Castlereagh is renowned for his temper.

"He refused all the Seconds' attempts to mediate," Henry persisted, "and could not be satisfied until he had fired twice, and winged Mr. Canning in the thigh. I have it on excellent authority that poor Canning had never held a pistol before in his life! —Compared to the wilful attack upon the Foreign Minister, the cutting of a woman's throat is as nothing."

"But why should Castlereagh put himself to the trouble?" I demanded. "Recollect what Eliza's friend said last evening: *Lord Castlereagh has only to conduct himself as usual, to silence the impertinent.* Why should he resort to violence at all?"

"The *Post* ascribes the Princess's end to self-murder," Eliza interjected, "and self-murder it undoubtedly was! Retire to your book room, Henry, and leave us in peace. We shall *never* be ready for our musical evening, and we do not make haste!"

IN ALL THE WORRY OF PROCURING A SUITABLE QUANTITY of Naples biscuit, and tasting the ratafia syllabub we intended to serve once the music should be done, and colluding with Eliza's maid, Manon, in the fashioning of a cunning headdress—not to speak of a stolen hour spent reading through my printer's proof—I might have put the gruesome death in Berkeley Square entirely out of mind. I should thus have avoided a period of tiresome activity, meddlesome impertinence, and no little danger to myself; and I might have remained in happy ignorance of the depravity and betrayals of the Polite World, quitting London much as I found it: secure in my view that the Metropolis was replete with honourable and godly people, whose predilection for frivolity was no more to be despised than a child's affection for playing at spillikins. But it was not to be. The death of Princess Evgenia Tscholikova obtruded on my notice at a few minutes before two o'clock, with the arrival of the Comtesse d'Entraigues's carriage at our door.

The Comtesse, as I have said, was not to be of our party that evening. Eliza had solicited her old friend for the honour of her song, but Anne de St.-Huberti affected humility; she never sang before strangers, she protested, but only in the intimacy of her own home, and only before chosen friends. Having heard her in voice on Sunday evening, I will confess to relief that the Comtesse was *not* to sing for Mr. Egerton and our guests; her instrument cannot now be what it was.

I hastily stowed the pages of my book beneath a circulating novel that lay discarded on the drawing-room table, and rose to greet the visitor.

"*Mes chères amies,*" the Comtesse sang out as she sailed into the room, a swansdown muff negligently disposed on one arm, "what dreadful weather you have for your evening, *non?* It comes on to rain! You will be fortunate indeed if half your guests venture out into the streets! And my dear Eliza, how swollen and red your nose!"

I foresaw a similar vein of conversation, richly mined by the Comtesse's malice; and being unable to explain Eliza's attachment to Anne de St.-Huberti—unless it be an affection for some memory of her own glorious career at Versailles, before Louis's fall—I determined to salvage what I could of the day and my own peace.

"Eliza is decidedly unwell," I observed, "and ought to be laid down upon her bed, with hot lemonade and sticking plaster. Indeed, I was just upon the point of quitting the house for the apothecary. You will forgive me, Countess, if I go about my errand..."

"But of course," the lady said earnestly, her gloved claw clasping my fingers. "It is always the office of the spinster sister, *non,* to sacrifice herself to her wretched family? You are admirably suited to the role, my dear Jane. You will darn the socks to perfection, and nurse other people's children without a thought for yourself. Run along while I amuse *la pauvre* Eliza with every sort of scandalous nonsense."

If I did not utter a retort that should set the harpy's ears to flaming, I may say it was from a sense of what I owed my brother Henry: those precious typeset pages carefully concealed beneath an overturned book. He is the most excellent of brothers, Henry—however many dubious females he may admit into his house.

I DID NOT HAVE FAR TO SEEK FOR MR. HADEN, THE APOTHEcary and surgeon, as his shop was directly next to Henry's home—at No. 62 Sloane Street. I might have despatched my errand with alacrity, had I been desirous of returning to the Comtesse d'Entraigues and her repellant conversation; but I had been within doors all day, and fretted at my confinement. For nearly two years now I have been accustomed to walking the lanes of Chawton, in mire or dust, in pursuit of the post, or acquaintance, or the broader delights of neighbouring Alton. I rejoice in the daily revelations of the garden in such a season as this: the tentative spurt of sunshine; the first daffodils waving in the stiff breeze; the inadvertent torrents; the appearance of the bluebells. London, with its fashionable throng, its noise and dirt, its persistent and impenetrable fogs, its rackety business of carriages and midnight hours, is a type of enjoyment to which one must be schooled. I might in youth have relished the heady excitement of money and power that is here everywhere on parade; but in my more sober years—in the fullness of my womanhood—I cannot ignore the immense want I see in the pinched faces of the streets, nor the gin-soaked decrepitude of the women and men who beg at every corner. There is a ruthlessness to London life perfectly in keeping with its glittering masters: I thought once more of the Princess Tscholikova, her blood running down the steps of one of the most exalted residences in Town—and shivered in my pelisse.

A brisk walk was required—a filling of the lungs, even if it be with sulphurous air—and so I ventured across Sloane Street into the pretty little wilderness of Cadogan Place, where nursemaids sat in careful watch over their infant charges, who played at battledore and shuttlecock upon the greening lawn.[3] Hans

---

[3] This part of the fashionable West End is now Cadogan Square. Hans Town was named for Sir Hans Sloane, whose daughter married the first Earl of Cadogan in the 1770s, uniting the two families' estates. Architect Henry Holland leased the area and built the original brick houses, many of which were altered in subsequent centuries. —*Editor's note.*

Town, as this village on the edge of the city is called, is by no means a fashionable abode, being fully a quarter hour's brisk walk west of Hyde Park; but it will do for such gentlemen of business as my banker brother Henry, for hopeful families of second sons, who regard the country air as more healthful than that of the city generally; and for those shabby-genteel members of the *ton* whose fortunes have been gambled away. We are a heterogeneous lot, part pretension, part vulgarity; but I cannot repine, or wish my brother returned to Upper Berkeley Street. His rooms are more commodious, and his neighbours infinitely more colourful, than I should discover elsewhere.

I was swinging with energy along the gravel path, when a "Good morning, Miss Austen" rang brightly in my ear, to be seconded by a chorus of little voices; and I turned to find Mrs. James Tilson some ten paces behind me, with her maid and a collection of children bestowed about her, bent upon their exercise.

"Fanny!" I cried. "I should expect you to be laid upon your bed, with a warm shawl about your shoulders, recruiting your strength for the dissipations of this evening! You cannot fail us, my dear! We depend upon you, however much it should come on to rain!"

Frances Tilson is the wife of my brother's chief banking partner in London, Mr. James Tilson, and the mistress of just such an household as is everywhere to be found in Hans Town. A boy of twelve is presently away at school; but no less than *seven* daughters fill the drawing-room in Hans Place, the youngest not above a year of age. Mrs. Tilson's excellent sense and tolerable understanding make her an attractive companion for these walks about the square, while her children—in small doses—provide amusement. Eliza will say that Fanny Tilson has no sense of humour, and that her taste for the exalted—her air of piety and sober reflection—are tiresome in the extreme; but I cannot abuse goodness, tho' I lack it myself. Such abuse must smack of envy.

"But of course we shall not fail," Fanny replied simply as the party came up with my position on the path. "We have been eagerly anticipating the party a fortnight at least. I have promised the older girls they may help me dress."

Squeals of delight greeted these words, and as we fell in together, and began to pace the gravel path, I observed, "It is as well, perhaps, that you have some frivolity to distract your thoughts. You have lost a neighbour, I understand."

"I do not care to speak of it," Fanny said, turning her head away. "Everything to do with *that person* is repugnant to a lady; and however much we may deplore the manner of her end, I think I am safe in stating that it was not unfitted to her mode of life."

I considered of the Princess, lonely and friendless as I had observed her the previous evening, her throat slit and her body cast upon the streets; and thought her death totally at variance with a life of privilege and indulgence. I apprehended that Fanny wished me to draw a *moral* from violent death, and being surrounded by her tender daughters, did not chuse to pursue the subject. My companion surprised me, however, by continuing the debate with vigour.

"Her body has been returned to the house," Fanny said, "and black crape hung from the doorway. There is a coat of arms—quite foreign—suspended above the door, and the knocker removed. I should have thought that the world would shun the remains of one so wretched as to take her own life, but in point of fact a succession of carriages has been coming and going all day, for the leaving of cards and condolences. I am sure there is no one to read them. She lived quite alone, as one would expect of a woman so lost to propriety as to abandon her husband, and desert all her friends."

"Not all, it would seem, from the succession of carriages," I replied.

"They say there is a brother," Fanny confided in a lowered tone. "A prince of some kind, tho' what that may signify among Russians, who can tell? He is said to be travelling even now from Vienna. The husband does not appear. The obsequies must be suspended until the brother arrives; and indeed, what sort of burial shall she receive? She cannot be a member of the Church of England. And then there is the fact of self-murder. Perhaps they will remove the body to Paris, where I understand she lived until lately..."

At that moment, a woman I judged to be a maidservant cut across our path, her chin sunk upon her breast and her expression abstracted. She was so near I might have brushed her arm, had I not pulled up short; and she quite ran into little Charlotte, a stout girl of seven, who cried in pain at the trodding of her foot. The maid never deviated, or lifted her head, or acknowledged our presence in any way—and as I gazed at her in consternation, I saw great tears slip unheeded down her cheeks. She moved as one bent upon an unholy errand, or in the grip of a horror so profound that no human voice might penetrate it.

"Druschka," Fanny Tilson said in some irritation as she bent to chafe her daughter's foot. "The Princess's maid. Perhaps it is *she* who reads the condolences. —If, indeed, she is able to read."

The woman had crossed Sloane Street and paused before the door of the apothecary, Mr. Haden. It was time, I thought, to fulfill Eliza's errand.

Chapter 3

A Queen's Ransom

~

MR. HADEN WAS NOWHERE IN SIGHT AS I ENTERED HIS SHOP. It was clean and commodious, which must inspire confidence in the healthfulness of the man's wares: a high-ceilinged space, lit by suspended oil lamps, and lined with shelves. Rank upon rank of glass jars held every conceivable tincture and herb, simple and poison; earthenware bowls stood ready for the pestle; a set of brass scales graced the front counter, along with a volume in which the apothecary recorded the names of his clients, the nature of their complaints, and the remedies he had prescribed. With so many children in Hans Town, Mr. Haden was never wanting in work, and Eliza—who is prone to illness as the years advance—finds it a great comfort to be lodged so near a capable quack.

The maid Druschka was standing next to the counter, her gaze fixed upon the scales as tho' she might read her future there. I had thought her countenance forbidding in Cadogan Place—an impression derived, perhaps, from the grim force of misery. Under the light of the oil lamps, however, I saw that age had deeply etched her visage. This woman could have known the Princess Tscholikova from her cradle.

So lost in reflection was she that my broaching of the door, and the faint tinkle of the bell suspended over it, might have been soundless for all the response they drew. Still as a statue, Druschka waited for Mr. Haden.

"There you are," he said briskly, appearing from the rear of his premises with a slim purple vial. "Tincture of laudanum. I would advise you to use it sparingly. Do you understand?" He held aloft three fingers. "No more than three drops each night."

Druschka reached wordlessly for the bottle, her aged hand swathed in a fingerless black mitt. If she comprehended the apothecary's speech, she made no sign.

"Here," Mr. Haden said impatiently. "You'll have to sign my book. *Here!*"

But the maid was already halfway to the door, and did not chuse to regard the apothecary behind his counter—an inattention born of a lack of English, I must suppose, or a misery so profound it no longer considered of a stranger's expectations. As she brushed past me towards the street I summoned courage and said, "Pray accept my condolences on the loss of your mistress, Druschka."

She turned upon me a pair of fathomless eyes and muttered, *"C'est tout des mensonges."*

"What did she say?" Mr. Haden demanded, as the maid stepped out onto the street.

"It's all lies," I repeated thoughtfully, and procured Eliza's draught.

The Comtesse d'Entraigues had quitted the house by the time I returned, but she had left Eliza no gayer for all her promised scandal.

"The poor creature is beside herself, Jane," my sister confided.[1] "Never knowing where her next shilling is to come from, looks and voice quite gone, the years advancing—and who can say how many light-skirts that old roué of a husband has in keeping? I thank God I was fortunate enough to consider of dear Henry's offer when I was at low ebb myself. You can have no notion how comforting it was, to know I might drop my handkerchief at any moment, as the saying goes, and he should come running to pick it up! When I think of his goodness—"

At this, she buried her reddened nose in a square of cambric and said nothing audible for the space of several moments.

It is true that Henry was besotted with Eliza, who is almost ten years his senior, when he was a callow youth and she a young mother fresh from a *château* in France. She was infinitely captivating in those days, black-haired and exquisitely-dressed, with jewels at her throat and a delightful penchant

---

[1] In Austen's day, a sister-in-law such as Eliza de Feuillide would be referred to as a "sister" once she married Jane's brother Henry. The fact of Eliza's being also Jane and Henry's first cousin makes for a tightly knit relationship.—*Editor's note.*

for shocking conversation. Even our elder brother James, destined for the Church and a prig from infancy, was wild for Eliza. It became a sort of game for Henry and James to vie for my cousin's favour when they were both up at Oxford, and she living in London far from the protection of her husband; but by the time the self-styled Comte de Feuillide was guillotined, and Eliza free, James had buried his first wife and was the father of a child. He courted Eliza for months, allowed her to toy with his heart and his future, and took her eventual refusal to become a clergyman's wife in good part. The idea of Eliza—who at five-and-thirty was still the girlish beauty she had ever been, carrying her pug about Town and riding in the Park—as the mistress of James's parsonage, was not to be thought of. Henry offered himself *twice* to my cousin, with a heart that had always been her own, and to the relief of the entire family—Eliza at last accepted him.

It was feared that such a rackety and volatile pair—one with more hair than wit and the other possessed of more charm than is good for him—should be run off their legs by debt. Dire predictions of a frivolous end—desertion or debtor's prison—my brother's affections elsewhere engaged as Eliza inevitably aged—were bruited about the family with ruthless disregard for the feelings of this junior son. But the Henry Austens have jogged along steadily in tandem harness for more than a decade now without disaster; and the family must declare Eliza much improved. It cannot be wonderful that a lady so intimate with death—of a mother, a husband, a son—could fail to be sobered by the prospect of eternity; but I must credit my brother with excellent sense, and the uncanny ability to manage his wife by never attempting to manage her at all. It was he who supported my cousin through every loss; he who travelled to France in the wake of revolution to demand recompense for the Comte de Feuillide's confiscated estates; he who bore with Eliza's extravagant tastes and exalted acquaintance. As a French countess, she had been much in the habit of attending Court Drawing-Rooms and the exclusive assemblies at Almack's; she saw no reason to leave off doing so now that she was become the wife of a mere banker. There are still few in London who fail to address Eliza as *Comtesse,* rather than *Mrs. Austen;* but it is Henry who franks her style of life.

"You would tell me the d'Entraigueses are embarrassed in their circumstances?" I enquired now as Eliza emerged from her handkerchief. "But that muff—! Her opera dress of last evening! The furnishings of the house in Surrey!"

"As to that—it never *does* to betray one's poverty to the milliner or modiste. You must know, Jane, that when one is in debt, the only sure course is to order another hat or gown; it keeps such encroaching persons dependant upon one's custom. My sainted mamma never did any differently; but Henry prefers to be beforehand with the world, and naturally I would not deviate a *hair* from his wishes." Eliza, despite her fifty years, looked as conscious as a girl as she uttered this palpable falsehood. "But the d'Entraigueses are quite at a stand. He cut a dashing figure in the early days of revolution, and escaped the guillotine by playing every side false; denounced his friends and turned traitor to the world; but when at last he was obliged to flee the country, his *château* was burned to the ground and his property seized. He has never entirely come about, and relies upon the kindness of friends—the gratitude of the various governments he has served—and something in the way of a pension from the present forces in France—in short, I do not know how they contrive to live. But that is not the worst, Jane." Eliza leaned closer and dropped her voice to a whisper. "He has lost his heart to a hardened Cyprian—a High Flyer of the most dashing order—a Demi-rep of the worst kind—and is demanding of Anne a divorce!"

"But he must be *sixty* if he is a day!"

"He is not above five years older than myself," she returned, a trifle nettled, "and there is quite as much of *that* in one's mind at our age as in the youngest stripling's. The Comte thinks, perhaps, to reclaim his youth by taking a bride likely to be mistaken for his daughter. Every kind of folly may be imputed to a man in love. But consider of Anne! She has long known what her husband is—she became his mistress while performing on the Paris stage, and cannot expect fidelity from one who seeks solace in such places—and *yet*! To be setting up her own establishment at her age, and without the slightest hope of a suitable settlement from the Comte—for, in truth, he has not a pound to give her!"

"She told you all this?"

"In strictest confidence, of course. I do not consider myself as having violated that confidence by reporting the whole to you," Eliza said comfortably. "You are almost my second self. But *Jane*—she has begged me to assist her, and I am sure I do not know what Henry would say if he were to learn of it!"

"She requires a loan? From Henry's bank?"

"If only it were that." Eliza plucked diffidently at the shawl draped across her knees. "Anne wishes me to sell her jewels for her. At Rundell & Bridge. She is convinced that a true English lady, as she is pleased to call me, will never be cheated by the most reputable jewellers in London—whatever nasty turn such a firm might serve an impoverished French opera singer."

"You did not *agree?*" I faltered, as the breathless image of Rundell & Bridge rose in my mind. "Good Lord, Eliza— Henry should be appalled to find his wife despatched upon such an errand! What if the jewellers should assume that *his* circumstances are embarrassed? Consider of the damage to his reputation! The possible loss of custom at his bank! The spurt of rumour and innuendo in the clubs of Pall Mall— and the consequent run upon his funds as clients shift their money elsewhere! You cannot seriously contemplate such a thing, even in the service of a friend!"

"No-o," Eliza conceded faintly, "tho' poor Anne *did* be-seech me most earnestly, and I suffered the greatest pangs in the knowledge I must disappoint her. I only succeeded in forcing her from the house, Jane, with the suggestion that *you* might be willing to oblige."

"Me? Eliza—!"

"It is not such an abominable notion, after all," she said. "You observed only yesterday that you wished to step into Rundell & Bridge. You might find a pair of earrings for your niece Anna, or perhaps a brooch for Cassandra. If you have nothing better to do, you might very easily slip into Mr. Bridge's back room and negotiate the sale—"

"Indeed I might not!"

"But only *look* at them, Jane." Eliza unfurled the paisley shawl. "Is it not a queen's ransom poor Anne left behind?"

I stared wordlessly at the gems winking in my sister's lap: earrings of ruby and emerald, a diamond tiara, a sapphire necklace. There were brooches in the shape of peacocks and tigers; jewelled ribands as might represent the honour of foreign orders; a spangle intended for dressing the hair; a quantity of rings. It was as tho' a treasure from an exotic clime, redolent of incense and intrigue, had sprung from the carpet at our feet. The glory of the fiery stones caught the breath in my throat.

"Eliza," I whispered. "What in Heaven's name are we to do with them?"

"Secure them among the dirty linen," she said briskly. "Else we shall certainly be murdered in our beds this night."

Chapter 4

Lord Moira Shares His Views

Tuesday, 23 April 1811, cont.

~

"ARE YOU AT ALL ACQUAINTED WITH THE PRINCESS Tscholikova's maid?" I asked Manon.

She was arranging my hair for the musical evening with her usual deft grace: a Frenchwoman of exactly my own age, with snapping dark eyes and a firm, thin-lipped mouth. Dressed in a charcoal gown with a starched white collar and cuffs, she is always precise as a pin, and terrifies my sister Cassandra with her swift step and haughty air. Manon and her mother, Madame Bigeon, fled the south of France during the Terror, and have been with Eliza ever since—Madame as nurse to Eliza's son, Hastings de Feuillide, and after the poor boy's early death, as general keeper of the household. Manon—whose given name is Marie Madeleine, too difficult a mouthful for daily usage—is in some sort Eliza's dresser, with the superiority natural to such an upper retainer; she is also Eliza's most loyal confidante, a soul to be trusted with matters of life and death. Not even a brief marriage to a soldier from Périgord—who gave her his name and a certain dignity before disappearing back to France—could detach her from the Henry Austens.

"You would mean Druschka?" she returned as she bound the bugle band about my forehead, and affixed the stem of a flower just above my left ear. "But of course I am acquainted with her. She is not French, you understand, but speaks our tongue to admiration. I know all the women in London who speak French, me. And most of the men also."

I studied her inscrutable reflection in the mirror, and understood there was another life entire behind Manon's picture of perfection: seething with hope and desire, perhaps, or tormented by loss; a human epic replete with character and incident, of which I knew nothing.

"Have you spoken with the maid today?"

"Non et non et non," she said crisply. "Today I have procured a pair of soles for Mr. Walter and Mr. Egerton to eat, I have swept the back parlour and the front, I have arranged the flowers for the mantelpiece and directed the setting of the glass which is lent by the cabinet-maker, I have dressed Madame Henri and yourself—all this I have done, and it is not yet five o'clock."

"Naturally," I murmured.

"You are wondering about the death of the Princess," Manon surmised. "It piques the interest, no? How such a one—with everything at her command, all the world in her favour—should do herself a violence. It is the artist in you. I perfectly understand."

"The artist?" I repeated. I had never considered of myself in such exalted terms.

"*La romancière,*" she explained. "Madame Henri, she has told me of this book you have written. I have a great envy to read it one day soon, when the pages they are printed."

There are times when the charming Eliza is too much of a rattle. "I had not wished my authorship of the novel to be known," I faltered. "It is a *great secret,* Manon—"

"But of course," she replied. "You should rather ride the horse bareback at Astley's Amphitheater, *non,* than be seen to ridicule all your acquaintance so acutely with your pen? I shall say nothing, me. I shall be dumb as a post. But all the same, I comprehend your interest in the dead one *et ses affaires.* It is in the nature of writers to paint life in all its violence and glory. Naturally you wish to know why it was necessary that the Princess should die."

The branch of candles on my dressing table sent flickering shadows across Manon's face, but her eyes were firmly fixed on the task at hand—the taming of the short front curls about my temples—and her countenance was serene, as tho' she talked only of the weather, and not my soul. It is true, nonetheless, that all my life I have wished to plumb the workings of the human heart—have sought to know the inner yearnings of my fellows through word and observation—and have found a sort of command of nature, in my ability to dispose of my acquaintance with the swift composition of an acid line. Was it mere vulgar curiosity, then, that animated my thoughts on the subject of the maid and her mistress? Was I to be self-condemned as no better than the Comtesse d'Entraigues, with her endless rapacity for gossip?

An image of Evgenia Tscholikova as I had glimpsed her in life—the earnest gaze fixed upon Lord Castlereagh's box—and the idea of the lady grown rigid in a pool of her own blood on the London street, arose before me as tho' reflected in the shifting candlelight. An echo of the maid Druschka's words, guttural with misery, rang in my ears: *It's all lies.* All lies.

"What do you know of the Princess?" I enquired.

Manon shrugged. "What everyone must know. She was born to the *noblesse*—she graced the Tsar's court at fifteen—she married a man of exalted position whom she knew not at all, and was miserable as a matter of course. She travelled with Prince Tscholikov to Vienna, where he was envoy to the Court; and there she fell in love with a man. Disgrace and ruin followed. She journeyed to Paris, alone and almost without means. Her brother succored her. And so, at the last, she came to this country—her bloom fading, her hopes gone, a woman not above thirty who must establish her credit amidst a sea of foreign faces and tongues. It has happened, *vous savez*, to others before."

"I suppose such a history might well end in suicide."

"Bah," Manon said briskly. "That is like your Englishness. Always the propriety, *oui*? But I, who have seen the world—I tell you that nothing, not even the shameful letters published without warning in the newspaper—is so terrible as death, mademoiselle."

I thought of the Terror: of the young girl Manon had once been, of an entire world lost to the guillotine.

"The man in Vienna—was that Lord Castlereagh?"

"Who knows? He is but the most recent in a string of lovers, perhaps. A woman denied all happiness will snatch at anything. But me, I should not snatch at Lord Castlereagh. He is ... *du glace.*"

Ice. I recollected the studied indifference of the former

Minister of War: he who had nearly killed a fellow Cabinet member defending his honour; he who could brave the ridicule of the press with insouciance. Ice was required of a man who must send entire regiments to their deaths; had he also sent the Princess to hers?

Manon's hands stilled, and she smiled into the mirror. "There," she said. "*C'est fini.* Does it please you?"

She could not restore lost youth, or conjure me a Beauty; but she had accomplished, all the same, something on the order of a miracle. My dowdy cap was discarded, my locks brushed with pomade until they shone, and my headdress as smart as my means would allow. The band of bugle beads bound about my forehead exactly matched those on the flounce of my dress. I would never be mistaken for an Incomparable—but as a secret scribbler of novels, a Bluestocking of a certain age come upon the Town—I would certainly do.

"Thank you, Manon."

She curtseyed, once more the modest servant. "I shall call in Hans Place tomorrow," she said with a sidelong glance, "to pay my respects to the Princess Tscholikova's household. Who knows what Druschka may tell?"

"Who knows, indeed?" I replied.

OUR DINNER GUESTS ARRIVED AT HALF-PAST FIVE: MR. Henry Egerton, whose principal virtue appears to be that he is the son of a clergyman resident in Durham; and Mr. Henry Walter, a serious young man of philosophic and mathematical stamp, who ought to have quitted London this morning, but stayed to eat sole in my brother's house. Eliza would wish to have nothing to do with Mr. Walter, as he is the nephew of her cousin Philadelphia—a prudish woman whose disapproval of Henry's wife is rooted in envy—but the most common family feeling dictated that Mr. Walter being in London, Mr. Walter must be invited to Sloane Street. And so he was placed at Eliza's right hand, and Mr. Egerton at mine, with the Tilsons to balance the table.

Mr. Egerton fell to my lot, and as he was barely half my age, and fatally tongue-tied, I found him heavy work. Having enquired where he had studied, and what poets he preferred, and whether he hunted a good deal or even at all—I left him to demand how I liked my visit to London, and whether I had yet penetrated the British Museum, or been favoured with a glimpse of Mrs. Siddons. This last bow, drawn at a venture, struck home—and I was able to speak with animation of *Macbeth* until the covers were removed and I turned with relief to the partner on my left, Mr. Tilson.

"You have won an admirer, Jane," he observed. "Mr. Egerton is overflowing with admiration—to the extent of apparent apoplexy. But do not be throwing yourself away upon a man with so little conversation; you would be sadly wasted. You require a partner whose cleverness equals your own—and not half a dozen exist in the entire Kingdom."

None, I thought, *since Lord Harold's demise;* but said only, "Flatterer. I could wish that your praise did not depend upon the abuse of my neighbour—for there can be no harm in him; he has not lived long enough to run to vice. If you must abuse somebody, let it be my cousin Mr. Walter—whom I cannot love, however worthy his achievements may be. He is a scholar, you know, dedicated to the education of Youth—and will bore the unfortunate Eliza to distraction."

"A prosy individual," he agreed, "and unbearably full of

consequence for a sprig of his years—he cannot be more than four-and-twenty. But his relation to yourself I may comprehend. Mr. Egerton I do not comprehend at all. Why is he of the select few invited to dine this evening?"

I saw that for all his playfulness, James Tilson was anxious. "I believe him to be nothing more than the son of an old family friend. What is it you fear, Mr. Tilson? That my brother is got among thieves and adventurers?"

My companion said nothing for a moment, his brow faintly furrowed. "You hold your brother in esteem and affection, my dear Miss Austen—as certainly do I. I will not scruple to say that Henry Austen is dearer to me than any but my own family. But I will also state that his judgement—so sound in most cases—has of late seemed wanting. There is a sort of recklessness in Henry...a desire to circulate among the Great...and if this fellow Egerton is another of them, I thought—"

He faltered, lips pursed.

"This is speaking seriously, indeed!" I rejoined, all fear of self-exposure forgotten. "Do not trifle with me, Mr. Tilson. Is my brother on the brink of ruin?"

"If he were, I should never betray him." Tilson's countenance eased, and he reached for his wine glass. "I could wish his friend Lord Moira at the ends of the earth, that is all. Henry may chuse to style his lordship as a great and useful patron—a name that lends tone to our banking concern—but the Earl is importunate in his demands for money, and a Whig besides. One might as well throw silver down a hole as lend it to a member of the Carlton House Set! Our thousands are gambled away in a single hand of whist! But Henry will not be brought to see it."

"Do you wish me to use my influence with my brother?" I asked.

"Have you any?" James Tilson enquired flippantly. "I assure you I have not, and we have been friends and partners these many years. Nor can I bring Eliza to the point; she is persuaded that all manner of good fortune will result from a connexion with the nobility, and encourages Henry to make Lord Moira his debtor. Try if you will to sound your brother on the matter, Jane; I acquit you of all responsibility if you fail."

"This troubles you, Mr. Tilson," I said, "and I am sorry for it. It is not like Henry to cause anxiety in the breasts of those he loves."

"Henry has no children," Tilson observed ruefully, "while I am possessed of more than enough for both of us; naturally I am the more provident, having so many mouths to feed. I leave it to you, Jane—and will cease to worry the matter. The musicians have arrived!"

THEY APPEARED AT EXACTLY HALF-PAST SEVEN O'CLOCK, in two hackney coaches hired for the purpose: a harpist with her instrument, bulky in flannel wrappings and requiring the services of two footmen to install in the front drawing-room; a pianist who would perform upon Eliza's beautiful little pianoforte; and a party of singers, led by a Miss Davis: quite short and round, with a flushed fair face, and a remarkable quantity of Voice to her small person. Half an hour passed in the arrangements of these people, and the necessary entertainment of our dinner party in the interval between the conclusion of the meal and the arrival of our guests for the evening—who began to appear by eight o'clock. Eliza had despatched some eighty invitations, and more than sixty people came: quite a rout for Sloane Street. I was relieved to find Mr. Egerton in the company of a Captain Simpson, of the Royal Navy, who possessed himself of the young man's sleeve and engaged him most earnestly in conversation pertaining to Whitehall; and saw James Tilson surrounded by gentlemen of his London acquaintance: Mr. Seymour, the lawyer; Mr. John-Lewis Guillemard, who has no business but to look smart and flirt with ladies young enough to be his wards; and Mr. Hampson, the baronet, who from strict Republican principles refuses to be called by his hereditary title. It was he who condescended to bring me a glass of wine—and abandoned me hastily at the descent of a thin, effusive lady in long gloves and a terrifying pink silk turban.

"Miss Jane Austen!" she cried, as though we two were met on a desert shore, the wreck of all hope tossing in the sea behind us. "How *well* you look, I declare! *Town bronze,* I believe they call it! You have certainly acquired *that* polish!"

"Miss Maria Beckford," I returned, and accepted her hand with real cordiality. "And Miss Middleton! Your father told me you were in London for your come-out!"

"We have taken a house in Welbeck Street," Miss Beckford replied, "and I serve as Susan's chaperone to all the smart affairs! You must certainly pay us a call. I long to hear all the Chawton news!"

Miss Beckford manages the household of her late sister's husband, Mr. John Middleton, who is my brother Edward's tenant at Chawton Great House—and thus my neighbour, when I am at home. She is a formidable woman, spare and abrupt and sensible, with a fund of learning and an enviable want of foolishness. I have long admired her ability to accommodate herself to circumstance. Lacking a husband, she entered instead her dead sister's household—and reared Middleton's children. She lacks for no comfort, is esteemed by all, and merits the respect due to an independent woman—without the necessity of submitting to a husband. I quite like Maria Beckford.

Her eldest niece, however, is another matter: a stout, well-grown girl of sixteen, who curtseyed with civility enough; but I detected boredom in all her looks, and guessed that to be dragged in her aunt's company to a Musical Evening—in a quarter of Town too far west to be considered fashionable, among a parcel of dowds—was to her an indignity tantamount to torture.

"It seems but a few months ago that you were playing in the long grass at Chawton," I told Susan, "and here you are, a Beauty in her First Season!"

She smirked, and muttered a nothing, her fingers plaiting the pink ribbons cascading from her bodice; an awkward child, with dull brown hair and coarse features, who will be dreaming of balls and private masques, of the assemblies at Almack's and the afternoon ride through the Park. But Susan, I fear, is destined for disappointment: Neither her fortune nor her beauty is great enough to figure in London. Almack's, and the breathless notice of the *ton*, will be denied her—as it was denied me.

"I must introduce you to my cousin, Mr. Henry Walter," I said, taking her hand firmly. "He looks as though he were in need of a dance."

My unfortunate cousin was engrossed in a discussion of Theosophy with Mr. Guillemard and Mr. Wyndham Knatchbull, a clergyman—and barely disguised his outrage at being so imposed upon, as to be forced to trade insipid nothings with a child. The harpist striking up an air at that moment, however, my cousin was spared the duty; and Miss Beckford and I left Susan in his orbit. She might, perhaps, serve as Mr. Guillemard's latest flirt. We retreated to the passage, so as to achieve the maximum degree of coolness with the minimum of crowding, and composed ourselves to listen.

ELIZA COULD TAKE PLEASURE, ON THE MORROW, IN THE fact that the last of her guests did not quit her house until midnight, and that the evening was deemed such a success— so much of a *crush,* in fact, an *intolerable squeeze*—that it merited a notice in the *Morning Post.* No less a personage than Lord Moira, the Regent's crony, condescended to grace Sloane Street with his presence; and it was thanks to the Earl that all my suspicions regarding Princess Tscholikova's end were animated long into the night.

"I own to some delight at Lord Castlereagh's discomfiture," his lordship confided to a group of five gentlemen arranged respectfully around him in the interval between Miss Davis's Airs in the Italian and the performance of Mozart upon the pianoforte. "There will be no talk of the Tories forming a government *now.*"

"But it can never truly have been under consideration," Mr. Hampson—the Republican baronet—protested. "The Regent is known to espouse the most radical principles! As his intimate these many years, my lord—and a partisan of the Whigs yourself—you can only have expected His Majesty to approach Lords Grey and Grenville for his Cabinet! This Tory posturing is all rumour, with the paltry object of disconcerting the Regent and elevating the star of Mr. George Canning—whose service in the furtherance of his own ambition is well known to men of sense!"

"Hear, hear," Mr. Guillemard intoned.

"Damn me," Captain Simpson exploded, "that's treason!" He lurched a little, as tho' he felt the roll of a deck beneath his feet. It must be said that the good captain—who had disconcerted me earlier in the evening with the news that my sailor brother, Frank, was superseded in his command—had been drinking deep of Henry's claret. "Would you have us turn over the Kingdom, aye, and all the Continent, to Buonaparte and his crew? That's what a Whig Cabinet will get ye!"

"Naturally I would have us do so, if it meant peace," Mr. Hampson rejoined equably. "The cost of this war—ceaseless and senseless as it has been—is bleeding the country and the poor to the point of annihilation! Peace, I say, at any cost—and if the Whigs will help us to it, I felicitate them with all my heart!"

Lord Moira raised his glass in approval, but a heated argument immediately broke out, as to the merits of Tory governance, which should stand firm against France to the dying breath, versus the Whig desire to conciliate the Monster and withdraw Lord Wellington from the Peninsula before the rout of French troops should entirely be achieved. There was mention of our ally, Russia, and the clauses of treaties published and secret; and while I lingered near Fanny Tilson, who talked of her children, my ear trained to the more interesting conversation of the gentlemen—the trend of remark circled back to the strange death of Princess Tscholikova.

"The poor lady could not have done away with herself in a better fashion, nor at a better hour," Lord Moira observed. "I am no ghoul, and must feel for the unfortunate creature in her misery—but if the woman must slit her throat, thank

God she chose to do so at the present moment, and at Castlereagh's door! It has been a close-run thing; we might almost have had Canning and Castlereagh returned to the Cabinet, and a host of Tories beside, and no end to the war in sight. The Regent, for all his Whig friends, has been considering of an approach to Canning and Castlereagh—His Highness regards them as likely to inspire publick confidence, and he is desperate to marshal the same in support of his Regency. Earls Grey and Grenville cannot offer him *that*."

"I cannot believe George Canning would ever consent to serve again with his greatest enemy," my brother Henry observed quietly. "Recollect, my lord, the duel."

"George Canning would serve with Satan himself, if the Prince of Darkness offered him power," Mr. Hampson returned scathingly.

"But now that the breath of scandal has touched Castlereagh," Lord Moira said, "all hope of a Tory Cabinet is fled. There are even those who speak of a Publick Enquiry in the House of Lords! I say it in confidence—but some would suggest—with the utmost delicacy, I assure you—that the Princess may *not* have died by her own hand. It is even suggested that the one who struck her down was Lord Castlereagh himself..."

"Good God!" Captain Simpson exclaimed. "That we should come to this! The governance of the land and the conduct of war determined by *paramours*!"

"It has always been thus," Lord Moira told him kindly, "but I will admit the present case to be positively Providential."

Providential, I thought, *to the enemies of Lord Castlereagh*— and scented in the phrase the iron smell of blood.

Chapter 5

The Warmest Man in England

Wednesday, 24 April 1811

~

. . . The Dashwoods were now settled at Barton with tolerable comfort to themselves. The house and the garden, with all the objects surrounding them, were now become familiar, and the ordinary pursuits which had given to Norland half its charms, were engaged in again with far greater enjoyment than Norland had been able to afford, since the loss of their father. . . .

I confess that I sighed as I read through those first few lines of Chapter Nine—that peculiarly interesting chapter in which my Willoughby must first emerge, like a questing knight of old from his dripping wood, and Marianne his Holy Grail. I sighed because the words seemed to me to be stilted past all bearing as I sat in Henry's book room this morning, lapped in the quiet of a house not yet recovered from the previous evening's exertions; sighed at the perversity of the printed word, which must appear as distinctly less lovely in its shape and significance than that same word set in flowing script. There is a clumsiness to typeface, I find, that strips from my prose its elusive mystery; I am revealed as a cobbler of letters as rigid and austere as the lead from which they are stamped.

—Or so I felt this morning. I may have experienced some lingering fatigue from Eliza's party, so great was my concern last evening to delight all those with whom I met, and to ensure their comfort lacked nothing. Or perhaps my attention was drawn from the story on the page—so innocent and familiar—to the story taking shape in my thoughts: a collection of vague suspicions given an alarming trend by Lord Moira's conversation. Whatever the cause, I could spare but half my mind to Willoughby, as he strode towards the hapless Marianne and her twisted ankle; the better part of my wit was sorting furiously through rumour, fact, and innuendo.

> ... *His manly beauty and more than common gracefulness were instantly the theme of general admiration, and the laugh which his gallantry raised against Marianne, received particular spirit from his exterior attractions.*——

Which is to say: Had Willoughby been short, fat, and ill-favoured, Marianne would rather have limped home.

I twitched the typeset proofs together with impatient fingers.

"Mademoiselle," Manon said from the doorway. "Do I intrude on your peace?"

"Not at all. I was just considering of my toast."

"Monsieur is already in the breakfast parlour. Madame Henri takes her tea in bed today."

"Thank you, Manon."

She glanced over her shoulder, then shut the book room door very quietly behind her so that we should not be disturbed. "While the house was yet asleep, I walked in Cadogan Square for nearly half an hour. The maid Druschka was there."

"Indeed?"

"She would not at first discuss the Princess or her death. But after a little—a period of quiet sympathy—she chose to confide."

I waited for what would come.

"Druschka would have it that the Princess Tscholikova would never *se suicider*," Manon said firmly. "She insists that her mistress was killed by another."

"Deliberate murder?"

"The most deliberate, but yes. Druschka vows she will not rest until justice is done."

I thrust aside the small table on which I had been writing and rose from my chair. "This might be the loyalty of a devoted servant, Manon—one who cannot bear the Princess to be dragged through the mud."

"A servant so devoted, mademoiselle, that she was admitted to her mistress's confidence."

"We cannot know that! The woman might claim anything in her grief!"

"One truth Druschka holds as absolute, look you: that Princess Tscholikova knew milord Castlereagh not at all."

I stared. "But the Princess's intimate correspondence with that gentleman was published in the *Post*!"

Manon shrugged. "Simply because a thing is printed, it must be true? In France we know better than to believe this. The principals were never named, in any case. A matter of initials only."

I revolved the maid's words in my mind. *All lies.* Not just the manner of her lady's death, but the scandal that led up to it: a fabrication entire. Impossible to say whether the scandal was invented to pave the way for murder—or whether murder was the inadvertent result of a botched attempt at scandal. Certainly the notion of the lady's suicide—and the plausibility of its occurring on Castlereagh's doorstep—were accepted solely *because* of those damning letters. But if Evgenia Tscholikova had never known the minister...?

Why was it necessary for a Russian princess to die in so sordid a way? And whose hand had held the knife that cut her throat?

"What you say interests me greatly," I told Manon.

"Like a *vignette* from a novel, is it not?" she said.

I WAS COLLECTED FROM THE BREAKFAST PARLOUR BY A SIS-ter so divinely habited as to appear every inch the Countess, from her spencer of willow green embroidered with cream knots, to her upturned poke bonnet. Gloves were on her hands, half-boots on her feet, and a reticule dangled from one arm. Eliza held a square package wrapped in brown paper; she did not quite meet Henry's gaze as she said, "I cannot waste another moment, my love, before returning this wretched soup tureen to Mr. Wedgwood's establishment; I declare I was miserable last evening, for being unable to place it in a position of honour on the supper table. It must and shall be repaired."

"Eh?" Henry replied, glancing up from his morning newspaper. "Ah, yes—the tureen. Very proper you should attend to it yourself, Eliza; I daresay Madame Bigeon has much to do this morning, in clearing the household of last evening's effects. But is your cold improved enough to permit of going out? Are you wise to expose yourself to the ill-effects of this spring wind? I had expected you to keep to your room this morning, and had quite resolved to dine at my club, rather than incommode the weary household."

"Dine at your club by all means," Eliza said hurriedly. "Jane and I shall step round to Ludgate Hill, and feel no compunction as to the hour of our return. We may content ourselves with the remains of last evening's supper, and perhaps some cold chicken."

"But does Mr. Wedgwood's shop lie in Ludgate Hill?" Henry enquired, rather puzzled. "I had thought it to be in St. James's."

"To be sure," Eliza amended, her gaze fixed on the Turkey carpet. "I am *forever* confusing the two. Come along, Jane."

My brother opened his mouth in bewilderment, but I silenced him with a look. Eliza's eyes were feverish and her nose quite red, but I knew her determination of old. Had the heavy box not already apprised me of the nature of our errand, her slip of the tongue confirmed it: We were bound for the elegant premises of Rundell & Bridge, jewellers to His Majesty the Regent and other sordid characters—to haggle over an opera singer's baubles.

LUDGATE HILL WAS USED TO BE THE SITE OF ONE OF THE City's ancient gates, before these were demolished to ease the passage between the tradesmen's square mile of London and the gentry's fashionable quarter. Here the ways are narrower than in the neighbourhood of Hyde Park, and the hired hack that served as our conveyance was jostled by carters and draught horses. The City, as it is known, is not a part of Town the Comtesse de Feuillide is accustomed to frequent; but the pollution necessarily derived from such quarters is as nothing to the privilege of entering Mr. Rundell's select establishment.

"He is a spare little man," Eliza said as we jostled over the cobbles in our coach, "much ridiculed as a miser, who rose from the merest silversmith's apprentice to the foremost goldsmith of our day. Do not expect a gentleman's manners, Jane—but pray treat him with absolute courtesy. He has the Regent's ear. I have it on excellent authority that Rundell provides His Majesty with the diamond settings for the Royal portraits—which you must know Prinny bestows upon each of his mistresses, at the outset of an *affaire*."

"Does His Majesty consider his image a form of payment?" I enquired drily.

Eliza's nose wrinkled. "His flirts are always gently-born, Jane, and possessed of husbands capable of franking their households. I should not call it *payment*. The Regent himself refers to Rundell's confections as *trinkets*—and is forever showering his female acquaintance with jewels, even those among them who are entirely respectable. It is his way, you see. He is rather like an overgrown child, delighting in the distribution of presents."

Overgrown is a kindness in Eliza; for the Regent is immensely fat, so gross indeed that he may no longer mount his horses. But something in her tone—half-awed, half-indulgent—brought to mind James Tilson's confidences of last evening, and his anxiety at Henry's reckless loans.

"Are *you* intimate with the Regent, Eliza? I cannot like the connexion. His way of life—indeed, that of the circle he supports—is utterly dissolute."

My sister gave a shrill little laugh. "Now you *are* the country cousin, Jane! To be sure the Prince is wont to gamble, as are all the members of the Carlton House Set, and their morals are not too nice; but where the hand is lavish and the taste of the very best, there will always be a need for funds. Funds are precisely what a banker provides, my dear. Old Thomas Coutts made a fortune in backing the highest names in the land—and I have advised Henry to take Coutts for his model."

"But Henry cannot command a particle of Coutts's resources," I exclaimed. "To urge him to lend to Coutts's extent is to goad Henry to ruin!"

"One must start somewhere," Eliza observed reasonably. "Coutts was not born to an easy competence, of that you may be sure—and no more was Henry. Indeed, none of you Austens have a farthing between you—else you would not be making such a push for independence, Jane, in the publication of your novel! Are we all of us to settle for uneasy penury, when with a bit of speculation we might be comfortable?"

"My brother Edward does not live in penury," I objected, "nor does he speculate."

"No. Edward lives on a fortune he could never have looked to claim," she retorted sharply. "I do not speak of your Kentish Knights, and their bequests; we cannot all be so fortunate.[1] Moreover, Edward has been very willing to place several thousands of his own funds in Henry's bank—and I hope

---

[1] Jane's elder brother, Edward, was adopted by his distant cousin, Thomas Knight, who bequeathed extensive estates in Kent and Hampshire to Edward.—*Editor's note.*

I am not an ungrateful creature. But we must make a *push*, Jane, to secure a nobler patronage—or Austen, Maunde & Tilson will never be more than a paymaster to an assortment of militia. That was Henry's introduction to the banking business, and very fine it was—but it must not be his end also."

I could not agree with Eliza—my heart misgave me when I thought of James Tilson's warning, and his numerous cares; but knowing less than nothing of my brother's affairs, or finance in general, I hesitated to voice too decided an opinion. I resolved to sound Henry on the subject when the next opportunity for privacy offered.

"I think, Jane, that you had better take charge of this parcel," Eliza suggested. "It would look well for us if you entered upon the scene as the owner of the jewels from the outset. I suppose your literary talent extends to the concoction of fibs?"

What else, in short, is literature?

"I shall present these pieces as the spoils of Stoneleigh," I told her. "You will recollect that my cousin, Mr. Thomas Leigh, inherited Stoneleigh Abbey from Lady Mary Leigh when she died some years ago; and being a widower, and quite childless, it should not be wonderful if he were to give Lady Mary's jewels to his nearest relations. Having no occasion to wear such showy finery, the Austen ladies—being of a practical turn—determined to find what price the jewels might fetch; and you, our worldly friend, were good enough to consider of Rundell & Bridge."

Eliza weighed this confection of lies with a pretty air of judiciousness. "Your Leighs are all descended, are they not, from a sister of the first Duke of Chandos? I think it should serve. But recollect, Jane, that in the telling of falsehoods, simplicity is *all.*"

"I cannot claim your degree of experience," I returned in Cassandra's most prudish manner; and we achieved Ludgate Hill in silence.

IT WAS TOO EARLY AS YET FOR MOST LADIES TO BE ABROAD, and we were fortunate to find the shop barren of custom when we descended from the hack. One cannot be too careful, when bartering valuables, to go unobserved by one's acquaintance—lest rumours spread as swift as contagion. The jeweller's door was opened by a liveried footman, and Eliza swept into the room with all the *éclat* of a grande dame, glancing imperiously about as tho' an Unknown had offended her. I followed with the large box in my hands, more in the role of paid companion than sister of the bosom; my mouth was dry and my heart pounding.

The room was narrow and long, lit by oil lamps suspended from the ceiling; display tables lined with velvet were set against the walls. A few gilt chairs were arranged near these, to accommodate selection; and a neat clerk in a dark blue coat and buff breeches stood alertly at the far end of the shop. When we failed to glance to either side, ignoring the settings of miniatures, the eye portraits cunningly lapped in draperies, the parures of emeralds and diamonds, or the amethyst bracelets that are everywhere the mode—this person came forward immediately and bowed.

"May I be of service, ma'am?"

"Pray present my card to Mr. Rundell," Eliza replied briskly. "We wish to speak with him privately."

She had barely concluded the words when a door at the rear of the shop opened, and a white head was thrust out. A pair of bold blue eyes, aloof and calculating, swept over us, missing nothing of the significance of the parcel I held.

"Comtesse," the apparition said, "good day to ye. Will ye be so good as to step back?"

Eliza inclined her head, motioned for me to go before, and the quiet elegance of the premises was exchanged for a spare room graced only by a desk and a strong oil lamp, a ledger and a quill to one side.

"I have brought my sister Miss Austen to you, Mr. Rundell," Eliza said without ceremony as the jeweller held out a chair. "She requires an opinion as to the value of certain heirlooms come down through the Austen family, and being upon a visit to my husband in London, could do no better than to consult the foremost jeweller of the day—or so I urged her. 'Mr. Rundell will never toy with you, my dear, for he knows his reputation to be founded on honesty and discretion.'"

"Did you say so, indeed?" He glanced from my countenance to Eliza's, his own impassive. "Obliged to ye, Countess. Let us see what you've brought then, madam."

I opened the parcel, lifted out the velvet roll the Comtesse d'Entraigues had left us, and unfurled it before Mr. Rundell's eyes. The myriad stones flared and danced under the light of the oil lamp, wickedly alive.

There was the briefest silence.

Mr. Rundell raised a quizzing-glass and bent low over the jewels, staring deep into their depths, passing with decision from one to another, lifting now this brooch and that ring, intent as a hound on the scent. An eternity might have passed thus, the room filled with the laboured sound of the old man's breathing and the sick feeling of deceit growing in my stomach; but that Eliza said, with the barest suggestion of doubt, "I believe these came to you through your mother's family, Jane? Some relation of... the first Duke of Chandos, was it not?"

The spell was broken; Mr. Rundell sighed, dropped his glass, and looked me accusingly in the face. "These were never made in England."

"No." I glanced swiftly at Eliza. "My knowledge of their origin is imperfect, but I believe many to have been acquired from certain jewellers in France... before the Revolution."

"Oh, aye," Mr. Rundell agreed drily; "you'll not be finding the like o' *these* among the Corsican set what rule France now. All for swans and bees, they are, and twaddle out of Egypt. No, these are the true gems of my old master's day, long before either of you ladies was thought of."

He lifted a ruby necklace in his fingers, and studied it intently with his glass. "I believe as tho' I've seen this before," he mused. "For cleaning, maybe—or to have reset. Dook o' Chandos, ye say?"

He reached for his ledger and my heart sank—for if he determined to place the jewels, we were entirely undone—but Eliza interposed hurriedly, "If my sister wished to sell, Mr. Rundell, what price should these stones fetch?"

"Sell?" he repeated, as tho' bemused. "Well, now, Countess—that would depend upon the interest of the buyer."

"And what is *your* interest, sir?" I demanded boldly—for I felt it incumbent upon me to act as principal in the transaction. "I am, as the Comtesse says, in London but a short while—and should be glad to despatch this commission. I confess I am hardly easy in having such a treasure by me, in Sloane Street."

"What lady would be?" Mr. Rundell agreed. The ledger was allowed to languish in its place; his entire attention was fixed upon me. "The premises of this shop are very secure, ma'am—very secure, indeed. I might venture to hold these stones on your behalf, until such time as a price is agreed upon between us, if indeed you are determined to part with your...heirlooms."

"I have no occasion to wear such precious stuff." I dropped my eyes demurely, the picture of spinsterly deprecation. "My dear father is dead, Mr. Rundell, and my brothers much preoccupied with their hopeful families—I am quite alone in the world—in short, I find that this princely bequest would serve me far better if transmuted to a different form. I hope I make myself clear?"

"Perfectly, ma'am. But I cannot hope to offer you a reasonable price without an interval of reflection. I should be cheating you else."

"Could you put a round figure to the whole, Mr. Rundell?" Eliza asked.

He pursed his lips. "The settings are decidedly out of mode, Countess—none but a dowd would be seen to wear them now without they was reset—and the price of gold has sadly fallen in recent weeks—"

"Tush." I made as if to rise from my chair. "You were mistaken, Eliza, in your opinion of Mr. Rundell. I think perhaps I should have followed my own inclination, and consulted Mr. Phillips in Bond Street."

"Not so hasty, if you please," he said, lifting one hand. "The settings are old and the price of gold is fallen sadly—"

"—At the height of *war*, Mr. Rundell? That is not what we hear from my brother the banker. The price of gold has, if anything, risen—"

"But it is undoubtedly true," he continued as tho' I had not spoken, "that the gems themselves are of the finest, and should fetch a pretty penny. If you will trust me with the lot for a matter of two days, I will undertake to state my very best price. You won't get as good from Phillips in Bond Street nor Gray in Sackville Street neither. They're warm men, but they haven't Rundell's means."[2]

"Very well," I answered, with just the faintest suggestion of unwillingness. "Write out a receipt for these items, if you please, and I shall return in two days' time."

"Done." Mr. Rundell scrawled his name on a square of hot-pressed paper and handed it to me with a flourish.

Eliza was so relieved to have the business concluded, that it was quite an hour before I could tear her from the contemplation of the amethyst bracelets strewn about the shop's casements.

---

[2] To be "warm" in Jane's day was to be wealthy. According to Charles Greville, a contemporary of Austen's, Rundell was so rich he was able to lend money to his bankers during the financial panic that followed Waterloo. When he died at the age of eighty, Greville notes, Rundell left the largest fortune then registered under a will at Doctors Commons—some million and a half pounds.—*Editor's note.*

Chapter 6

The Cyprian on Parade

Wednesday, 24 April 1811, cont.

~

OUR ERRAND HAPPILY CONCLUDED AND THE WEATHER holding fine, we ordered our hackney carriage to Gunter's establishment, and regaled ourselves with pastries and tea, followed by a thorough debauch among the volumes of Lackington's book shop—a vast room lined with shelves and clerks poised on the steps of ladders necessary to reach them, a vision so replete with the printed word that I stood as one stunned, incapable of voicing a request for full seven minutes. Mary Brunton's *Self-Controul* then offered as the ardent object of my writer's soul—it being the only novel talked of in London this April—but in vain; among all that wealth of books, not a copy of Brunton was to be had. Eliza quitted Lackington's with a volume in the French, and I with some poems of Cowper and a dissatisfied heart. Of what use is it to reside for a time in the very centre of the world, surrounded by every possible whim or comfort, if one cannot obtain *Self-Controul*?

Having spent all our money, we made a virtue of necessity, and extolled the benefits of exercise in walking the remainder of the way to Hans Town.

"Only think, Jane," Eliza observed as we bent our steps towards Hyde Park, "what it shall be to find *your book* in Lackington's window! I am sure I shall faint!"

"It could never be deemed worthy of such prominence," I said despairingly. "It shall be thrust with the other lamentable publications beneath the counter, there to languish unread—or abused by every rational critic as the most vulgar and silly effusion yet offered by an ill-educated ape-leader. What can I have been thinking, Eliza, to throw Henry's money after such folly? —When there are already so many books in the world!"

"But none can boast a creature half so entertaining as Willoughby, I assure you, nor half so . . . so *improving*. . . as Elinor. Jane—" She stopped short, shading her eyes with one hand. "Is not that the old Count I espy before us? In animated conversation with the ladies in that *very dashing* perch-phaeton? I wonder if he is forever speaking to them in French!"

I should judge it to be nearly three o'clock in the afternoon—a fashionable hour to promenade in the Park, whether by foot, horse, or carriage; and the parade was thronged with parties of young ladies in open carriages, Corinthians astride their showy hacks, and sedately strolling misses in the company of chaperones. There was also, I may add, a quantity of those persons commonly known as the Muslin Company: showy hacks of a different kind of animal, also intended for a gentleman's pleasure. My mother should have called them Bold Pieces, and abhorred their display of charms; but the present age held such women in something like admiration, as might be divined from the euphemisms commonly applied to them: High Flyers, Fair Cyprians, Birds of Paradise, Snug Armfuls, Barques of Frailty, Demi-reps. These were not the common women of the streets, but mistresses of the highest order, who lived under the protection of a variety of swains to whom they offered a fidelity commensurate with the quantity of gold laid out to secure it. The dashing perch-phaeton Eliza had espied was certainly commanded by one of these: a golden-haired, ringleted creature of perhaps seventeen, who tooled the ribbons of a very fine pair of matched greys. The phaeton was of a sort usually driven by a gentleman rather than a lady; and this daring, coupled with the extraordinary cut of the girl's habit, must draw the attention of every male eye.

"It does not do to stare, of course," Eliza observed reprovingly, "when a gentleman of one's acquaintance is in conversation with such a person; one ought to affect an interest in the opposite side of the parade. But do you think it possible, Jane, that we see before us poor Anne's rival? The agent of all her fears? The girl is very lovely, I daresay—but barely out of the schoolroom!"

I did not immediately discern Comte Emmanuel-Louis d'Entraigues, who was supported by an ebony walking cane, his grey hair surmounted by a showy beaver. But an instant's study revealed the elegant scholar of Barnes, Surrey: a man in his middle fifties, well-dressed but with something foreign in the cut of his coat; a figure once elegant and strong but now tending to corpulence; a Gallic beak of a nose and a pair of lips that might be judged either sensual or cruel. The hands alone were still very fine: untouched by labour or traf- fick with the world, accustomed to the handling of leather- bound volumes and *objets d'art*—such as the girl who now dimpled down at him, a confection of innocent beauty and knowing vice.

I studied the creature's complexion of rose and cream, straight line of a nose, and wide sapphire eyes; there was breeding as well as beauty there, if one chose to find it, yet the girl would never be taken for other than an adventuress. Her carriage dress was too formed to her body, and the décolleté plunged as deep as a ball gown's. A dark blue hussar's cap was set at a raking angle over her brow, and guinea-gold curls clus- tered at the nape of her white neck. There was something fa- miliar in her looks, tho' she was entirely a stranger to me ... and then I had it: in figure and countenance, she might have been Anne de St.-Huberti's younger self.

"I cannot put a name to that little Bird of Paradise," Eliza whispered, "but her companion is none other than Harriette Wilson, the most accomplished Cyprian in London. You will recollect the box at the Opera House—the Ponsonbys and Mr. Canning ..."

At that moment the Comte laughed in appreciation of some saucy remark; the girl in the phaeton lifted her whip carelessly over her horses' backs; and the equipage surged forward. I am no judge of horsemanship, having never mas- tered the art—but the girl handled the ribbons well. Cer- tainly Miss Wilson was in easy looks as the pair flashed by, upright and animated with two burning spots of colour in her cheeks; but it is not in the nature of a Cyprian to betray fear or doubt. Her style is bound up in confidence, she does not lay herself open to criticism or rebuke.

"I used to dash about myself in that way," Eliza said wistfully. "I kept a neat little gig—a two-seater, Jane—and put Pug on the seat beside me. I daresay the equipage should be accounted unbearably dowdy now, but it was all the crack when I was a young widow, and had the leisure to consider of such things. I was used to take up a gentleman of my acquaintance for a delightful coze, and then set him down when another presented himself; one might spend an hour very agreeably in flirting about the Park. But Henry is so tiresome—he actually refuses to keep a carriage in London. To be setting up one's stable is so very dear!"

It was a fair description of Harriette Wilson's way of life, I thought—the taking up and setting down of gentlemen—but one cannot tool round the Park forever and ever. Age advances. Younger women appear to attract the gentlemen's eye. One finds oneself no longer the driver, but the companion— grateful to be offered a place even in a rival's perch-phaeton. I supposed this was, in a sense, Anne de St.-Huberti's fate—she who had been both performer and mistress in her salad days; but having achieved a measure of respectability, was it remarkable that she remained at her husband's side?

"Would not it be preferable for the d'Entraigueses to part," I suggested doubtfully, "than for your friend to endure the Comte's vicious propensities?"

"Lord, no," Eliza countered. "You must know, Jane, that gentlemen will have their amusements. You are not a married lady, and indeed it is highly improper in me to be telling you this—but in the general way men are not formed for the marriage vow. I do not speak of your brother, mind. Henry is a jewel past price, for all he is so pinch-penny as regards horses. But my mother was wont to observe: *Eliza, so long as your husband treats you with tenderness, you have no business nosing into his affairs.* The Muslin Company are of a piece, you know, with their gambling debts—their clubs—their cockfighting and sport— We cannot be expected to understand it."

Advice in this vein from Eliza's mamma—the late Philadelphia Hancock—was not to be lightly put aside; she was commonly believed to have formed a liaison while in India with so exalted a personage as Warren Hastings, the former Governor-General of Bengal, who had settled a fortune on Eliza. Indeed, my cousin was generally assumed to be Hastings's natural daughter. Such easy habits of intimacy among the Great went unmentioned in the Steventon parsonage of my childhood; unquestionably, Eliza was more conversant with the habits of the *ton* than I should ever be.

"If the Comte has actually demanded a divorce, however...?"

"—Then he has flouted every rule of a gentleman's conduct," she replied indignantly, "and that will be the Frenchman in him, I daresay. One may offer a woman *carte blanche,* Jane—one may indulge in every kind of ruinous expence... bestow high-bred cattle and equipages of the first stare... the lease of a quiet little house in a good part of Town...but one does not *marry* a Cyprian. If d'Entraigues cannot be brought to understand this, then we must assist poor Anne, as we did this morning, to provide against the dreaded future. *Lord!* —He is upon us, Jane—school your countenance to welcome!"

"*La petite Elis-a!*" cried the Comte d'Entraigues, his arms opened wide and the ebony stick dangling; "*comme c'est beau d'encontre mes amies!*"

I curtseyed at his bow; allowed him to kiss my gloved hand; and resigned myself to an interval of conversation entirely in the French. But my thoughts were running along different lines. If the Comte could violate every rule, why could not *Jane?* The old roué had done nothing to attach *my* loyalty.

"What a very charming young woman you were speaking with just now, Comte," I said with an air of benign vacancy. "An accomplished one too! Such an air of dash! And such command of the reins! I was quite overpowered. Pray tell me her name—I long to know it."

Eliza gave a tiny squeak, and for an instant I thought the old Frenchman would pretend not to understand me.

"You have not been very long in London, I think," he observed in heavily-accented English. "It is most improper in you to enquire, Miss Austen. But me—I have never been one to observe the proprieties. Her name is Julia Radcliffe—and if she were not the Devil's own child, I should call her *une ange!* Now forget the name, if you please—or your so-good brother Henri will accuse me of corruption!"

I affected a look of bewilderment, and Eliza turned the conversation; until at reaching the tollgate at the western edge of the Park, the Comte bowed, and went his own jaunty way.

"Julia Radcliffe!" Eliza burst out once the Frenchman was beyond hearing. "No wonder he insists upon divorce! Marriage is the only card he holds!"

"What do you mean, Eliza?"

"I have it on certain authority, Jane, that Julia Radcliffe—for all she is the merest child—is the Highest Flyer in the present firmament, the most sought-after Demi-rep in the Beau Monde—and that she should even look at d'Entraigues is beyond wonderful! Our Comte has never been very plump in the pocket, you know, since the Revolution—and it is certainly not *he* who pays for those matched greys. Marriage is all such a man may offer—and indeed, all Julia Radcliffe might value! Money she has; the hearts of a legion of Bond Street beaux are already in her keeping; but *respectability*, my dear—the certainty of a name and protection to the end of her days—is a prize no Demi-rep may command. Harriette Wilson once thought to be the Duchess of Argyll, I believe— but in the event, Argyll considered of what was due to his station, and dropped his handkerchief elsewhere."

"Men are such fools, Eliza," I said, gazing after the old Count.

"To be sure, my dear. Else they would never be so amusing. Only consider of your Willoughby! He should be enslaved to a Julia Radcliffe—she was a girl of very good family, you know, until just such a young gentleman gave her a slip on the shoulder. There is a child, I believe, somewhere in Sussex— However, none of the Radcliffes will notice her now."

"She does not seem to pine for the lack," I observed, and stepped through Hyde Park gate.

Chapter 7

The Man Who Did Not Love Women

~

THE SPRING RAINS DESCENDED UPON LONDON AN HOUR before dawn, sluicing across the roof tiles and gurgling in the gutters, so that I dreamed I lay at the edge of a country brook in the wilds of Derbyshire. As is common with such dreams, I lived and breathed the air of the place while yet cognizant I was but a visitor—that my time and purpose were not of that world. I knew full well that I dreamed. When the elegant figure of Lord Harold revealed itself, therefore, under the shade of a great oak—silent yet welcoming, completely at its ease—I perceived with anguish that this was a memory: for we two had walked once through the woods and fields near Chatsworth. He fell into step beside me, companionable as ever; restful in all he did not need to say. When I told him impulsively that I loved him still, he kept his eyes trained on the middle distance, a derisive smile on his lips.

I awoke with a start, seared with thwarted yearning, and the dissatisfied knowledge that I should have preferred to walk forever in that enigmatic presence. He had offered no word; the beloved voice was silenced. I stared out despondently through the bed-curtains at the windowpanes streaming with rain. There would be no walks in the Park this morning, no rejoicing in the fresh sprays of lilac; this was a day for the nursing of colds, for books by the fire and the industry of the needle— for bemused scavenging in the lumber-rooms of memory.

The clatter of carriage wheels in Sloane Street below— unusual for the early hour—then drew my attention: a train of vehicles, of the most sombre black, was wending its way east. The second equipage bore a device on its door that was tantalisingly familiar—a gryphon's head chained to an eagle's, in red and gold. I knit my brows, endeavouring to recall where I had seen it before; and at that moment the carriages came to a halt. The lead horses stamped fretfully, coats steaming in the rain; a sleek black head was thrust out of the magnificent travelling coach, and a question barked in a foreign tongue. Something guttural and exotic in the consonants—it must, it could only be, Russian. Princess Tscholikova's family had descended upon London at last.

The harsh words achieved their effect; the train of carriages slowly turned the corner into Hans Place. Would this potentate of the steppes bury his dead Princess with all possible speed? Or would he demand a full enquiry into the nature of her death?

And why did I persist in believing the suicide was false—a bit of theatre for the credulous *ton*?

Theatre. The Theatre Royal, where the Princess had sat, elegant and composed, her countenance earnest as she gazed at Lord Castlereagh's box. But a few hours before her bloody end at his lordship's door, the woman I'd seen was hardly on the brink of madness. I did not think she had ever been. I pulled the bed-curtains closed, and went back to sleep.

"Henry," I said as we hastened up the steps of the British Gallery a few hours later, intent upon the watercolour exhibition, "what do the members of your club say, regarding Princess Tscholikova's death? How does the betting run—for or against Castlereagh, and murder?"

"We do not have the kind of betting book you should find at White's, Jane," my brother tolerantly replied; it is Henry's great virtue that nothing I may say will ever shock him. "Nor does it approach what you should discover at Brooks's. Your Lord Harold was a member of both clubs, I believe—but such company will always be far above my touch. The members are more careful of their blunt when they have earned it themselves. All the same, I have laid ten pounds upon the outcome's being suicide—and know the odds to be rising steadily in my favour."

"Had I ten pounds to wager, I should challenge you," I instantly replied. "I had no notion you were such a pigeon for the plucking, Henry! There has been no mention of a weapon in the papers; and if none was found, depend upon it, the Princess was killed by another's hand. It remains only to determine whether Castlereagh's was that hand."

"By no means," Henry countered, as we paused before a

delightful picture of the sea that my Naval brothers should have roundly abused, for its ignorance of the properties of both warfare and nature. "It is probable that the coroner charged with the lady's inquest prefers to keep the particulars of the case to himself, until such time as the panel is assembled."

"When is the inquest to be called? I have seen no mention of it in the papers."

"Ah! In this you will find the true worth of the clubman," Henry replied with satisfaction. "Tho' it was thought the affair would be hastily managed—a verdict easily returned—there was some little delay, I collect, at the request of the Princess's family. A representative desired to be present; a brother, I believe. The inquest is called for ten o'clock tomorrow morning—in the publick house next to the Bow Street magistracy. Any number of bets ride upon the outcome; most of your Pall Mall loungers will be crammed into the room."

"Would you escort me there, Henry?"

"Good Lord, Jane!" he cried, startled. "I cannot think it proper. However many panels you may have seen in recent years, they are as nothing to a Bow Street affair."

"But the magistracy is only a step from your bank! You know you will never resist the temptation to look in upon the proceedings."

"What has that to say to *your* presence?"

"Do not play propriety with me, Henry," I told him warningly. "I am no more broken to saddle than Eliza. If you do not agree to escort me to Bow Street, I shall walk the whole way by myself."

Henry stopped still in the middle of the gallery, the

stream of visitors flowing around us like rainwater round a pebble. "Jane, I cannot think you a victim of vulgar curiosity. Why does the lady's self-murder trouble you so?"

"I cannot credit it."

"—Tho' she was a stranger to you? Tho' you are entirely unacquainted with her history, her morals, her character?"

"I might learn more of all three from the coroner's inquest," I observed.

Henry lifted his hands in amazement. "A formality, merely! The whole business cannot demand above an hour—and will conclude as it began, with the judgement of suicide!"

"You do not credit Lord Moira's opinion? —That the lady was killed by another, and Castlereagh must certainly fall under suspicion?"

"I do not. The Earl is a Whig, Jane, and should wish calamity upon all Tories even had the Princess never been born."

I strolled towards a depiction of Attic ruins. "Tell me about Lord Castlereagh. What sort of man is he?"

"Respected by many, but loved by few. A cold fellow of decision and despatch, but pig-headed by all accounts and incapable of compromise. Lord Castlereagh must and shall be judged correct, in all his dealings, and will brook no criticism. Such a man may command well enough in the field— but may swiftly bring disaster on his government colleagues at home."

"You describe the arbiter of policy, Henry. I would learn more of Robert Stewart, the man. What are his passions? His attachments? His loyalties?"

My brother hesitated. "I cannot rightly say. I am hardly intimate with his lordship; I know only what I read of him in the papers, and what Eliza may tell me. She is a little acquainted with Lady Castlereagh, who is forever throwing open the house on Berkeley Square to all the world."

"Has he any children?"

"None."

"Perhaps there is no love between the lord and his lady."

"I cannot undertake to say. The marriage has endured for many years, and no breath of scandal has attached itself to the principals—until the *Morning Post* chose to publish the Princess Tscholikova's private correspondence. Indeed, had she written to anyone other than his lordship—George Canning, perhaps, or another Tory member—I might have been less surprised. It is a part of Castlereagh's coldness to find little of beauty in any woman. He prefers the society of gentlemen."

"What! He does not frequent the Muslin Company?"

"Jane!" Henry replied, with an expression of distaste. "What has Eliza been teaching you?"

"Nothing I did not already know."

"To my knowledge, Castlereagh is singularly disinterested in women of that order."

"—And our Henry is all astonishment! Is a Barque of Frailty so necessary to a gentleman's comfort?"

"In one way, at least: the company such a woman attracts is vital to any man of policy. You can have no notion, Jane, of the gentlemen who assemble in Harriette Wilson's salon each evening—both Whigs and Tories may be found there. Lady Cowper's drawing-rooms—or Lady Castlereagh's—are as nothing to it. Some of the most powerful movers in the Kingdom meet at Harriette Wilson's feet; and I do not scruple to say that more decisions of moment are taken in her company than in the House of Lords. One is neither Whig nor Tory in Miss Wilson's circle; one merely worships at the altar of the divine Harriette."

"I have it on excellent authority that her star is on the wane," I said. "Julia Radcliffe has supplanted her."

"Now you would speak of Canning's latest flirt," Henry said.

"Mr. Canning should never be adjudged *cold*, then, by his fellows?"

"Far from it. No less exalted a personage than Princess Caroline was once the object of Canning's gallantry, if you will believe; and tho' he is spoken of as a devoted husband and father, his family does not reside in London.[1] The eldest son is sickly, and must be often in the care of a particular physician; Mrs. Canning is quite a slave to her child, and neglects her husband. Canning was used to be met with often at Harriette Wilson's—and I understand it was she who introduced Julia Radcliffe to his society."

"Eliza would have it that Radcliffe is beloved of the Comte d'Entraigues."

"Indeed?" Henry stared at me in some amusement. "Canning and d'Entraigues were once great friends—tho' I do not see them go about together so often now that Canning is out of government. Perhaps the Barque of Frailty has come between them."

"Princess Tscholikova was also acquainted with d'Entraigues," I mused, "for his wife told us as much; but I cannot see how *that* is to the point."

"None of this *highly* diverting gossip will have anything to say to the murder—self-achieved or otherwise—of the Princess," Henry observed. "You had better seek for your information in Bow Street, Jane."

---

[1] Princess Caroline of Brunswick was the estranged wife of the Prince Regent, later George IV.—*Editor's note.*

"And yet—the rumour surrounding a man may reveal so much of his character," I returned. "I am endeavouring to make Castlereagh's out. He is, after all, at the centre of this business. If all you say of his lordship's probity and coldness is correct—then the idea of his entanglement with the Princess is absurd. But there on his doorstep she was found! Can this be *Canning's* revenge, perhaps? Having been worsted in a duel, did he think to ruin Lord Castlereagh with scandal—and sacrifice the Princess to his ends?"

Henry snorted. "George Canning's ambitions are everywhere known, Jane—but not even Canning would risk hanging in the service of such a cause. You indulge the worst sort of lady's fancy, and make of a gentleman an ogre."

"I wish it were more the fashion for ladies to study politics, Henry," I said despondently. "I am persuaded the answer to the Princess's death lies *there*—with the powerful men surrounding her—and yet the web of faction is so tangled, I cannot see *how*."

"You are missing Lord Harold, Jane." My brother slipped my hand through his arm, and led me further into the gallery. "What do you think of that portrait? I cannot admire a likeness taken in watercolour; I am all for Mr. Lawrence, and his oils."

Chapter 8

The Lumber-Room
of Memory

Thursday, 25 April 1811, cont.

~

HENRY HAD SPARED MORE THAN AN HOUR FROM HIS BANK-ing concern to guide me through the exhibition, which be-ing newly mounted, was the object of the Polite World's interest for a fleeting time; so numerous were the patrons, that I confess I was nearly crushed in navigating the nar-rower passages. Picturesque landscapes, and vignettes of the sea; portraits of beauty and youth—they each had something to recommend them; but in truth my attention was equally held by the personages I saw everywhere around me. In a Hampshire village as intimate as Chawton, the society is un-varying; its delights are to be found in the small but telling transformations of personal character over time. In London, however, the richness and variety of the spectacle—in dress, equipages, retinues, and remarks—is an endless enticement to the ear and eye. I could not divide my time equally between the gallery walls and the opulent crowd milling about me; and so at length professed myself exhausted, and ready to quit the place.

Henry saw me safely into a hackney cab, being intent upon his offices in Henrietta Street; and tho' the day was advancing, and I was a little tired, and considering of the last few pages of my book yet to be proofed, I let down the window of the coach and directed the driver in an entirely opposite direction to Hans Town.

"Pray convey me to the chambers of Mr. Bartholomew Chizzlewit," I told him, "in Lincoln's Inn Fields."

Henry was correct. I *was* missing Lord Harold.

I first made the redoubtable Chizzlewit's acquaintance nearly two years ago, in the cottage at Chawton which is now my home. Mr. Chizzlewit had journeyed from London for the sole purpose of putting into my hands a strange and enduring legacy: the private papers, correspondence, and journals of Lord Harold Trowbridge, second son of the fifth Duke of Wilborough: intriguer, man-about-town, and government spy. The Gentleman Rogue, as I was wont to call him, had long been an acquaintance of mine—having fallen in my way some years before, at the home of a friend newly-widowed and beset by unpleasantness. Lord Harold progressed from an object of suspicion to one of profound attachment; his virtues being almost indistinguishable from his vices, his character one of iron tempered by great sorrow, his scruples unexacting as to means and almost wholly taken up with ends—he was, in short, the agent of my instruction in the ways of the Great World, and the most cherished friend of my heart. He was killed by a Buonapartist agent some three years ago; and I have not yet learned to supply his loss. But his papers, when I have the time and means to consult them, are a great comfort to me—reviving, for a little, the impression of his voice and mind, in the very signature of his hand.

They are also, I may add, a dangerous repository of intelligence, which any number of personages might do violence to obtain. There is enough matter stored in Lord Harold's Bengal chest to end careers, induce violent hystericks, urge divorce or pistols at dawn—and having encountered the murderous effect of his lordship's legacy in my own quiet Chawton, I resolved to despatch the chest to the security of Bartholomew Chizzlewit, who had served as his lordship's solicitor almost from the cradle. Mr. Chizzlewit accommodated me with alacrity, and refused all my attempts at payment—remarking, in his enigmatic way, that it was a privilege to serve one who had merited his lordship's trust, there being so few yet surviving in the world.

I drew a veil over my face—as behooved a lady reckless enough to consult the Law quite unattended even by her abigail—and paid off the driver at the door of the chambers. The rain had dwindled to a fine mist, but the aspect of the day was lowering and gloomy; Eliza would be dozing over her French novel, and never remark upon my absence. I was impatient beyond reason to settle down with a lamp, the panelled oak door thrust to behind me, and reach once more for the beloved wraith I had glimpsed by that Derbyshire brook only this morning.

A clerk, dressed all in black, suspended his quill as I entered the chambers. These were sensibly, if not richly, furnished with mahogany bookshelves and high tables laden with ledgers; a fire burned merrily in the open hearth; and the scent of cloves, heated by the flames, laced the air. There was no sign of the footmen in green livery who had attended the solicitor in all his state, at his descent upon Hampshire; but perhaps they were employed in Chizzlewit's domestic establishment.

"How may I be of service, ma'am?" the clerk enquired.

"Miss Jane Austen, if you please, to see Mr. Chizzlewit."

The fellow's eyes ran from my bonnet to my boots. The coloured muslin I had chosen for the British Gallery was newly made up, a prize won of this trip to London; but I had been long enough in Town to learn that I presented a neat but hardly dazzling appearance. The usual run of the chambers' patrons were of the cream of nobility, and quite above my touch. The clerk was not impressed.

"Are you expected?" he demanded impatiently.

"No. Is Mr. Chizzlewit within?"

"I cannot undertake to say. If I may send in your card..."

The truth is that I possess none. Country ladies of modest means and uncertain age do not leave their cards at each other's houses; all such formality belongs to Town, and the society of the fashionable select, or such gentlemen of trade as are required to offer their names as surety of respectability. I had never squandered the contents of my slim purse on hot-pressed squares engraved with black ink—but the insolence of this clerk was causing me to regret my providence.

"Pray enquire whether Mr. Chizzlewit is at leisure to receive Miss Jane Austen," I rejoined, my voice overly-loud, "and if he is not—I shall engage to appoint an hour convenient to us both."

"Is there some difficulty, Edmund?" a mild voice enquired—

and I glanced over my shoulder to discover a gentleman younger than myself, in buff pantaloons and a well-made coat of dark blue superfine, his cravat dexterously tied. One of the noble patrons, no doubt—who possessed a card, and was expected, and should never be made to feel shabby-genteel by a person of little manners and less birth.

"This lady is wishful to see you, sir," the clerk answered woodenly. "I was informing her you was engaged."

"But happily you were mistaken," the gentleman said, with the ghost of a smile in his eyes. "I am quite at leisure to consult with . . . Mrs. . . . ?"

"Miss Austen," I said quickly. "But I believe there is a mistake. It is Mr. Chizzlewit I require to consult."

"I am Sylvester Chizzlewit," he returned. "But perhaps you are better acquainted with my grandfather—Mr. *Bartholomew* Chizzlewit?"

"Indeed! He once informed me that the firm's service to the ducal House of Wilborough dated from *his* grandfather's time— and I perceive now that the tradition is an enduring one."

"Wilborough!" The lurking smile broke fully on the gentleman's face, transforming it from polite indifference to the liveliest interest. "And your name is Austen. I believe I may divine your errand, ma'am. Pray allow me to convey you to the private patrons' chamber."

BEFORE DESPATCHING THE BENGAL CHEST TO LONDON nearly two years ago, I had spent any number of hours in organising its contents. Lord Harold had pursued no particular method while amassing his accounts. He had merely tossed his correspondence and journals into the depths of the chest as tho' it were a diminutive lumber-room. Over time his records of travels in India, his schoolboy missives from Eton, his maps of Paris scrawled with marginalia, and his passionate letters to ladies long mouldering in the grave, formed an incoherent jumble. During a succession of winter days in my Hampshire village, I had established my own system of classification as rigourous as any natural philosopher's: at the bottom of the chest I placed the childish scrawls of letters written to his beloved mother; next, his first desperate entanglement with a lady and the dissolute accounts of young manhood: gaming hells, club debauches, meetings at Chalk Farm at dawn.[1] The squandering of a second son's income could be traced in the piles of old debts, the dunning letters of tailors, wine merchants, chandlers, and gunsmiths; the sale of a string of hunters at Tattersall's. The inevitable exile to India filled the next layer, and the layer after that; the fifth Duke's death and his lordship's accession to an uncle's fortune; his investments in the Honourable Company; the Revolution in France and the demand for his talents as a secret government envoy. It was in this guise I had finally encountered him: the Gentleman Rogue at the height of his powers—polished, cynical, adept, and aloof. He caught and held my interest precisely because the greater part of his mind was always withheld from me— who had never found it very hard to understand everybody.

"My grandfather will be pleased to learn that you have paid us this call," Sylvester Chizzlewit told me. "I hope I may assure him of your continued health and happiness, Miss Austen?"

"I am well enough," I replied, "but I collect that Mr. Chizzlewit is not. He no longer sits in chambers?"

---

[1] This was the traditional meeting ground of duelists, outside London.— *Editor's note.*

"He was much beset by an inflammation of the lung this winter, and undertakes a trial of the waters at Bath. We are hopeful they may prove beneficial. Miss Austen, I must beg you to remain where you stand, and avert your eyes, as the measures we have adopted for the concealment of our keys will admit the confidence of no one."

The words were uttered with as much courtesy as the intelligence of his grandfather's indisposition, or his wishes for my continued health; but there was a firmness in tone that brooked no question or delay. I turned my head away, and heard a soft *click* under Sylvester Chizzlewit's fingers, as tho' a panel in the wainscotting had slid back on hidden springs.

"Very well," he said, raising a formidable ring of keys; "we must now seek the mates of these from Jonas."

Jonas, it was presently revealed, was an elderly clerk whose white hair sprouted in tufts about his head, and whose back was stooped with a deformity of the spine. He smiled vaguely when roused from his ledgers in the room adjoining Sylvester Chizzlewit's; his myopic pale eyes roamed over my figure.

"Keys," he murmured, as if to himself. "But can she be trusted? His lordship thought so, aye—but his lordship's dead, isn't he?"

"That will be quite enough, Jonas," Chizzlewit said sharply. "Pray bestir yourself."

The old man sighed, and eased his arthritic frame from the high stool on which it was perched. "None too young, is she, and *not* what his lordship might be expected to favour. A lady-bird, they said, as was in his keeping, but I cannot credit it. Too long in the tooth by half..."

I was put to the blush, and knew not where to look, but

Mr. Chizzlewit preserving a perfect gravity, I attempted in-
sensibility, and followed in Jonas's muttering train.

The clerk led us down a corridor lit by flaring lamps set
into the woodwork, and into a pleasant room devoid of company. A handsome table held down the centre of the room,
and several easy chairs were scattered about, but no fire
burned in the imposing hearth.

Jonas crossed to the chimneypiece, and took up a position on one side. Mr. Chizzlewit stood at the other. Without a
word, the two inserted their keys into indiscernible holes in
the woodwork, and at the count of three, sprang the locks in
a single motion.

The chimneypiece swung outwards, as tho' it were a
door: revealing a considerable chamber behind, inky with
blackness. Sylvester Chizzlewit coolly reached for a taper that
lay on the false mantel, and lit it in the flame of an oil lamp.
Then he held it aloft.

"I must beg you, Miss Austen, not to attempt to look
within. Jonas, we require the Bengal chest."

To be left alone with my treasure was to find again
the comforting embrace of a familiar friend. When the door
of the patrons' chamber had closed behind the solicitor and
his clerk, I ran my fingers over the raised figures carved in
teak (most of them grossly improper), the heavy iron hasps
and hinges, and the sloping initials cut on the lid. Then I
drew an ornate key from my reticule and—glancing over my
shoulder with apprehension, for Jonas's air of mystery was
infectious—set it in the lock.

There were too many riches within. I might have been

tempted to peruse the journals that described his lordship's trek by horseback into the wilds of Central Asia; his visits to the court of St. Petersburg, and his views on the murder of the present Tsar's father; his abduction of a lady from a harem near Jaipur; or his tête-à-tête with Napoleon Buonaparte, in a Paris prison from which he subsequently escaped, in lowering himself through a series of drains—but I had not come to Chizzlewit's chambers solely to indulge in memory. Lord Harold was killed in the autumn of 1808, and if memory served, he had been much taken up with government policy at that time, being newly returned from the Peninsula. George Canning had then held the Foreign Ministry, and Robert Stewart, Lord Castlereagh, the Ministry of War. Lord Harold must certainly have been acquainted intimately with both.

The journal I sought was a slim one bound in bottle-green calf, the chronicle of the Rogue's final year—begun in January of 1808 and ending abruptly with the first few days of November. I skimmed rapidly through several passages; his lordship had been writing from Oporto. The relevant entries spanned several months.

> *... unfortunate that Gustavus IV should be quite mad, as he is the sole ally on which His Majesty may depend in the region of the Baltic ... my man writes from St. Petersburg of the Tsar's threats to our Swedish King, to suggest that if Gustavus prefers to keep Finland, he had much better join with Russia and drive Britain out of these waters ...*
>
> *... seems clear that our intelligence of the Tsar's intentions is wide of the mark. I cannot make out why the reports I obtain are so transparent on the matter, and those that Castlereagh reads directly contradict them ... Thornton*

signs his treaty in Stockholm, and two weeks later Russian troops cross the Finnish border... there is duplicity in all this.

Castlereagh's ten thousand men are sailing north to Gothenburg, with no clear orders and no one but Sir John Moore to save them... he is to defer to a mad king, who wishes to use British troops to seize Zealand from the Danes...

...I am sick at heart that when we most need troops here in Portugal and Spain, they are sent on a fool's errand instead, to bait the Baltic tiger...I cannot make my voice heard in Canning's ministry... he is all for helping the Spaniards to help themselves, but ordnance and funds are lacking... here, where we most require troops to face Marshal Junot, our attention is divided. Do we fight Napoleon, or the Tsar?

...Moira tells me of disputes between Canning and Castlereagh, and fears it will end badly...Canning is everywhere known to be less of a gentleman than Robert, and it is not to be wondered at, his father dead in his infancy and his mother upon the stage, the kept mistress of a dozen men—but one would have thought he would learn loyalty during his days at Oxford...

...this abortive campaign shall be adjudged a failure of Castlereagh's, and a discomfiture to Portland's government...

I could make little of all this; the web of policy, again, too entangled to comprehend. Certainly the abortive defence of Sweden had been followed by the even more ignominious expedition to Walcheren, an island in the Scheldt, which

Lord Harold had not lived to see—forty thousand troops, thirty-five ships of the line, more than two hundred smaller vessels, and very little to show for it, while behind our backs, the French arrogantly installed Buonaparte's brother on the throne of Spain. Again, the pressing need to crush the Enemy in the Peninsula had given way to a fool's errand in the northern seas. Lord Harold was clearly disturbed by a discrepancy in intelligence—but he wrote to himself in these pages, as a man does when he ruminates upon anxieties in his mind: elliptical and reflective, without the need for explanation. Not for the first time, I wished acutely for his living presence.

One name, however, had leapt out at me from the journal's pages: *Moira.* Lord Harold had known Henry's intimate friend, the debt-ridden Earl. I should have expected it; both men had been bred up as Whigs from infancy.

The plaintive sounding of a clock somewhere in chambers alerted me to the fact that the day was much advanced; Eliza would be wondering if I were lost. I slipped the bottle-green volume into my reticule and locked Lord Harold's chest.

ELIZA WAS, INDEED, ANXIOUSLY AWAITING MY RETURN— but it was Madame Bigeon who informed me of the fact. Manon's aging mother answered my pull of the front doorbell. When I would have stepped into the hall, she urged in a rapid undertone, "Pray, mademoiselle, do not for the love of Heaven delay, but go for Monsieur Henri at once!"

"Is it Eliza? She is—unwell?" I managed.

Madame shook her head. "It is the Runners. Bow Street is in the house!"

Chapter 9

The Gryphon and the Eagle

Thursday, 25 April 1811, cont.

~

"FETCH ME INK AND PAPER, AND I SHALL REQUIRE THE HACK-ney to carry a note to Henry," I told madame—but before she could hasten on her errand, a barrel-chested fellow in a dull grey coat and a squat, unlovely hat had barred the passage behind her.

"What's all this?" he demanded, surveying me with a pair of eyes both sharp and small in a pudding face. "Are you the mort what's visiting from the country?"[1]

"I am Miss Austen. This is my brother's house. And who, my good sir, are you?"

The question appeared to surprise him. Perhaps the better part of his interlocutors were too stunned at the awful

[1] *Mort* was a cant term for woman.—*Editor's note.*

sight of a Runner—the terrible gravity of the Law, and New-gate's dire bulk rising before their eyes—to enquire of the man's name.

"Clem Black," he said. "Of Bow Street."

"So I understand." I took off my bonnet and set it carefully on the table in Eliza's hall. "What is your business here?"

I spoke calmly, but in truth was prey to the most lively apprehension on the Henry Austens' behalf. There could be only one explanation for the presence of a Clem Black in the house: my poor brother was even more embarrassed in his circumstances than his partner James Tilson could apprehend. Perhaps there had been a run on the bank. Perhaps Austen, Maunde & Tilson had discovered a discrepancy in the accounts. Perhaps Henry—so recently installed in this stylish new home, with its furniture made to order and its fittings very fine—had felt his purse to be pinched, and had dipped into the bank's funds without the knowledge of his partners.

But at this thought my mind rebelled. Not even Henry—lighthearted and given over to pleasure as he so often was—would violate the most fundamental precept of his chosen profession. When it came to the management of another man's money, Henry was wont to observe, a banker must be worthy of his trust.

"You're a cool one, ain't ye?" Clem Black said with grudging admiration. "The other gentry mort is indulging in spasms and such. If you'd be so good, ma'am, as to come with me—"

I bowed my head and preceded him into Eliza's front drawing-room, where so recently the crowd of gentlemen and ladies had stood, in heat and self-importance, to listen to Miss Davis and her brood in the singing of their glees. Eliza was reclined upon a sopha, Manon engaged in waving a vinaigrette beneath her nose; but at my appearance my sister reared up, her countenance quite pink, and said, "Ah—*not* Henry. I had hoped— Still, it is probably for the best. We may delay the unhappy intelligence as long as possible. Jane, I have wronged you—and I cannot rest until I have assured you that the injury was unknowingly done."

"Hush, Eliza," I murmured, and joined her on the sopha. "What has occurred?"

"That man"—she inclined her head in the direction of a second Runner I now perceived to be nearly hidden by the drawing-room draperies, his gaze roaming Sloane Street as it darkened beyond the window—"that man has quite cut up my peace. Indeed, indeed, Jane, I should never have undertaken the errand had I suspected the slightest irregularity!"

"Eliza, pray calm yourself. Manon—leave off the vinaigrette and fetch some claret for *la comtesse*. You, sir—can you account for the extreme distress and misery you have occasioned in a most beloved sister?"

The man at the window turned. At the sight of his face I drew a sudden breath, for its aspect was decidedly sinister. Two pale agates of eyes stared full into my own; a pair of bitter lips twisted beneath a lumpen mass of nose; and the left cheek bore the welt of an old wound—the path of a pistol ball, that had barely missed killing him. He was not above the middle height, but gave an impression of strength in the quiet command of limbs that might have served a prizefighter.

"You are Miss Jane Austen," he said.

"I am. But you have the advantage of me, Mr.—"

"Skroggs. William Skroggs. I am a chief constable of Bow Street. Do you know what that means?"

"I am not unacquainted with the office—"

"It means," he said softly, advancing upon me without blinking an eye, "that I have the power to drag you before a magistrate, lay a charge, provide evidence, and see you hang, Miss Austen—all for the prize of a bit of blood-money, like. I've done the same for thirteen year, now, give or take a day or two, and I find my taste for the work only increases."

He was trying to frighten me. I stared back at him, therefore, without a waver, my hands clasped in my lap. "Do not attempt to bully me in my brother's house, Mr. Skroggs. His friends are more powerful than yours. Be so good as to explain your errand and have done."

The corners of the cruel mouth lifted. "With pleasure," he said, and lifted a wooden box onto Eliza's Pembroke table.

I recognised it immediately. I had carried it myself into Rundell & Bridge, playing country cousin to Eliza's grande dame.

"How did you come by those jewels?" I demanded sharply.

Bill Skroggs—I could not conceive of him as William— halted in the act of opening the lid. "Amusing," he observed, with a leer for his colleague Clem Black—"I was just about to pose the same question to Miss Austen myself."

I glanced at Eliza in consternation. She was propped on her cushions, eyes closed, a handkerchief pressed to her lips. It was possible she had fainted; but certain that she had no intention of crossing swords with the Runners. It was left to the novelist to weave a suitable tale.

Manon appeared with her wine and began to coax a little of the liquid through her mistress's lips.

"The jewels were given to me," I told Skroggs with passable indifference, "and being little inclined to wear them, I resolved to consult Mr. Rundell, of the Ludgate Hill concern. Was it he who required you to call in Sloane Street?"

"You might say so." Skroggs chuckled. "He's no flat, Ebenezer Rundell—and well aware as how a receiver of swag is liable to hang. You won't find *him* going bail for no havey-cavey mort with a load of gammon to pitch. He come to Bill Skroggs quick enough."

I studied the man's pitiless countenance, and for the first time a chill of real apprehension curled in my entrails. I understood little enough of the man's cant to grasp the full meaning he intended, but had an idea of Mr. Rundell consulting his voluminous ledgers, so close to hand, and finding no record of the Lady Mary Leigh or the Duke of Chandos's ancestral jewels.

"If you would ask how I came by such a fortune in gems," I answered calmly, "I am ready to admit that the tale I told Mr. Rundell was false. There is a lady in the case, who does not wish it known that she desires to sell these pieces. I cannot offer you her name, as I should be betraying a confidence."

The Bow Street Runner threw back his head and howled with laughter. Clem Black joined him in expressions of unholy mirth. I stared at the two men, bewildered. What had I said to send them into whoops?

"Betraying a confidence!" Skroggs repeated, almost on the point of tears. "A lady in the case!"

I rose from the sopha. "Pray explain yourself, Mr. Skroggs. This deliberate obscurity grows tedious."

He left off laughing as swiftly as tho' a door had slammed closed. "You had these gems off a dead woman, Miss Austen, and we mean to know how."

"A dead woman?" I repeated, startled.

He reached into the box and drew out an emerald brooch, in the figure of two mythic beasts locked in combat:

the gryphon and the eagle. I had glimpsed the device only a few hours before—on a stately black travelling coach bound for Hans Place.

"Good God," I said, and sat back down abruptly, my legs giving way at the knees.

"Now," Bill Skroggs said softly, "why don't you tell us all about it, eh? What's this *confidence* you don't care to *violate?* —That you slit the Princess Tscholikova's throat, and left her for my lord Castlereagh to find?"

Chapter 10

Banbury Tales

~

ELIZA GASPED AT THE RUNNER'S WORDS, AND BURST INTO tears; Manon broke into a torrent of French, gesticulating with wine glass and vinaigrette; and as she advanced on Bill Skroggs, his partner moved to the drawing-room door and closed it firmly, his broad back against the oak.

"It was you gave the jewels to old Rundell," Skroggs said, pushing Manon aside as he approached me, "and you who have a story to tell. I'll give you a quarter-hour, Miss Austen, by my old pocket watch; and when the time's sped, it's off to Bow Street."

I have rarely found occasion to wish that among the myriad professions pursued by my brothers—clergyman, banker, sailor, and gentleman—at least one had embraced the Law. In truth, the few country attorneys thrown in my way have been prosy individuals, devoid of humour, exacting as to terms and precise as to verbiage, with a lamentable relish for disputation. In this hour of desperate peril, however, I yearned devoutly for a hot-headed barrister in the family fold: one who might knock Bill Skroggs on his back with a single blow, before serving notice that his sister was not a toy for the magistrate's sport. What I detested most in the Runner's manner was his easy assurance of my venality—no hint of sympathy or doubt lurked in those hard, pale eyes. Innocence was unknown to Bill Skroggs; in his world every soul was guilty of *something*. His exultation was like a hound's that has caught the fox between its teeth. In this I understood the depth of my danger.

Some fleeting thought of Sylvester Chizzlewit coursed through my brain—but such an exquisite gentleman would surely be dining in his club at this hour, and beyond the reach of supplication. Eliza was no support in my hour of need: a lady who has had recourse for fifty years to fits of the vapours, hartshorn, and burnt feathers cannot be expected to show steel in extremis. I should have to attempt to offer Skroggs the truth, and turn the snapping dog on a rival scent.

"You labour under a grave misunderstanding, Mr. Skroggs," I observed, "and one that is likely to cost you your prize money.[1] I know nothing of Princess Tscholikova or her death—"

---

[1] Bow Street Runners were not public servants but professional thief-takers more akin to our present-day bounty hunters. They typically worked for a percentage of the value of any stolen goods recovered; this was their "prize money." As the jewelry belonged to Princess Tscholikova, presumably her family would pay the reward once the gems were recovered. This pursuit of gain made Bow Street Runners typically less interested in justice or the guilt or innocence of those they pursued, and more intent upon the simple recovery of goods. Although they were empowered to arrest suspects and bring them before the magistrate, justice was for the court to determine.—*Editor's note.*

"But you know these rubies and emeralds, and you were cool enough to tell a Banbury story to old Rundell. Isn't that right, Mr. Black?"

"Acourse it is," Clem Black agreed.

"Miss Austen purported to have inherited the swag from the Duke of Chandos, only Rundell had seen the jewels before, and noted the occasion in his ledger. The jewels belonged to Princess Evgenia Tscholikova, who departed this life on Tuesday last. Rundell had the cleaning and resetting of her gems four months since."

"Acourse he did," Clem Black agreed.

"I have already admitted I told Mr. Rundell an untruth," I interjected unsteadily. "I regret the necessity that argued such discretion. An acquaintance begged my sister, Mrs. Austen, to broker the valuation and sale of these gems—and I agreed to stand as their owner. We assumed them to be solely and entirely the property of our friend."

"This would be another Banbury story, Mr. Black," Bill Skroggs intoned wearily.

"Acourse it is," Clem Black agreed.

"Oh, you *stupid* man," Eliza burst out. She sat up as swiftly as a cork bursting from a champagne bottle. "Can you not see that Jane and I are distinctly unsuited to the murdering of the Princess? She was a Long Meg of a woman—built on queenly lines—and neither Jane nor I is much over five feet! We should have had to stand on a footstool to cut the poor creature's throat, and the idea of either of us possessing the nerve—"

"Ah, but there is a *Mr.* Austen to be considered," Skroggs said with avuncular kindness. "It's a gang of thieves I think of, Mr. Black, with murder on the side."

"Acourse it is," Clem Black agreed.

"The Austen party is ideally situated in the neighbour-hood of Hans Town, a hop and a skip from the Princess's door—Henry Austen being known to the lady, perhaps, as a man of business much inclined to lend his blunt to nobles whose purses are to let. Let us suppose he visits the Princess in Hans Place to discuss the matter of a loan, sympathises with the poor lady's embarrassed circumstances, so far from home—kills her when her back is turned, makes off with the jewels—and puts his respectable spinster of a sister and his jumped-up countess of a wife on to the job of selling the loot."

Eliza gasped. "Jumped-up countess! I'll have you know I am everywhere received, Mr. Skroggs, among the highest members of the *ton*! The friends who might end your career in the wink of an eye are legion—"

"Yes, yes, yes," I said crossly, "but none of this is to the point. What you suggest is absurd, Mr. Skroggs, because the jewels were given to us by a Frenchwoman of our acquain-tance, the celebrated opera singer Anne de St.-Huberti, and if you wish to understand how she came by them—I suggest you enquire of *her* husband, rather than Eliza's. I can well imagine the Comte d'Entraigues slitting any number of throats."

"D'Entraigues?" Skroggs gave the name a passable pro-nunciation, as tho' he had heard it before. "Old Royalist fled from the Revolution? White periwig, brocade waistcoats? Fond of walking in Hyde Park of an afternoon, ogling the fe-males?"

"The very same."

Bill Skroggs whistled faintly, and jerked his head at Clem Black. The junior Runner thrust himself away from the drawing-room door. Skroggs gestured with a blunt hand towards Eliza's delicate Louis XV chairs and said, with sur-prising restraint, "May we?"

"But of course," Eliza returned disdainfully. She had left off hiding her face in her handkerchief, and was meeting the Runner's gaze with furious dark eyes. "But if you dare to suggest that *my husband* is capable of slitting any woman's throat—"

"I don't say as I believe you, mind," Skroggs offered judiciously, "but I'm willing to listen to the whole story, even if it is a Banbury tale. How did the Countess come to give you these jewels?"

Eliza told him the sordid history: how the aging singer had seen her power wane over the Comte d'Entraigues; how she had feared for her future, and confronted the demand for divorce; how she had turned to a friend from her salad days, Eliza Hancock Austen, Comtesse de Feuillide, because of the memories the two ladies shared of glittering nights at Versailles. Eliza threatened to veer off at this point into a side-lane of reminiscence, regarding a prince of the blood royal and a musical evening in the Hall of Mirrors; but a delicate kick from my foot returned her to the thread of her tale. She explained how she had considered of her husband's reputation—the probity of his banking concern—the ubiquity of rumour—and urged her sister *Jane* to pretend to ownership of the Frenchwoman's jewels.

"We know no more than you, sir," I added when Eliza had paused for breath. "It would seem incredible that Anne de St.-Huberti is in ignorance of the gems' origin, for she certainly cannot pretend to have held them for years. But perhaps she thought to profit by the sale, did the pieces go unrecognised—and avoid all connexion, if their owner should be divined."

"But, Jane," Eliza protested, "that cannot explain how Anne came by the Princess's jewels. You cannot believe her cognizant of . . . of . . ."

"...Murder?" I supplied. "Any woman who has survived the Terror with her neck intact, must have grown inured to bloodshed. But it is possible, my dear, that she knew nothing of the jewels' origin—but was given them to sell by her husband, and enacted a Cheltenham tragedy for your benefit, replete with Barques of Frailty and threats of divorce. It is all a farrago of lies, naturally."

"I shall *never* receive her," Eliza declared mutinously. "I shall offer her the cut direct, when next we meet!"

"Begging your pardon, Comtesse," Bill Skroggs broke in, "but I'm afraid it will not do."

I stared at him. "Will it not? Whatever can you mean? It must be evident that we speak nothing but the truth! Indeed, sir, we are as much victims of this rapacious scoundrel as the Princess Tscholikova!"

"But you have no proof." He looked from Eliza to me. "One mort's story is very much like another's: part Devil's own malice, part fear of the nubbing cheat. If I was to take any of it as gospel, I'd be the laughingstock of Bow Street."

"Nubbing cheat?"

Skroggs lifted his hand close to his ear, head lolling in a horrible caricature of a broken neck. "Hangman's rope. You'd say anything to escape it, I reckon."

He rose regretfully. "I'll have to lay charges. This tale's all very well, but there's an old saying about the bird in hand being worth two in a bush—and I've got you both to hand, so to speak. Come along, now."

"Mr. Skroggs," I said firmly—Eliza had gone white, her handkerchief pressed once more against her mouth—"what if you were to grant us a measure of liberty, so that we might obtain certain... proofs?"

He laughed brusquely. "As a sort of side-show to your flight to the Continent, ma'am? I do not believe there is any proof *you* could discover that would interest William Skroggs."

"—Not even if we were to learn how the Princess ended on Lord Castlereagh's doorstep? And who, *exactly,* put her there?"

The Bow Street Runner went still, and shot me a rapier look through narrowed eyes.

"Come, come, Mr. Skroggs," I said smoothly. "You cannot be interested merely in the recovery of the stones—for those you have. If it were only prize money you held in view, your end should be satisfied, thanks to Mr. Rundell. Something else draws your interest. You were hired, I collect, not by the Princess's connexions—but by Lord Castlereagh himself, were you not?"

Eliza hiccupped with suppressed excitement.

Skroggs cast a venomous glance at his colleague, Clem Black, as tho' accusing that unfortunate man of betraying him.

"It seems quite obvious," I continued, "from the few words you have let slip, that Princess Tscholikova did not die by her own hand."

The Runner smiled thinly. "Forgive me, ma'am—but you cannot possibly know that."

I shrugged. "No murder weapon has been mentioned in the newspapers. I collect that none was found by the lady. Do you think it was a knife, Mr. Skroggs, or a gentleman's razor that slit the wretched Princess's throat?"

"Either would serve," Skroggs replied with ruthless precision, "but I will not be led into an admission I am enjoined not to make prior to the convening of the coroner's panel. I cannot allow you to spread rumours in this way, Miss Austen. —Being but a suspect criminal, prattling for her life."

"If indeed the poor creature was deliberately and coldly taken," I continued, oblivious to his scruples, "then her killer chose to place her *directly* on Lord Castlereagh's doorstep. The scandal that has followed is everything an enemy of his lordship could desire. I do not for a moment entertain the notion that Castlereagh was himself responsible for striking the Princess down, and leaving her where she fell; such careless disregard for convention is not in his character. Therefore, he was the object of a plot. I have an idea that Castlereagh would wish to know *who* was the party that set out to destroy his reputation and career."

"Naturally!" Eliza cried, "So that he might challenge the fellow to a duel, and put a ball through his heart!"

"Mr. Skroggs refuses to say yea or nay," I mused. "And in his very silence we may read a fatal admission. He *is* in Lord Castlereagh's hire, and the Princess's jewels are merely a foothold on the greater slope he must climb. But how, indeed, shall such a man as a Bow Street Runner penetrate the holy of holies—the inner sanctum of the British *ton*—where, without doubt, Lord Castlereagh's enemy hides?"

I paused for effect. The countenance of William Skroggs was slowly flushing scarlet.

"I hold myself as good as any of them," he said hoarsely.

"No doubt you do." I ran my eyes the length of his figure. "But I fear, my good sir, you will never come within an inch of your killer. You do not possess the air or address—or forgive me, the birth—that distinguish a Bond Street lounger. His native ground will be barred to you. Whereas my sister—*that jumped-up countess...* is everywhere received."

Clem Black snorted derisively. I observed Bill Skroggs's hands to clench.

"You require our help as much as we require your mercy," I declared. "Come, Mr. Skroggs—shall we strike a bargain?"

Chapter 11

Lord Castlereagh Condescends

Friday, 26 April 1811

~

THE MORNING OF THE PRINCESS'S INQUEST DAWNED FAIR and bright, more May than April, with a frivolous breeze that set the horse chestnut leaves to fluttering. I had no share in the innocence of the day, however; I was wrapped around in deceit, the chief object of it my brother.

Upon Henry's return from his bank, Eliza and I had said nothing of the Bow Street Runners' calamitous call. We had enjoined poor Madame Bigeon and Manon to secrecy, and their love for Eliza was so great, that at length they acquiesced—tho' Madame was all for recruiting Henry's wit and stoutness in foiling the brutal intent of the Law. The Frenchwomen's experiences in their native country, and the troubles that occasioned their flight to England, had taught them to trust neither in plots nor constabulary—but to avoid all such authority as might sever their heads from their necks. In this I detected good sense and hard courage, and resolved to employ the two ladies' talents whenever my own should fail me.

I had managed, in the end, to bring Bill Skroggs neatly round my thumb. The Runner had been taught to see the sense of my argument—that Eliza and I should penetrate where he should be barred—and had agreed to accord us our liberty for the space of one week: a mere seven days to defeat the object of a most cunning and subtle killer. I found the constraint of the brief period immaterial; I had always intended to quit London by the end of the month in any case. The imperative to clear my name in the interim merely added a fillip of interest to the waning days of my Season. I had much to do, if I were not to hang.

While Manon ushered the two men to the door, and Skroggs issued his final cold-blooded warnings, I was busy enumerating in my mind the chief points that must be addressed, in an undertaking such as this:

Firstly, did Anne, Comtesse d'Entraigues, know to whom her jewellery in fact belonged, or was it a treasure that had fallen into her lap as chancily as she deposited it in ours?

Secondly, had the Comtesse participated in either the theft of the Princess Tscholikova's jewels, or her murder?

Thirdly, if the Princess had been killed—or her dead body deposited—on Castlereagh's doorstep, who should most benefit from the ruin of his lordship's reputation?

And fourthly, were that person and the Princess's murderer in league—unknown to each other—or were they one and the same?

Eliza went up to her room directly the outer door was

closed on the offending emissaries of Bow Street. She pled her tiresome cold—and when at length Henry returned, he forbore to disturb her. I uttered falsehood after falsehood as we two sat down to a cold supper, furnished without apology or explanation by Madame Bigeon. Henry drank his wine, enquiring idly of my afternoon, and I was free to divert my anxiety by imparting every detail of Chizzlewit's chambers— for my brother had known of Lord Harold's Bengal chest nearly as long as I.

"It would seem, from what you say, Jane, that his lordship was most unhappy with Sir John Moore's conduct of the Swedish campaign," Henry observed. "I believe that gallant general was in fact arrested by King Gustavus, and only escaped Stockholm by donning a peasant's clothes, and making his way through the gates of the city in a labourer's cart."

"Lord Harold utters no criticism of Moore," I said thoughtfully, "and indeed, I have always reflected that Moore's subsequent death in the retreat from Corunna would have deeply grieved his lordship, had he lived to know it.[1] I took the import of his text to mean, rather, that he disapproved of the Government's diversion of force and attention from Peninsular affairs, to those in the Baltic."

"That is perhaps the case," Henry said cautiously, "but I cannot find that troop dispositions made two years since, can have any bearing on the death of a woman in Berkeley Square. Recollect, Jane, that the Prince—rather than serving as unofficial leader of the opposition—now holds the reins of government as Regent; that Mr. Perceval's government is

[1] General Sir John Moore was killed in the British evacuation from Corunna in January 1809.—*Editor's note.*

in flux; that Lord Castlereagh and Mr. Canning came to such blows that they are no longer invested with considerable powers in the Cabinet—as they were when Lord Harold wrote his entry—and thus, that the case is entirely altered! You cannot be forever seeking illumination in those old papers, my dear—tho' it pains me to say as much."

"All the same—I should like to have a little conversation with Lord Moira, Henry. I would be most grateful if you could put me in the way of speaking to him, as soon as may be."

"I should be very happy, Jane." My brother appeared startled. "But why this impatience?"

An idea of the gallows rose in my mind. "My time in London . . . grows short."

"As does mine." He glanced at me ruefully. "I am expected in Oxford on militia business for much of next week. I quit London on Sunday—but rest assured that Egerton will proceed with his printing whether I am present to spur him, or not. Eliza shall be Egerton's taskmaster in my absence."

Would that my novel were all that occupied my heart in the interval!

"You are very good, Henry." I kissed his cheek as I rose from the table. My brother clasped my hand a moment in his before releasing it.

"I need not say how much your presence at such a time must gratify me, Jane. I cannot like leaving Eliza alone when she is in such a case."

A tremor of guilt suffused me. "You would mean . . . her cold? But it is very trifling."

He thrust his chair from the table. "She is hardly as young as she once was. Her indispositions of late have only increased, no matter how many remedies she seeks for them. I will not scruple to disclose that our removal to this house in

Sloane Street was due in part to a desire for a more salubrious neighbourhood. The air in Hans Town is very fresh—it might almost remind one of the country."

"Indeed it might. And now that May is upon us—"

"You do not find Eliza much altered?" my brother demanded. "I tell myself it is only the ravages of the winter, but her health has always been indifferent, Jane—you know her for a most delicate creature."

I perceived that this trouble had been growing upon him, in the quiet evenings of early dusk, through December and January; such is the fate of a man who marries a lady ten years his senior, to be staring always at the prospect of a grave.

"Nonsense," I said. "Eliza is very stout. And I am here to nurse her, with mustard plasters and flannel if necessary. Go to Oxford."

When he would have smiled, and turned for his library door, I added swiftly, "But make my introduction to Lord Moira first, I beg!"

"Is it so important?" The satiric twinkle of my Henry of old was returned once more to his eyes. "I might almost believe you in fear for your life, Jane—so ardent is your desire for instruction in politics! We might look for Lord Moira to attend the inquest into Tscholikova's death on the morrow. Most of the Upper Ten Thousand[2] will have squeezed into the publican's rooms before nine o'clock has tolled."

"Then I shall certainly accompany you," I said swiftly, and bid him goodnight.

I confess I was relieved to learn that my brother would be

[2] The Upper Ten Thousand were the aristocracy of England; the *haut ton.—Editor's note.*

absent for the better part of next week; I had too much to accomplish in those swiftly declining days, and too little guile to manage the business without a full confession. I might expect Eliza to emerge from her sickroom the very moment her husband's hired mare had clattered away from Sloane Street; we would all of us move in greater ease once the ignorant were absent from the house.

For my part, I employed a quarter-hour in writing a brief missive to Sylvester Chizzlewit, Esquire, before snuffing out my candle. It should be sent round to the solicitor's chambers no later than eight o'clock in the morning, with a discreetly-worded plea for his attendance upon me in Sloane Street. I foresaw the need of a gentleman in the coming days—one with an acute and subtle mind—and my brief acquaintance with the Chizzlewit family assured me that the youngest scion should possess such qualities.

As for the inquest itself—I had no fear of being called as witness by the coroner, to account for my dubious brokering of a dead woman's jewels. Bill Skroggs had assured me that the magistrate would permit no mention of the curious theft to be introduced at the proceedings. Death alone was the panel's province; Lord Castlereagh's subtle investigations into a murder were a matter of stealth, to be conducted in the shadows.

THE BOW STREET MAGISTRATE'S OFFICE SITS DIRECTLY OPposite the Theatre Royal, where Monday evening I had obtained my sole glimpse of Princess Tscholikova in life. It is also aptly located hard by a publick house: the Brown Bear, capably run by one Steptoe Harding. On these premises the Runners are wont to rest their weary limbs at the close of the day, and trade tales of the ardours of crime, under the influence of a can of ale or a measure of Blue Ruin. This morning, however, as Henry and I made our way towards Covent Garden, the narrow passage of Bow Street was clogged with carriage traffick that all but prohibited entry to the Bear. It was as my brother had predicted: the cream of London Society had come to learn why a Russian princess had breathed her last on Lord Castlereagh's doorstep.

It was but half-past eight o'clock in the morning, and the inquest was not to be opened until the hour of ten; yet already seats were claimed towards the front of the publican's main taproom, and the knot of persons by the door was five deep, all of them discoursing at the top of their lungs on every subject from movements in the Peninsula to a nobleman's losses in one of the more fashionable gambling hells. Most of the interested parties were gentlemen: some of their faces I recognised. None were of Henry's intimate circle—indeed, these were the Great of London Society: Lord Alvanley, who was extremely wealthy and deplorably intimate with the Prince Regent; Earl Grey, who might hope to lead a government in time, if the Regent deigned to remember his Whiggish friends; Henry, Lord Holland—another Whig, but one for whom I held an indescribable fondness, as having been the object of Lord Harold Trowbridge's trust and esteem for thirty years at least. I have no acquaintance with Lord Holland or his fashionable lady; I shall never dine among the twenty or thirty Select who are summoned nightly to take potluck at Holland House; but I shall always bear him a depth of affection, for having supported Lord Harold in his darkest days.

The scene should have been offensive, were it not so benignly familiar: a crowd of elegant clubmen conversing at their ease in the Brown Bear, while beyond the door of the publick room, the body of Princess Tscholikova must even then await the scrutiny of the coroner's panel: blue and cold, her neck ravaged by a knife or a razor, the remains already giving off a putrid smell at the passage of four days' time. I felt a wild impulse to go to her—to protect this unknown woman from the callous riot of hunting and pugilism, *on-dits* and cockfights, the formation of governments and Perceval's discomfiture . . . I thought to look for Earl Moira, in the hope that I might profit from this interval in furthering acquaintance—but as Henry squeezed politely past a gentleman who must, who could *only* be the ambitious Tory minister, George Canning, I glimpsed the Comte d'Entraigues.

He did not observe me; indeed, I am certain the Comte believed himself ignored. He was standing at Canning's elbow, like an acolyte or a servant; his hands clasped behind his back, his head humbly bowed. I remembered something Henry had said: that Canning and d'Entraigues were intimate once, until *la belle cocotte*, Julia Radcliffe, had divided them. It did not appear as tho' they were divided now.

It was possible the Comte d'Entraigues would offer the cut indirect to so insignificant a person as his despised wife's acquaintance, regardless of the fact that we had met only two days before in Hyde Park—but as I gazed at his raddled countenance, I perceived that the piercing eyes were studying an image behind me. I turned, and saw the sleek black head of the nobleman who had peered from the carriage window through the rain of yesterday morning: the Russian Prince who must be Tscholikova's brother.

He wore black, as did all those in his party—two gentlemen and a figure I recognised as the maid Druschka. All four might have been alone in the room, for all the notice they gave the curious. I did not wish to betray a vulgar interest, and looked instead for my brother.

Henry was already surging forward to claim a pair of seats at the middle of the room. He had no reason to find a foreign grandee of particular note; his attention was drawn, rather, to the suddenly paralysed clubmen behind us. They stood as tho' cast in stone, all their eyes riveted upon a single figure as he paused in the now empty doorway: a tall man, with a pronounced nose and penetrating eyes, and the disordered locks of a fashionable exquisite: Robert, Lord Castlereagh, the dread object of a dead woman's love.

Chapter 12

Dead Letters

~

SIR NATHANIEL CONANT IS MAGISTRATE AT THE BOW STREET office, and it was he who brought the publick room of the Brown Bear to order.

"*Gentle*-men," he sonorously intoned, pounding with the flat of his hand on a scarred oak table, "gentlemen... *and* ladies, *silence* if you please. The enquiry into the shocking and lamentable death of Princess Evgenia Tscholikova in the early hours of Tuesday last, is now called to order—Thomas Whitpeace, coroner for the districts of Covent Garden and Queen Square, *presiding*."

I settled myself in the seat Henry had procured for me, aware that the better part of the fashionable bucks arrayed in the doorway would be forced to stand for the duration of the proceedings. But Robert, Lord Castlereagh, ignored the crush of gawkers and strode regally to the very front of the room, where a scarlet-faced individual promptly offered his own seat to the former member of the Cabinet. His lordship looked neither to left nor right, and might have been alone in the assembly for all the notice he gave his fellows—including particularly George Canning, and the old French nobleman who lingered in his shadow. Castlereagh was exquisitely dressed in a coat of dark green superfine that even I could judge was cut by one of the first tailors of the day—Weston, perhaps, whose quiet elegance should exactly suit his lordship—and kerseymere breeches. His boots shone; but it was his lordship's bearing that inevitably drew the eye.

"I must say, Henry," I whispered to my brother, "he is exceedingly handsome, even for one well past his first youth. Such compelling dark eyes! Such a sensitive line to the mouth! And the turn of countenance, tho' haughty enough, is not unpleasing. It suggests a high courage—which must serve his lordship well in such a place."

"I should give a good deal to learn his knack of tying a cravat," Henry returned. "He wears the *trône d'amour*, Jane. You will observe the creases to be sublime—and requiring no absurdity in the collar-points to achieve the first stare of fashion. His lordship disdains the dandy set, being rather a Corinthian in his tastes—that is to say, that he prides himself on matters of sport. His ability to drive four-in-hand, his patronage of the Fives Court, his precision at Manton's with a pistol..."

My brother's confidences died away. Castlereagh's talent for marking his targets was already too well known.

He was followed at perhaps a half-pace by a gentleman in the neat dress of a political servant. But here all resemblance

to the common herd must end—the gentleman's countenance called to mind the angels; his form, the Greeks. A
paragon of beauty, where most men might prefer to be
called handsome—and I noted more than one indrawn
breath, of surprise and admiration, as his figure made its way
in Castlereagh's wake.

"And *who*, Henry, is that?" I murmured.

"Charles Malverley—third son of the Earl of Tanborough.
He is devilish astute in the upper works, I understand—
serves his lordship as private secretary. Ambitious, and a
great favourite with gentlemen and ladies alike."

At that moment, a communicating door from the far side
of the publick room opened, and a man I judged to be
Thomas Whitpeace paced swiftly towards the coroner's chair.
He was diminutive and spry, a balding man of middle years
blessed with the bright eyes of a bird; and I observed him survey the august crowd with a slightly satiric look.

He cleared his throat, well aware of the devices of
theatre—and there it was again, I thought: the sensation of
being *played to,* in a grotesque drama whose ending was beyond my knowledge. Whitpeace offered no welcome, no
recognition that this was an inquest quite out of the ordinary
way—but announced the names of the panel without further
ado. These appeared to be men of trade for the most part—
citizens of the neighbourhood surrounding Covent Garden,
and thus purveyors of market goods, or the labour that sustained them: wheelwrights, carters, a butcher, and a poul-
terer. Several looked decidedly ill-at-ease; but one, a squat,
red-haired individual with powerful arms, glared contemptuously at the lot of us. Samuel Hays was a smithy, and foreman
of the panel, and *he* was not to be put out of countenance by
a deal of *ton* swells, up to every grig.

I was interested to see whether the man's expression altered after he was conducted, along with his fellows, to view the Princess's decaying corpse—which must have been placed in the room Thomas Whitpeace had just quitted—but upon his return Hays appeared, if anything, more defiant than ever. He was alone in this; the rest of his panel looked quite green.

"Let it be known that Deceased is one Princess Evgenia Tscholikova, so named and recognised by two persons here present who have sworn before the magistrate as to Deceased's identity. We are to consider," Thomas Whitpeace said quietly into the well of expectant faces, "in what manner Deceased came by her death, in the early hours of Tuesday, the twenty-third of April, 1811—whether by mishap, by malice aforethought, or by her own hand. The coroner calls Druschka Molova!"

A stir filled the closely-packed room as the black-clad figure of the maid moved heavily towards Thomas Whitpeace. She kept her eyes trained on the floor, and was followed by one of the men who had accompanied the Russian Prince.

"I am Count Kronsky," this personage said, with a dramatic bow and clicking of his heels, "and I will speak for the maid, as she does not understand the English."

His own accent was so impenetrable that the coroner had to request him to say his piece again, before comprehending it, Druschka following the exchange all the while. When it came to the swearing of the oath, the maid refused, as being contrary to her Orthodox faith; and at length, exasperated by the complexities of multilingual persuasion, the coroner proceeded to his questions.

The story that unfolded was a simple one. Druschka had been raised from a child on the estates of the Pirov family, and was employed as the Princess's personal maid at the time Evgenia turned fifteen, and was presented to the Tsar's court. At the Princess's wedding—which occurred when Tscholikova was seventeen—Druschka had accompanied her mistress to the home of her husband; and from thence she had journeyed to Vienna, later to Paris, and lastly, to London. The maid's fierce loyalty and love for the dead woman was transparent, even through the voice of her interpreter.

"On the night in question," Mr. Whitpeace said, "you last saw your mistress...when?"

At eight o'clock, Count Kronsky relayed, when the Princess had entered a hackney bound for Covent Garden.

"She did not return home that evening?"

No indeed, tho' Druschka had waited faithfully in the hall from midnight onwards, intent upon undressing her mistress and seeing her to bed. She had still been sitting in the hall of the house in Hans Place when the Runner had come from Bow Street, and taken her to view her mistress's corpse.

The coroner had only one further question to put—and this was of so curious a nature, as to give rise to speculation among the audience. He held aloft a fragment of porcelain, perhaps as large as a man's hand, jaggedly broken, and asked whether the maid recognised it.

The elderly Russian turned the fragment over in her fingers, her lined face crumpling. She gave way to racking sobs, quite horrible to hear—and no further communication was possible. Count Kronsky spoke sharply in his native tongue, and seemed on the point of striking Druschka; but Mr. Whitpeace ordered him to let the maid stand down.

As she did so, she raised a streaming countenance and said in guttural English, "It is milady's."

Count Kronsky put a short and brutal question, received his answer, and said, "This porcelain box once held the Princess's jewels."

If a flush suffused my entire body at this, my discomfiture was lost in the general murmur of interest that swept o'er the publick house at the Russian's words. Henry, being too captivated by the drama, paid no heed to my momentary lapse of composure.

"I now call one Joshua Bends," Whitpeace said, "watchman of the Berkeley Square district, to be duly sworn."

Joshua Bends was an elderly person, much afflicted with rheumatism, and so nearly bent double that I wondered how he managed to sit in the narrow wooden box that served the charleys for shelter. He placed a palsied right hand on the coroner's Bible and spoke his oath from a toothless mouth; and when he turned to face the room, I detected the hallmark of senility in his bleared and ill-focused eyes.

"How did you come to be present in Berkeley Square on the morning in question?"

"Hey?" Joshua Bends muttered, his hand cupped around his ear. "What's that, Yer Honour?"

Mr. Whitpeace repeated his query with commendable patience; and Bends lisped through his toothless mouth, "Doing me work, Yer Honour, as is expected. Allus walks right round the square I do, and calls out the hour, as regular as church bells. I've been charley in the square coming on thirteen year, and there's some as says I'm like to die in my box, I am—but I hope as the Good Lord preserves me from the sort o' death that there Princess had. Pale as snow she was, in a crumpled heap on the paving-stones, and me thinking she was in a dead faint, until my boot slipped in the deal o' blood she'd lost in dying."

Mr. Whitpeace made a moue of irritation—his witness had got well beyond him—and said abruptly, "Let us begin as is proper, with the first hour of your labour, my good man. When did you relieve your colleague in the watchman's box near Berkeley Square?"

"At midnight, same as allus. I clapped old Amos Small on the shoulder and woke him from a sound sleep, I did, and sent him off home to his daughter's. The bells of St. George's had just called out the hour. I'm a prompt man. I don't like to keep a fellow waiting, even if he do be asleep."

"And so you took up your place in the box near Berkeley Square as close to midnight as makes no odds," the coroner underlined. "Did you make note of the carriage and foot traffick that passed during your watch?"

"Not partickular," Bends said, once the question had been repeated in order to satisfy his indifferent ears. "I may have seen a deal o' carriages, in and around the square, but as to most of 'em—they lets their cargo off at the door, and pulls to the stable yard. I don't pay no mind. There's allus a gentleman or two on foot, but they comes nearer to dawn, from they hells and clubs in Pall Mall, and the gentlemen is allus jug-bitten—et of Hull cheese—bless 'em."

When asked to explain this descent into the vernacular, the good Bends explained that he meant *drunk as a wheelbarrow.*

"Did you not observe one equipage, at least, to pull up before No. 45, Berkeley Square, and discharge its occupants?" Mr. Whitpeace enquired.

"That'd be his lordship's residence," Bends said, with an eye cast shiftily at Castlereagh. "Happen I did see his lordship's coach at a stand afore No. 45."

"At what time was this?"

"Nigh on one o'clock, by the bells. They rang out but a notion afore the coach came clattering over the stones and pulled-to."

"And did you observe anyone to quit the coach?"

"I saw her ladyship step down from the carriage, and a gentleman I took to be his lordship," Bends said carefully.

"*Took* to be his lordship? Are you suggesting Lady Castlereagh was accompanied into her house in the small hours of morning by a gentleman not her husband?" Mr. Whitpeace enquired smoothly.

The foreman, Samuel Hays, let out a hoot of laughter; and Lord Castlereagh half-rose from his chair, as tho' to fling a protest—or perhaps a glove—in the offending black-smith's face. A hand from Charles Malverley, however, eased his lordship back into his chair; tho' I observed his entire form to stiffen with outrage.

"I can tell a lady from a hundred paces," Bends volunteered affably, "from her way o' dressing the hair and carrying herself—and Lady Castlereagh is allus so outlandish in her modes, I'd never mistake. Known for it, she is—makes a point of drawing notice to herself. It's her way o' cutting a dash, I reckon."

If Castlereagh was not already purple with indignation, I should be greatly surprised; for it is true that Emily, Lady Castlereagh, is known for her outré habits and eccentricities of dress; but as she is perhaps the foremost political hostess of our day, much is forgiven her. The quiet propriety and elegance that characterise her husband's habit are not for Lady Castlereagh; she prefers to shock.

"Let us say that you observed a gentleman we may *presume* to be Lord Castlereagh enter his lordship's abode in company with his lady," Mr. Whitpeace said evenly, "at a little after one o'clock in the morning. And did you observe anyone to quit the Castlereagh residence later during your rounds?"

"I cannot say as I did."

"Did you observe a second equipage to pull up before No. 45, Berkeley Square, at any later hour?"

"I did *not*," Bends said quaveringly, "and how that pore lady came to be a-laying there at the foot of his lordship's steps, with her throat cut and her great dark eyes beseeching of the heavens—"

"Joshua Bends!" the coroner said with great decision, "If you cannot confine your remarks to the questions put, I shall not allow you to offer testimony! Pray tell us what else you observed during the course of your rounds, in the interval between the Castlereaghs' arrival home, and your discovery of Deceased."

In a series of verbal perambulations, the aged charley related how he had discouraged a woman of the streets from plying her trade on the corner of Charles Street; how he had watched Mr. St. John Westbrook weave his inebriated course from Lord Sutherland's private card party to his lodgings in the Albany; how he had walked round the square at three o'clock by St. George's bells, and heard what he took to be a pair of lovers *in extremis* in a closed carriage, pulled up in the mews behind No. 43; and how, having taken a catnap between the hours of three and four, he set out after the sounding of the church bells with his lantern raised, to call out the weather and the o'clock, among the shuttered houses of Berkeley Square.

"What direction did you then take?" Mr. Whitpeace enquired.

"Towards Covent Garden—me meaning to nip over for a can of ale and a bit of bread and cheese, like, as is my custom, afore the breaking of the day. A man can get a bite and sup in Covent Garden all night long, if he's so inclined, what with the carts coming in from the country and the folk setting up for market day. I allus have my bread and cheese after St. George's tolls four o'clock, I do, me being bred up in the country and used to them hours."

Joshua Bends stared defiantly in the direction of the magistrate, as tho' he expected a reprimand from Sir Nathaniel; but the fact of a charley's playing truant in search of sustenance was as nothing to the grosser crimes with which such men are usually charged—everything from the taking of bribes, to the abetting of thieves and the corruption of young women. Sir Nathaniel made no sign he had noted a dereliction of duty.

"You walked to Covent Garden at four of the clock," Mr. Whitpeace observed, "and cannot have been returned to the square much before five."

"Heard the tolling of the bells, I did," Bends retorted triumphantly, "and went about my rounds to call the weather."

"In what direction?"

"Clockwise, Yer Worship. Walked right round the square, I did, on the pavings that runs alongside they great houses. And there she were lying, like a heap of old clothes."

A murmur of unease ran through the room, and Lord Castlereagh shifted in his chair.

"Where, exactly, did Deceased lie?" Mr. Whitpeace asked.

"Across the paving, slantwise, in front of No. 45," Bends replied. "His lordship's house."

"Was Deceased lying on her face, or on her back?"

"Her back. I went to her, o' course, and felt for her life—but as soon as I knelt down beside her I knew it was no use. The blood was that thick on the ground—"

"Was it liquid?" Mr. Whitpeace demanded. "Or congealed?"

Bends stared, uncomprehending.

"Was it thick upon your hands," the coroner amplified, "or akin to water? Speak, man."

"Her neck was wet, but not so wet as to be like water." The charley glanced about the publick room, as tho' in search of aid.

"She had not, then, died in the last few seconds."

Bends shrugged.

"Did you observe any sort of weapon near the Princess?"

"No-o," Bends said falteringly, "but for the piece of china."

Thomas Whitpeace leaned towards the charley avidly. "What sort of china?"

"It looked like the lid of a dish. Or maybe a lady's box," Bends offered, "such as she might keep treasures in. About the size of a loaf of bread, it was. I've never seen the like afore, except in the windows of they shops on Jermyn Street. Very fine, with gilt edging and all manner of birds painted on top."

"Where did you find this . . . lid?"

"Smashed on the ground beside the lady."

"Smashed? How, then, did you know it for a lid?"

"It was broken in three great pieces, and when the Runner come, he fitted 'em together and showed me what it was. One of the pieces had blood along the edge."

I glanced at Henry. His countenance was very pale: imagining the scene, as I had done, of the Princess Tscholikova standing in the night, and dragging the jagged edge of porcelain across her luminous white neck. *A lady's box, such as she might keep treasures in.* The emerald brooch, gryphon and eagle, rose before my mind's eye.

"There was no sign of jewels scattered about the pavement?" the coroner demanded sternly.

"Yer Honour!" Bends cried. "As God is my witness—"

Count Kronsky rose smoothly from his place. "Prince Pirov would assure the coroner that his sister's jewels are in his possession."

"Very well," Mr. Whitpeace said. "What did you then, Joshua Bends?"

"Set up a hollerin' fit to bust."

"And the result?"

"The lights went up in No. 45. Fair deal o' candles they must've lit—sparing no expence even for the serving folk. That's a gentleman's household, that is."

"Who appeared first from No. 45?"

"His lordship's man." Bends gestured towards Charles Malverley. "Full dressed he were, as tho' 'twere broadest day!"

"You may step down, Bends," Thomas Whitpeace instructed. "The coroner calls Mr. Charles Malverley!"

CHARLES MALVERLEY'S BEATIFIC FACE WAS QUITE PALE UNder his fashionably-disordered curls as he swore his oath. But his gaze did not waver as he submitted to the coroner; he was a self-possessed creature, schooled from infancy in matters of conduct. I judged him to be in his early twenties—a man just down from Oxford or Cambridge, perhaps, with no inclination for Holy Orders. Younger sons of earls can be dreadfully expensive; bred up to the world of *ton* with only the slimmest of expectations, they face a life of sponging on their more affluent relatives—or the distasteful prospect of a profession. Charles Malverley must be breathlessly expensive; but rather than descending into debt and vice, he had done the honourable thing—and put himself out for hire.

"You serve Lord Castlereagh in the capacity of private secretary, I believe?" Mr. Whitpeace said.

"I do."

"And for how many years have you fulfilled that office?"

"A matter of months, rather. His lordship was good enough to take me on in the autumn of 1809."

"The autumn—that is a vague term, Mr. Malverley. Was this before or after his lordship resigned from the Cabinet?"

"I cannot see that it makes the slightest difference," Malverley rejoined with asperity, "but if you will know—it was perhaps a fortnight after his lordship determined to enter private life."

I glanced around the room for Mr. Canning: He was seated a little in front of me. His countenance betrayed no undue sensibility regarding Lord Castlereagh's retirement: the private accusations of misconduct and stupidity Canning had circulated in Cabinet, and the furious culmination of pistols at dawn.

"Let us say, then, that you went to Lord Castlereagh's in mid-October, 1809," Mr. Whitpeace persisted.

"By all means, say so," Malverley returned impatiently.

"Thus you have been very much in his lordship's confidence, I collect, for full a year and a half?"

"I have attempted to serve Lord Castlereagh to the full extent of my abilities," Malverley said, as tho' the coroner had uttered an impertinence. "I aspire to nothing more."

"Very well. We shall return to the *exact* nature of your services in due course. On the evening in question, Mr. Malverley, you were first to answer the watchman's summons."

"I was."

"And yet, it was past five o'clock in the morning. Do you reside in Lord Castlereagh's establishment?"

A wave of colour rose in the young man's cheeks. "I have rooms the Albany. But on the evening in question I . . . had not yet found occasion to return there."

"You were working on his lordship's behalf until dawn?" Mr. Whitpeace's expression was politely incredulous.

"In a manner of speaking." Malverley shot a quick look in Castlereagh's direction. "His lordship required me to escort Lady Castlereagh home after the conclusion of the play at the Theatre Royal, as her ladyship was greatly fatigued. His lordship, I believe, intended going on to one of his clubs. I saw Lady Castlereagh home in her carriage. At our arrival, the hall porter informed her ladyship that the Princess Tscholikova had called a few moments before our arrival, asking for his lordship, and had been refused the house— owing to the lateness of the hour, the imperfect understanding the porter had of the Princess's standing, and the family being from home."

"The Princess Tscholikova had called in Berkeley Square? But the watchman said nothing of this!"

Malverley shrugged. "I can only relate what the porter told me."

"Had the Princess been much in the habit of calling on Lord Castlereagh in the small hours of the morning?"

"She had never done so, to my knowledge." Malverley's eyes dropped. "I do not believe she was on terms of acquaintance with either of the Castlereaghs."

"And yet, the porter would have it that she came to the house after midnight—for so it must have been—but a few hours before her death!"

"That is so. I cannot account for it."

"What happened then?"

"Lady Castlereagh glanced at the Princess's card, and declared herself ready to retire. When she had ascended to her room, I told the porter to secure the front door and go off to bed."

"—Tho' his lordship was not yet returned?"

"His lordship possesses a key," Malverley said.

"You did not then quit the house for your own rooms?"

"I went into my office—an antechamber to his lordship's study. The room gives onto the square—which is how I came to hear the charley so distinctly."

"Your office?" Mr. Whitpeace repeated, a fine line between his brows. "What did you there?"

"I set about answering some of his lordship's correspondence."

"What hour would this have been?"

"Perhaps...half-past one o'clock in the morning."

"You undertook to answer his lordship's correspondence *in the middle of the night*?"

Malverley's gaze met the coroner's without hesitation. "I was not at all tired; and I find the quiet of the household at such an hour conducive to work."

"I see. How long were you at your writing desk?"

"I hardly know. Several hours, I should think."

"His lordship accords you a great deal of responsibility!"

"I am gratified to say that he does."

The secretary was very much on his dignity now; the implausibility of his story, and the publick imputation that should be put to it—that he was in *Lady* Castlereagh's service, rather than her lord's—appeared so far beneath his notice, as to be unworthy of question.

My brother Henry leaned towards me. "This begins to grow interesting, Jane."

"And dangerous," I whispered.

"Please describe for the panel what happened next, Mr. Malverley," Mr. Whitpeace said drily.

"I had just risen from my desk, preparatory to seeking my own lodgings, when a cry went up from the paving-stones below my window. I heard a cry for help, quite distinctly, and recognised the charley's voice. Thinking that perhaps he had been set upon by footpads, I unbolted the front door and peered out. It was then I saw old Bends kneeling on the paving, and the Princess."

"You knew her for Princess Tscholikova?" Mr. Whitpeace demanded sharply.

"Not immediately. I went to the charley's assistance, of course—saw from the great cut in the throat that the lady was dead—and summoned a footman from his bed, in order to despatch him to the magistrate in Bow Street. Only then did I have occasion to look again on the corpse's countenance, and understood that it was the Princess Tscholikova."

Malverley's pallor was remarkable now, and his lips compressed; but he did not falter, or raise his hand to his eyes. He was indeed a young man of considerable resolution—the sort who should have made an excellent cavalry officer, or a loyal aide-de-camp. I found occasion to wonder just how far his loyalty might extend, to those he loved—or feared.

"Were you acquainted with the Princess?" the coroner enquired.

"Only slightly. One might meet her often in certain

circles, and perhaps exchange a few pleasantries—but I should never say that we were *well* acquainted."

"In the course of your duties, Mr. Malverley, did you have occasion to answer the Princess's letters to his lordship?" Mr. Whitpeace asked it mildly.

Castlereagh started from his chair, with no restraining hand to save him. "I'll answer that, Charles," he said sharply. "You never answered the woman's letters, because she never wrote to me! It's all a pack of damned lies!"

The room went still. An hundred pairs of eyes were fixed on his lordship, except my own—which profited from the appalled silence, in a survey of my fellows. George Canning's looks were alert; Lord Alvanley's intrigued; the Comte d'Entraigues's—oddly exultant.

"You may step down, Mr. Malverley," Thomas Whitpeace said. "The coroner calls Robert, Lord Castlereagh!"

Chapter 13

Dark Horses

~

I WILL NOT ATTEMPT TO REPEAT LORD CASTLEREAGH'S testimony here in my journal; it is enough to say that he delivered it with his usual arrogance, coldness, and appearance of contempt for all the world. A lesser man than Mr. Thomas Whitpeace should have quailed before the duty of interrogating such an one, who has been accustomed to stare out of countenance the most formidable orators in the Kingdom— but the coroner proved equal to the task. He demanded to know where Castlereagh had gone, after quitting Mrs. Siddons's play at the Theatre Royal—and Castlereagh refused to tell him. His lordship produced no friend who might vouch for his presence at one of his numerous clubs; no hackney coachman who might swear he had delivered his lordship to a reputable address; and no explanation of his apparently solitary pursuits throughout the small hours of Tuesday morning. Castlereagh proved as impenetrable as the walls of Copenhagen he'd once ordered bombarded—and invoked the honour of his reputation, in his refusal to disclose his movements.

Mr. Whitpeace then turned to the matter of the Princess's appearance at his lordship's town house, and was informed, in scathing accents, that no intimacy whatsoever existed between his lordship and the unfortunate woman. When the matter was pursued—and the pregnant business of the lady's corre- spondence raised—Castlereagh displayed the hot temper for which he is justly famous, and insisted that he had never cor- responded with the Princess. He went so far as to suggest that Tscholikova had merely sought attention in throwing herself at a fashionable household—and that this mania for the world's notice had ended in madness and suicide.

When queried as to the cause of the Princess's despair, Castlereagh could offer no explanation—save that she had re- ceived no vouchers from his wife for admission to Almack's Assembly Rooms. As the better part of those present under- stood how exalted was the favour of inclusion at Almack's, and how rarely and whimsically it was bestowed by the Assembly's patronesses—among whom was numbered Lady Castlereagh— this notion appeared almost plausible. But it was my brother Henry who supplied a surprising bit of intelligence.

He was called to bear testimony before the panel, to my shock and consternation. I believe he must have expected the summons—that he had, indeed, attended the inquest in order to satisfy it—but had kept mum, rather than excite Eliza's interest.

There is nothing like the pair of them for shielding each other.

"You are Henry Austen, of Austen, Maunde and Tilson, a banking establishment in Henrietta Street?" Thomas Whitpeace enquired.

"I am."

"And you reside at No. 64, Sloane Street, in the area of Hans Town?"

"That is correct."

"Pray explain to the panel the terms of your acquaintance with Princess Tscholikova."

I studied my brother's countenance, which was unusually guarded, and felt the depths of my bowels twist with dismay. Henry! Acquainted with the Princess! When Bill Skroggs, the Bow Street Runner, had intimated as much the evening before—and I had rushed to disprove the very idea! My brother was a dark horse, indeed—and there was no knowing, now, what hidden paths he might pursue, when he was far from Eliza's society.

"My partner in business, Mr. James Tilson, was a near neighbour of the Princess in Hans Place. About a week since, she approached him with the request for a loan."

A murmur of interest rippled through the publick room. Mr. Whitpeace's eyes narrowed.

"And did your partner satisfy the Princess's needs?"

"He was loath to do so. Mr. Tilson is a most circumspect man. He lends money only when he is certain of securing its repayment."

"—He regarded the Princess as *uncertain*, then?"

"You may say so, if you like," my brother cautiously replied. "He placed the matter in my hands for determination."

"And what did you then, Mr. Austen?"

"I sent round my card to Hans Place, and was summoned to wait upon the Princess on the morning of Friday, the nineteenth of April.—I did not like to ask a lady to condescend to my place of business in Henrietta Street."

"Quite. How did the Princess seem to you?"

"Having no knowledge of her person or character prior to our meeting," my brother said, "I may only speak to the lady's manner that particular hour. She was greatly agitated, naturally—and seemed a prey to the worst kind of anxiety. She confessed to a considerable embarrassment of circumstances. I collect that the lady has—*had*—a taste for deep play. She disclosed that her debts were most pressing—and that she required a loan, of some seven thousand pounds, to satisfy her creditors."

"Seven thousand pounds!" exclaimed Mr. Whitpeace. "And did you make over such a sum?"

"I did not," Henry answered. "I could not immediately command so much, and was obliged to disappoint the lady. I offered her half the amount, but she told me flatly that nothing less than the full sum would do. I may say that my refusal appeared to appall her."

"Indeed?"

"Her countenance lost all colour, but she stopped me when I would have summoned her maid. I clearly recall her words as I took my leave: *Then all hope is ended. I shall have to steel myself to it.*"

"Have you an idea of what she meant, Mr. Austen?"

"When I heard of her death..." Henry paused. "I will say that I have carried a most terrible weight of responsibility. I feel myself to be culpable."

"—Believing that your failure to relieve her debts drove her to self-murder?"

Henry offered no reply but an inclination of the head.

Eliza's own dear apothecary and surgeon, Mr. Haden, was then called to say that the Princess had sought his help on several occasions, owing to sleeplessness and general agitation of nerves; that he had given laudanum in the case, and advised rest; and that upon viewing the body once it was returned to Hans Place Tuesday morning, he had found the arteries of the neck raggedly severed—as befit a half-hearted attempt to cut oneself with a broken bit of porcelain. He judged this consistent with self-murder. A determined killer should have employed a more potent weapon, and succeeded at the first blow, he avowed.

This final testimony all but sealed the panel's conclusion. The foreman, Samuel Hays, looked the sort of man to consider *any* woman—particularly a Russian princess—subject to fits of dejection and hystericks; I did not doubt he should persuade his men to a swift judgement of self-murder.

And so it proved: the panel quitted the publick room for an interval of perhaps twenty minutes, during which time they were happily supplied with ale; and returned forthwith to state what was expected. The foreign woman had killed herself. The question only remained of where and how she should be interred.

Lord Castlereagh did not stay to receive the well-wishes of the exquisites who had assembled to observe his martyrdom; neither did he offer George Canning the slightest notice. He strode from the room with an expression of injured fury on his countenance, and I had an idea of the targets at Manton's being riddled with balls at a later hour in the day.

"There is old d'Entraigues," Henry observed as we submitted to the crush surging about the door. "What interest can bring him here?"

"A secret he refuses to tell, no doubt." I glanced at my brother. "You are very sly, Henry. You have been labouring under strong emotion ever since Tuesday morning, and have sought no one's comfort. I shall never call your soul transparent again!"

"I am relieved to be done with the business," he admitted. "Guilt is an ugly master, Jane."

"But who now suffers under its whip, Henry?"

He frowned at me, the turbulent room suddenly receding. "What do you mean?"

"The business is hardly concluded—no matter what Mr. Whitpeace says. Where was Castlereagh that night, and why does he refuse to be explicit?"

"Because he is a gentleman," Henry said reasonably, "and can have no cause to satisfy the curiosity of the vulgar."

"The same compunction may be said to seal the lips of Mr. Charles Malverley—whom I cannot credit with answering correspondence at the dead of night, in evening dress! There is a want of openness *there* that must perplex the interested observer."

"Only when the observer believes the very worst of all mankind," my brother retorted. "Malverley seemed a frank and pleasant enough young fellow to me."

"Who owned the carriage pulled up in the mews of No. 43, Berkeley Square—and did the pair within, or their coachman, observe any violence in the street beyond?"

"You shall never learn the answer to *that,* my dear. From the description of the watchman, that pair were in no case to observe anything—and should never admit to their presence in such a circumstance, at any hour!"

"Where was Princess Tscholikova between the hours of midnight—when she left her card with Castlereagh's porter—and five o'clock in the morning, when her body was discovered at his door?"

"Wandering the streets of London alone, *steeling herself to it.*" Henry's tone bordered on contempt.

"Did she then dismiss her equipage at quitting Castlereagh's house, and proceed on foot? She certainly did not return to Hans Place—or Druschka would have informed the panel."

"That *is* singular," Henry agreed, his brows knit, "for she was discovered in evening dress. It seems a most unusual costume for a lady to employ in walking."

"And most singular of all: Why did the Princess carry the lid of a porcelain box about for some five hours prior to her death?"

"So that she might cut her throat with the fragments, Jane!" my brother retorted impatiently.

"Good God! She might as well have employed a knife! Are you so *blind*, Henry?"

"I simply chuse to be satisfied with what all the world accepts," he said. "You cannot seriously mean to question Bow Street—magistrate, coroner, and all."

The faces of Bill Skroggs and Clem Black leered at me in memory. It was possible that a verdict of self-murder should satisfy Lord Castlereagh—and that he would call off his hired dogs; but a something in his lordship's aspect taught me otherwise. He would regard himself as slandered, and Castlereagh was not the sort of man to rest under such an indignity.

But I said nothing of all this to Henry. I, too, may play the dark horse when I chuse.

Chapter 14

A Drawing-Room Cabal

~

THO' ALL THE WORLD HAD BEEN PRESENT AT THE PRINCESS'S inquest, Lord Moira was not—and the gentleman's failure to appear was felt to be a vexation.

"I cannot be certain the Earl has breakfasted," Henry said diffidently as we quitted the Bear, "and should hesitate to call in Brook Street at such an hour."

"But it is nearly noon!"

Henry glanced at me pityingly. "You do not know the habits of the Carlton House Set. Besides, Jane—I am the man's banker, not his intimate. I am in the habit of meeting him here in Henrietta Street—not in his drawing-room, of a spring morning."

"It is essential I should speak with him, Henry."

"Indeed?" There was mockery in his tone; he thought me a vulgar dabbler in Princess Tscholikova's misery.

"And not only under the impulse of curiosity," I persisted. "Recollect that Lord Harold's bequest charged me with drawing up his memoirs! Lord Moira was his lordship's *friend*—admitted to his confidence—cognizant of the intrigues of Whiggish life. It must be expected that I should wish to canvass the past with one who apprehended so much of Lord Harold's world."

"I suppose we might send the Earl a line." Henry's very stride suggested doubt. "But I cannot entirely depend upon him answering such a note—or indeed, failing to mislay it! It is Moira's custom to forget much of what he ought to remember, I dare swear."

"—Such as his obligations, in the matter of debt?"

"He should never fail to pay a debt of honour—one contracted in deep play. Such sums are the first to be satisfied among men of the Earl's cut. It is their tailors and tradesmen who are obliged to wait."

"And their bankers? I will not require you to disclose the exact figure, Henry—but how deeply is his lordship beholden to Austen, Maunde and Tilson?"

My brother attempted an air of amusement. "A very trifling amount, I assure you. But this is unbecoming, Jane, to nose so deep into a gentleman's pocket! Or do you hope to gain the upper hand by such knowledge, and have the Earl entirely in your power?"

"The Earl may ride deep into Dun Territory for all I care—but you may not," I returned.[1] "James Tilson is anxious,

---

[1] *Dun Territory* was a cant term for indebtedness, as those who owed money were "dunned" by bill collectors.—*Editor's note.*

Henry. He has many burdens to consider—and less affection for the Great than you or Eliza."

"I should never fail Tilson—tho' his circumspection does grow tiresome. You must believe me, Jane, when I say that all such anxiety is misplaced! To speak only of Lord Moira—his credit is unimpeachable. His lordship has the ear of the Prince Regent. He was a member of the Ministry of All Talents, and has twice since refused posts in Cabinet.[2] If His Royal Highness holds the Earl in trust, why should not I? What greater surety can a banker demand, than the friendship and esteem of the highest Influence in the Kingdom?"

If I considered privately of the staggering nature of the Regent's debts—how he had been pressed to appeal to Parliament for the satisfaction of them, upon the occasion of his marriage—how the publick cost of so expensive an Influence had surpassed some six hundred thousand pounds to date, over and above an annuity of sixty thousand pounds he had been granted as Prince of Wales, and the still larger income for which he hinted continuously, now that he was made Regent—I said nothing of my doubts to Henry. It is not for *Jane,* who must scrape and contrive on a mere fifty pounds per annum, to question a banker's calculation of the odds.[3]

"I must believe that the best and simplest manner of

[2] The Ministry of All Talents united notable Tory and Whig political figures under the leadership of Thomas Grenville and Charles James Fox in 1806.—*Editor's note.*

[3] The present-day equivalent of 1810 British pounds may be calculated roughly by a factor of sixty; the value in present-day dollars, by a factor of one hundred. Thus, Jane scraped by on an income roughly equivalent to three thousand present-day British pounds per annum, while the Prince's debts discharged by Parliament were roughly equivalent to thirty-six million present-day pounds. His annual income was in the neighborhood of 3.6 million.—*Editor's note.*

forming an acquaintance with Lord Moira would be to throw myself in his way," I mused. "What a pity I did not force the introduction at Eliza's party! But he was surrounded by gentlemen—appeared generally to be holding court—and I did not like to put myself forward. What are his lordship's habits, pray?"

Henry grimaced. "He prefers cards above everything—pound points at whist, naturally—tho' his luck has been devilish out of late. And he may always be found tooling his curricle in the Park—likes to be seen to exercise his blood chestnuts, and thinks himself an excellent whip. He is nothing, mind, to your late lamented Lord Harold. Now *there* was a horseman!"

We had come to a halt before the door of Henry's banking establishment, in Henrietta Street; here our ways must part. My brother, however, was in no hurry to be rid of me. "Such a string of hunters as were sold at Tatt's, Jane, when his lordship stuck his spoon in the wall! His matched greys went to his nephew the marquis, I believe."

This sudden glimpse of Town Life as the Rogue had led it—drives in the Park, no doubt with a string of females to equal his taste in horses, hunting parties in Leicestershire, mornings in a Belcher handkerchief among the members of the Four-in-Hand Club—was so vivid and painful as to bring a lump to my throat. I could not speak for a moment, then managed with tolerable composure: "At what hour would a fashionable gentleman of a certain age be likely to tool his chestnuts through the Park?"

"Let us say—four o'clock."

"It will do very well. Are you at leisure to stroll with me at that hour, Henry? Or shall affairs of business claim you?"

"I am always at leisure," he retorted as he hailed me a

passing hackney, "to watch you embroil yourself in trouble, Jane."

As my hired conveyance pulled up before No. 64 Sloane Street a quarter-hour later, I was gratified to observe a gentleman in the act of descending the few steps to the flagway: Sylvester Chizzlewit, neat and elegant as a pin. He helped me alight—insisted upon paying off the jarvey—and offered his arm as tho' the distance from street to threshold were too precarious for a lady to suffer unaided. The solicitor could not be more than seven-and-twenty, but his well-bred ease suggested a man long schooled in service to the *ton*. I felt an hundred years old.

"How fortunate that I was not a moment previous," he murmured. "I should then have missed you, Miss Austen, and left only my card."

I disposed of my pelisse and hat while Manon took Mr. Chizzlewit's walking-stick, her eyes decorously cast down.

"Is Madame Henri at home to visitors?" I asked.

"I shall enquire." Manon bobbed a curtsey; she was rarely so schooled in the rôle of servant, preferring to regard herself as a trusted lady's companion. Perhaps some odour of the Law clung to the solicitor's person, and urged her to appear the pattern-card of respectability.

I led Sylvester Chizzlewit into the front drawing-room, where the looking-glass Eliza had borrowed for her party still winked above the mantel. A fire burned in the grate, in defiance of spring. As Messrs. Skroggs and Black had left a palpable chill on the household, the crackling glow was comforting.

"Your haste in answering my plea is a mark of generosity I must regard with gratitude, Mr. Chizzlewit."

"The tone of your missive, which I read but an hour ago in chambers, suggested that haste was vital," he observed.

"Won't you sit down?"

He waited for me to take one of Eliza's Louis XV chairs, then disposed himself on a settee. "I collect you wish to discuss a matter of some delicacy."

"As the affair concerns not only myself, but my nearest relations—"

I broke off as the drawing-room door opened to admit Eliza, unwontedly correct in a sober gown of grey Frenched twill. A square of lawn was clutched in her right hand, and her countenance bore all the marks of a sleepless night; but she was, as ever, remarkably handsome. At the sight of Mr. Chizzlewit's elegant figure, her mouth formed a breathless O.

"I hope I do not intrude," she said with melting solicitude.

"Impossible, my dear Eliza. Pray allow me to introduce my acquaintance, Mr. Sylvester Chizzlewit, to your notice. Mr. Chizzlewit, my sister—Mrs. Henry Austen."

"My friends are permitted to call me *Comtesse,*" she said kindly, extending her hand. "You cannot be Barty Chizzlewit's son? I was used to know him very well, but we have not met this age."

"He is my grandfather, ma'am."

"Then we are in excellent hands," Eliza said. "I am excessively diverted! Barty Chizzlewit's grandson! He once served me nobly in a mortifying little affair—the attempted sale of a packet of my letters—but it does not do to be talking of my salad days. I was a sad romp, I fear. And has Jane *told* you about those horrid men from Bow Street that would have us taken up for murder?"

Sylvester Chizzlewit's eyebrows soared. "She has not, Comtesse—but I stand ready to receive your confidences! I have been bored beyond reason for the past twelvemonth at least—but I might have known that bosom friends of Lord Harold Trowbridge could never disappoint. I am at your service, ladies. Whom have you killed?"

"No one at all!" Eliza cried.

"Mr. Chizzlewit is merely playing off his humours," I said firmly. "Sit down, Eliza, and give him a round tale, if you please."

And so, between us, we imparted the whole: How a Frenchwoman of dubious morals had deposited a treasure in gems in Eliza's lap; how we had sought the opinion of Mr. Rundell; how he had betrayed us to Bow Street; and how astonished we were to find that the jewels belonged to none other than the late Princess Evgenia Tscholikova.

"I did not credit the tale of self-murder from the very moment I learned of the Princess's death," I confided to the solicitor, "but I regarded Lord Castlereagh as the object of scandal—that it was he who should be suspected of the lady's murder. I bent my thoughts to considering of Lord Castlereagh's enemies—"

"Did you, indeed?" Sylvester Chizzlewit's looks were satiric. "Yours is an unusual character, Miss Austen. Few ladies should have bent their thoughts to anything but repugnance. But I am forgetting: You were an intimate of Lord Harold's. Naturally you are unlike the common run of females."

I coloured. "Princess Tscholikova's killer ought to be hidden among the coils of politics—if, indeed, Lord Castlereagh is the scandal's intended victim—and it was under this spur that I consulted Lord Harold's papers in your chambers yesterday. I hoped he might have recorded a rogues' gallery of the Whig Party—those most likely to oppose Lord Castlereagh. But to discover, upon my return to this house, that it is *I* who am to be blamed for a stranger's violent death—!"

"We are granted a week—but six more days—to clear ourselves of suspicion," Eliza said mournfully. "And that man Skroggs was so bold as to suggest that my excellent husband might have cut the Princess's throat—when Henry was wholly unacquainted with her! It was *I* who met her some once or twice at Emily Cowper's, and chanced to nod when our paths crossed in Hans Place."

"I fear you are mistaken, Eliza." I clasped her hand. "Henry informed the coroner's panel that the Princess required of him a loan a few days before her death—and that he refused her. He blames himself for the lady's despair."

"No!" She looked all her consternation. "But he has said nothing to me of this."

"We have not been overly frank with Henry ourselves. You must know, Mr. Chizzlewit, that my brother is as yet in ignorance that Bow Street has come upon the house."

The solicitor gave a gesture of dismissal. His lively countenance had sobered during the course of our recital, and he appeared as one deep in thought, rising from the settee to turn slowly before the fire, chin sunk into the snowy folds of his cravat.

"I was used to know an intimate of the Viscount's household—one Charles Malverley," he mused.

"Lord Castlereagh's private secretary! He also was present this morning at the Princess's inquest." I straightened in my chair, all interest. "Did you know it was *he* who attended the discovery of the body—at five o'clock in the morning?"

"How very singular," Chizzlewit murmured. "In Berkeley Square so early?"

"Mr. Malverley would have it he was working through the night—Lady Castlereagh retired—Lord Castlereagh at one of his clubs—but his lordship will not disclose *which*!"

"Lies on the one hand, and obdurate silence on the other. How like Charles—he was always a creature of chivalry." The solicitor rubbed his nose reflectively. "Our firm has served the Earls of Tanborough—Malverley's family—for time out of mind, and Charles and I were a little acquainted at Oxford. Naturally, our paths have diverged in the days since— I am not the sort of man to seek membership at White's Club. But perhaps I should endeavour to renew the acquaintance."

"Then you will help us?" Eliza cried.

"I declared myself to be at your service, Comtesse—and time grows lamentably short." Mr. Chizzlewit ceased pacing and directed a searching gaze at my sister. "Bow Street would merely frighten you, and thus flush a larger game from the covert. We must give them what they seek. Why have *you* not already sought an explanation for the jewels from your bosom-bow? —This French opera singer who is married to d'Entraigues?"

"Because I am afraid," Eliza confessed. "Consider of the awkwardness of such an appeal! Am I to descend upon Anne's house in Barnes—accuse her of trafficking in stolen goods—demand a reason for her perfidy—and then be shown from the house without the slightest satisfaction? For Anne is certain to deny all knowledge of the thing, Mr. Chizzlewit. She must know the jewels were never hers to sell."

"But does she know to whom they belonged?" I demanded thoughtfully, "or were they dropped in her lap much as they appeared in yours? We cannot hope for a full confession from Anne de St.-Huberti if we mount a deliberate attack—but with a little policy we might learn much. Eliza, the Countess begged you to have the jewels valued— indeed, to have them sold outright. Might we not pretend that our mission has met with success—that Mr. Rundell is considering of a fair price—but that he requires more information? You might then enquire where the pieces were made—how long they were in her keeping, et cetera— without putting the bird to flight."

"An excellent scheme," Mr. Chizzlewit agreed, "but let me beg, Comtesse, that you summon your old friend to Sloane Street. I cannot like you calling in Surrey, and putting yourself in a murderess's power."

"I cannot think *Anne* a *murderess*," Eliza objected. "She is a creature of no little malice, to be sure, but depend upon it—her husband is to blame for this coil."

"The Comte d'Entraigues?" Mr. Chizzlewit glanced in my direction. "That would be *politics,* again. The Frenchman, tho' everywhere known for a scholar and a gentleman, was of considerable use to the Portland government in combating Buonaparte. There are those who call d'Entraigues *spy.*"

I smiled to myself, exultant that my understanding had not failed me—for Lord Harold should certainly have known of every intelligencer who moved in Europe during his days of intrigue; the ways of espionage were as lifeblood to him. "Does rumour name the spymaster in the late Portland government? To whom did d'Entraigues sell his information, Mr. Chizzlewit?"

The solicitor had the grace to look conscious, as tho' he

broached matters of State with the merest female nobodies. "It was said that George Canning was the Frenchman's confidant. You will know that the Foreign Ministry is charged with management of the Secret Funds—those monies disbursed for the gathering of intelligence—and Canning undoubtedly held the purse strings."

"But then I cannot make out the matter at all!" I cried in frustration. "Why should d'Entraigues be embroiled in a plot to throw scandal at Castlereagh's door—when it is Castlereagh and Canning—d'Entraigues's very patron—that the Regent most wishes to form a new government?"

Sylvester Chizzlewit threw up his hands; Eliza had recourse to her vinaigrette; and so we three parted for the remainder of our precious day—each of us bent upon securing the confidence of some one of those we suspected.

Chapter 15

A Calculated Misstep

~

WHEN MANON HAD CLOSED THE DOOR ON MR. CHIZZLEWIT, she turned resolutely and said, "He is too young, that one. It is to be setting *un enfant* against the likes of *ces salopards* of Bow Street, yes? But if you will not have Monsieur Henri to know—"

"Monsieur Henri is bound for Oxford on Sunday," I replied, "and cannot be troubled with this business. That young man is a solicitor—and naturally I should wish to consult with him, when under threat of the Law."

The maid lifted her shoulders in that most Gallic of gestures. "Do not talk to me of the Law! Do you know they have had poor Druschka to that inn in Covent Garden, and made her answer their questions? Bah!"

"You would mean the inquest? Indeed, I heard her

testimony myself. I cannot recall, however, that she was forced to an indiscretion—"

"It is the judgement she cannot abide! Suicide! And Prince Pirov—the dead one's so-Russian brother—has enjoined Druschka to silence; not a question, not a protest, may she utter in his hearing. She told me the whole, not an hour after the household was returned from the Brown Bear." Manon glanced at me under her eyelashes. "We have taken to meeting, *vous savez*, in Cadogan Place, for our exercise."

"Have you, indeed?" I regarded Manon with interest. "Would Druschka take flight if I were to accompany you—on your exercise tomorrow?"

The French maid folded her hands. "But no. What she desires is justice—and I have told her my mistress desires it too."

FROM HENRY'S DESCRIPTION, ONE WOULD THINK THAT Francis Rawdon Hastings, the second Earl of Moira, was an engaging buck of the first stare, slap up to the echo, and alive upon every suit. In truth he is a man of nearly sixty years of age, sadly given to corpulence, lacking in most of his teeth and hair—and is notable mainly for having survived such bosom-bows as Charles James Fox and my own Lord Harold. He is the indifferent father of a son and heir—the indifferent owner of a series of estates, all heavily mortgaged—and lives in contented alienation from his wife. It did not require Henry's circumspection to inform me that the Earl was in the habit of supporting a different High Flyer each Season—for what man of position and birth should do less, when convention required of him no more?

And indeed, when we came upon the Earl after a quarter-hour's desultory ramble along Hyde Park's gravel, it was to discover his blood chestnuts fretting at their bits, and his lordship pulled up near a woodland path of primroses in full flower. He was beaming down with avuncular fondness at a blushing picture of beauty—none other than the celebrated courtesan, Julia Radcliffe, whose matched greys were apparently languishing in their stables. The divine Julia had adopted a parasol, the better to twirl with indolence, and pursued her demure way in the company of Harriette Wilson. I had an idea of the two Barques sailing regally against the Park's current of respectable humanity, the better to stare the male half of the Fashionable World full in the face—and perhaps to be taken up in a curricle or two.

"There is the Earl now!" I declared brightly.

"But he is engaged," Henry said.

Poor Henry—always so solicitous of his sister's morals, and to such little purpose. He secured my hand—which was drawn through his arm—and would have dragged me past the blood chestnuts without a word of salutation to his lordship.

"Fiddlestick," I muttered. "It is only a bit of the Muslin Company. If he is a gentleman, he will bid them *adieu*."

"But if *I* wish to be taken for a gentleman," my brother muttered in return, "I should never carry my sister into the orbit of such a pair! You cannot know who they are, Jane. Walk on."

There was nothing to be done—my brother's scruples were too severe—and thus I was forced to rely on a woman's ingenuity. I gave a little lurch, and a soft cry, half broken-off—and sank to the ground as gracefully as my brother's grip would allow.

"Henry!" I cried in failing accents. "My ankle! Oh, pray that it may not be *broken*!"

He gave me a darkling look, but bent immediately to

examine the offending foot—and in another moment, I was surrounded by exactly the interesting party whose notice I had hoped to excite.

"Are you unwell?" Harriette Wilson enquired, without the least ceremony. "May we be of assistance?"

I do not suppose she can have been much above five-and-twenty; an intriguing creature whose looks were neither classic nor regular—but whose countenance was suffused with good humour and mischief. Her eyes snapped, her dimples were numerous; but I think I may say without prejudice that her bloom had begun to go off. I had known of Harriette Wilson's fame nearly eight years before, when in her teens she had figured as the mistress of our Hampshire neighbour, Lord Craven—who bored her so dreadfully, she abandoned him for Frederick Lamb; but the intervening years of high living and late hours had sadly ravaged her complexion.[1] She was looking hagged, not to put too fine a point upon it—and the paint she employed to supplement Nature, contrasted painfully with Julia Radcliffe's unblemished youth.

"My ankle," I said soulfully. "I turned my boot upon the gravel—just *there*—and felt the most tiresome spurt of pain.

---

[1] Jane refers obliquely to Harriette Wilson in a letter to her sister, Cassandra, dated Friday, February 9, 1801. Speaking of Eliza Lloyd Fowle, sister of the Austens' beloved friend Martha Lloyd and sister-in-law of Thomas Fowle, to whom Cassandra was engaged prior to his untimely death, Jane notes: "Eliza has seen Lord Craven at Barton, & probably by this time at Kintbury, where he was expected for one day this week. —She found his manners very pleasing indeed. —The little matter of his having a Mistress now living with him at Ashdown Park, seems to be the only unpleasing circumstance about him." It was this Lord Craven who carried off Cassandra's fiancé, Tom Fowle, to the West Indies as his military chaplain in 1795— indirectly causing Fowle's death of yellow fever in 1797.—*Editor's note.*

Pray do not concern yourself—my brother, Mr. Austen, shall do all that is necessary—"

"Austen?" exclaimed Lord Moira, giving his reins to his tyger, and easing his bulk from the curricle. "So it is, to be sure—your servant, Mr. Austen—and you have quite the look of him, my dear, quite the look of your excellent brother."

"It does not appear to be badly bruised," Miss Wilson observed, gathering up her jonquil muslin to crouch in the dust of the carriageway, "but ankles are treacherous, are they not? I once turned *mine,* while strolling along the Steyne in Brighton, and was forced to enlist the aid of Prinny."[2] Her black eyes sparkled suddenly with mischief. "In point of truth, I had not *entirely* turned my foot—but I did so *long* to see the interior of the Pavilion! Very naughty of me, was it not?"

"But then, you are the naughtiest of creatures," Julia Radcliffe volunteered, in a voice that held all the soft caress of finest silk. "You have all our concern and interest, ma'am— but I think perhaps we are *de trop* in such company. Come along, Harriette!"

Lord Moira lifted his hat to the two Cyprians as they swayed off down the gravel under a single parasol, then said, with delightful perspicacity, "You must be in considerable discomfort, ma'am. May I have the honour of conveying you to your brother's house—or anywhere else in the Kingdom?"

---

[2] "Prinny" was the nickname of the Prince of Wales, at this time the regent. In her memoirs, Harriette Wilson recounts her correspondence with the prince, in which he invited her to come to London so that he might look her over as a prospective mistress—at which she declined the trip as too expensive to waste on a mere possibility.—*Editor's note.*

I glanced at Henry, who was looking less anxious than resigned. "You are too good, sir. But the indisposition is very trifling—I am sure that if my brother will lend me his support—"

Henry lifted me to my feet and said, "Lord Moira, I do not think you met my sister in Sloane Street on Tuesday last—may I introduce Miss Jane Austen to your acquaintance?"

"Pleasure." The gentleman bowed over my glove with an audible creak of his stays, while I hung on Henry's arm and endeavoured to look wan.

"My sister is on a visit to London, sir, of several weeks' duration," Henry persisted.

"Indeed? And how do you find the Metropolis, Miss Austen?"

"It is everything that is delightful, sir. My sister, the Comtesse de Feuillide, is unceasing in her efforts to amuse."

"Little Eliza!" Moira's eyes creased with fondness. "I remember her in her first youth, my dear—such a winsome child, and so pretty even in her widowhood. . . . It was quite a feat, you know, that your brother brought off, in persuading such a flower to be leg-shackled to him. But I perceive that you limp—decidedly you are lame in the right foot—and I cannot allow you to strain the joint further."

"Perhaps a hackney . . ." I demurred.

"Where is such a conveyance to be found, at this fashionable hour in the Park? No, no—I assure you, it is not the *slightest* trouble. I should be very happy—know my way to Sloane Street in the veritable dark—"

I smiled tremulously. "Thank you, my lord. I confess I should be better for the rest. And then I might release my brother—who has been unflagging in his escort, but *most* anxious to reach his club, for at least an hour past!"

"Jane—" Henry began indignantly.

"Do not apologise, my dear," I assured him. "I know how tiresome females are to a man of affairs, such as yourself. But Lord Moira is all politeness—all consideration. I confess he recalls dear Lord Harold to mind!"

It was perhaps paltry of me to employ my love for the Rogue in such a mean service—but the idle chatter had its effect. The Earl halted in his steps, surveyed me acutely through his quizzing-glass, and said, "Not Lord Harold *Trowbridge?*"

"A very intimate friend, sir—and a sad loss. You were acquainted with him, I collect?"

"From our school days! By Jove! A friend of Harry's! Not that half the world was *not*—but still, I should have thought… What a wonder the world *is,* hey? Let me help you to ascend—"

And thus I was established behind a pair of blood chestnuts to rival the very Highest Flyer's.

Chapter 16

A Comfortable Coze

~

"I WAS NEVER MORE ASTONISHED THAN WHEN I LEARNED of Harry's death," Lord Moira observed, as he gathered up the ribbons and flicked his whip-point over the leader's ear. "I recollect exactly where I was at the time: entering a wager in Watier's betting book. There was Henry Vassall— Lord Holland, you know—with his face whiter than the piece of paper he held in his hands, and the news of Harry's death written on it. For a moment I thought old Holland had suffered a fit—whole family's prone to apoplexy, that's how his uncle Fox went—but no. 'Harry's gone,' he said. And, 'What, back to Oporto?' I returned. 'He's been done to death by his valet,' Holland said, 'somewhere down near Portsmouth.' And even then, my dear, I thought it the queerest turnout ever conceived for

Harold Trowbridge. He was the sort of man one expected to die on the duelling ground—not at the hands of some deranged servant."

For an instant, I could feel the Rogue's hands tightening about my own, and the smooth butt of a pistol nestled in my palm. The targets had been placed in the courtyard of the Dolphin Inn, and the ostlers were watching; the meeting was intended for the following dawn. Lord Harold could snuff the flame of a candle with a single ball, he could nick the suit from a playing card at thirty paces; but I had never held a gun before, and should have dropped the thing but for his hand supporting mine.

"He was too fine a shot to end on the duelling ground," I replied. "Treachery—not the defence of honour—was his undoing. Orlando was a Buonapartist spy."

Lord Moira turned his chin to stare at me, a feat all the more remarkable for the height and stiffness of his collar-points. "How well did ye know Harry, Miss Austen?"

"I watched him die, Lord Moira."

My companion uttered an ejaculation, and must have slackened his grip on the reins, for the blood chestnuts showed a disposition to bolt. The Earl was taken up with managing his high-bred cattle in all the confusion of a Hyde Park afternoon, and I was soon too breathless with fear and speed to do more than steel myself to the crash I felt must inevitably come—but after an interval, the whirl of scenery abated, and I unclenched my hands.

Lord Moira's countenance was red and his lips were clamped tight on all the oaths he must have suppressed; but at length, the severity of expression relaxed, and he said, "Never tell me you're the young woman to whom Harry left that extraordinary bequest?"

"If you would mean the collection of his papers—then yes, my lord, I am she."

"Good God! And to think that Wilborough—Harry's brother, the Duke—put up such a stink and fuss! He must never have set eyes upon you, my dear, for how he could think a slip of a female—"

Whatever he might have said, the Earl abruptly forestalled, his face growing if possible more crimson.

"—should be called a doxy? A jade? An unscrupulous vixen? I can well imagine the epithets His Grace might summon. And indeed, my lord, I cannot account for Lord Harold's decision to place his most vital records in my keeping—other than that which he disclosed in a posthumous communication: He wished me to compose his memoirs."

To my surprise, Lord Moira threw back his head and gave a bark of laughter. "His memoirs! In the hands of a delicately-nurtured lady! How rich! Only Harry could fob off such a bit of cajolery on the Great World! My dear Miss Austen—I *long* to read your account of all our dreadful pasts, indeed I do!"

I placed my gloved hand on the Earl's coat sleeve. "It was my sincere hope," I said earnestly, "that you would assist me in drafting the volume, through the explication of certain political matters I cannot comprehend at all. Tell me, sir— are you at all familiar with the bombardment of Copenhagen? Or the particulars of the Walcheren campaign?"

Lord Moira frowned. "What has any of that to do with Harry? He was in the Peninsula, surely, when the fool's errand was mounted?"

"—By which, I collect, you would refer to Lord Castlereagh's expedition."

"Each of Castlereagh's missteps is very like another," the Earl returned brusquely. "A waste of time, men, and opportunity in the pursuit of a chimera! But I repeat: What had this to do with Harry?"

"It afforded him a good deal of anxiety at the time," I said. "His journal entries for 1808 are replete with references to confusion at the highest levels—the need for arms and policy in Spain, and the diversion of both to the Baltic—disagreement between the intelligence he received of personal agents in Oporto, and that which was read by others in London—in short, an uneasiness and an apprehension of duplicity."

"Harry had always a nose for the treacherous," the Earl observed, "which is what makes his death such a confounded shame. But I misdoubt that anyone could divine the truth of Portland's government, my dear—it was notable for its confusion."

If his lordship expected me to be content with such pap, he was the more mistaken.

"Lord Harold refers directly to yourself in his private musings. *Moira tells me of disputes between Canning and Castlereagh, and fears it will end badly,* he wrote. From this I understood you were in some communication with Lord Harold . . . ?"

The Earl shot the Park gate with admirable precision, all his attention claimed. I did not press him for the moment, anxious lest we should be overturned—but when the curricle had achieved the relative order of the street, he said: "Do you know what it is to have two horses vying for pride of place in a team, Miss Austen? —Each one wishing to be leader?"

"I am no driver—but I think I may form an idea of the outcome."

"A runaway gallop—broken traces—the lynchpin smashed

and everyone in the carriage thrown into a ditch! That is what we very nearly had in government, while Harry was in Oporto."

"Mr. Canning and Lord Castlereagh being the cattle in question?"

"Naturally. George Canning—who held the Foreign Office—was devilish jealous of the conduct of war in Spain, which ought to have been Castlereagh's province as Minister of War. The two were forever despatching conflicting orders. They had each their own sources of intelligence, and would not admit the other's to be worthy of consideration. They favoured different generals, and sent them on private errands all over the globe. At last Canning encouraged Portland and his fellow Cabinet members to support Castlereagh's misguided campaign in the Baltic—in the hope it would occupy the War Minister, if not explode in his face. As, indeed, it did. There is a good deal of petty cunning in Cabinet intrigue, Miss Austen—and a good deal of personal vengeance exacted in the name of national cause."

"I thought, from Lord Harold's words, that something more lay behind the jealousy and disputes," I said. "A deliberate intent to confuse events and destroy the nation's chances—from an ardent desire to *see Buonaparte win*..."

Lord Moira's hands clenched on the reins, and his chestnuts jibbed at the cut of the bit.

"But what you would suggest, Miss Austen . . . is that someone in government is guilty of treason!"

"Exactly," I replied.

WE WERE ARRIVED IN SLOANE STREET WELL BEFORE I SUCceeded in convincing my gallant Earl that such perfidy as deliberate sabotage was possible among honourable men. Indeed, I do not think I convinced him of it. Lord Moira was inclined to regret his confidences—his freedom with both speech and memory—and to regard me as an interfering woman. It was only as he helped me to step down from the curricle—and I declared my ankle already mended as a result of his solicitude—that he said, with a visible air of trouble, "I should not regard our conversation, Miss Austen, as of the *slightest* consequence—the merest exchange of trifling incident between mutual acquaintances of a very singular gentleman. How I wish we still had Harry among us! But alas—"

"Indeed," I returned equably. "But allow me to confess, Lord Moira, that his lordship knew me for a close-mouthed creature of no mean understanding; else he should never have entrusted me with such a legacy, on the very point of death. I spoke to you, my lord, in the same spirit of trust I should have adopted in speaking to Lord Harold. The treason I intimated—"

I broke off, as the Earl glanced about us apprehensively, lest the child-strewn streets of Hans Town inform against him—"the treason I intimated, has in all probability continued unabated. Reflect that it has, in large measure, proved successful."

"What? Tush! The case is entirely altered with the Regent come into power—"

"Lord Castlereagh's desperate campaign in the north was foiled by lack of confidence," I continued implacably, "yet it drew off men and arms that might better have combated the French in the Peninsula—thereby achieving a double blow against England's hopes. But a few months later, two great

minds—Castlereagh's and Canning's—were forced from governance and allowed to prey upon each other as the objects
of frustrated ambition and policy. The Kingdom was the true
victim of that duelling ground, when the two ministers met to
defend their honour in the autumn of 1809. Neither has been
returned to high office since, and policy has floundered. And
now, as the Regent would take up his chance, and consider of appointing these two gentlemen once more—Lord Castlereagh's
reputation is besmirched by rumour and murder."

"Princess Tscholikova." Moira said it heavily, as tho' the
name were a curse. "But the coroner has declared that she
killed herself!"

"Pish! I no more credit the notion than you do. It was
here in Sloane Street, I think, that you remarked upon the
singularity of her death—and how it must delight Lord
Castlereagh's enemies. You are a Whig, sir—one of the most
highly-placed in the land—and can have no love for Lord
Castlereagh's politics. But you have served in government,
and comprehend the intrigues of those who place power
above all else—even country. Surely you might compose a
list of Lord Castlereagh's enemies?"

The Earl hesitated, his gaze focused on something beyond
my visage; I believe he saw in memory a pantomime of the
past, replete with images whose significance he only now apprehended. Then he bowed low, and said hurriedly, "You have
given me to think, my dear. May I call upon you—send round
a missive—hope to converse again of all we have discussed?"

"Certainly," I answered, and curtseyed. "I should be honoured."

It was enough to hope the Earl did not file my existence
away, among his notes of hand and tradesmen's duns.

Chapter 17

The Long Arm of the Tsar

Saturday, 27 April 1811

~

I WAS AWAKENED FROM MY SLUMBERS THIS MORNING BY A gentle scratching at the bedchamber door, and having donned my dressing gown and hurried my feet into slippers, discovered Manon in the upper hall. She was neatly arrayed in her customary charcoal gown, but she wore a cloak of blue wool and a straw bonnet trimmed with a bunch of cherries. When I would have spoken, she held a gloved finger to her lips and glanced down the hall towards my brother's room.

I motioned her within the bedchamber and closed the door.

"Druschka," she whispered. "She walks in Cadogan Place. I observed her from the scullery window, all hunched and miserable, and saw that she glanced continually at this house. She wishes to share a confidence—I feel it! Will you accompany me?"

"Allow me five minutes," I returned, "and I shall join you on the flagway."

The maid nodded, and slipped like a shadow back into the hall. I splashed water from the ewer onto my face, donned a simple walking gown of sarcenet, brushed my chestnut hair into a knot, and chose a pair of stout half-boots of bottle-green jean. I lost precious time in the fastening of these, and was forced to snatch at the serviceable but sober bonnet that served my country walks in Chawton. I hastened below with a minimum of noise, and found Manon awaiting me in the front hall.

"I did not like to tarry on the flagway, lest Druschka espy me and wonder at my failure to join her," she explained. "It is best, I think, if I approach her first; do you wait a few moments, mademoiselle, and then happen upon me as tho' the meeting were a matter of chance."

"Very well," I said, and wished I had time enough for the brewing of tea in the interval.

Manon quitted the house, as was proper, by the servants' entrance at the rear; and in a few moments I glimpsed her striding confidently towards the green. The clock on Eliza's mantel chimed seven; the Russian woman had escaped from her quarters on Hans Place at an early hour. For an instant I considered of her present existence: surrounded by powerful men—Prince Pirov and his followers—who kept their own servants and undoubtedly regarded Druschka as a pitiful old retainer, not worth the slightest consideration. Even her grief should be read as an offence—the Druschkas of the world were not allowed to feel. It was hardly wonderful that she sought comfort in solitary rambles.

Manon's mother, Madame Bigeon, was audibly moving about the kitchen; I ventured towards that region of the house and saw to my relief that tea was already in the pot. Madame Bigeon poured me out a cup, and offered me bread and jam, which I gratefully accepted.

"I am going out for a walk," I said brightly. "The weather is so very fine!" The old woman gave a brief nod of the head, and returned to preparing Eliza's breakfast tray. Several fowls lay upon a scrubbed oak table, ready for the plucking, and the sight of their limp necks instantly recalled to mind the Princess Tscholikova. I averted my gaze, the bread and jam lodging uncomfortably in my throat, and made my way to the servants' door.

THERE WERE TRADESMEN ENOUGH THE LENGTH OF SLOANE Street, but Cadogan Place was empty of life. The children of Hans Town preferred eggs and toast in the nursery to the early chill of an April morning. I did not immediately discover Manon and her Russian acquaintance; but a brisk stroll the length of the square's north and east sides revealed them to be established on a stone bench, all but hidden by greenery, their heads together in close conversation. I pursued my solitary way as tho' I had not observed them; but in drawing abreast of the pair, exclaimed, "What is this, Manon! Have you leave to desert your mistress at such an hour? You had better be building up the fires, and attending Madame Henri in her dressing room!"

Manon sprang to her feet as if conscious of her error,

then bobbed a curtsey. "I beg your pardon, mademoiselle—
indeed I beg it most earnestly—but I could not ignore such
misery in one who may claim my friendship. You who are so
wise—who possess the friends in high places—you cannot
fail to pity poor Druschka, when you have heard all."

"Druschka?" I repeated as I studied the Russian woman,
whose eyes met mine unflinchingly. She rose from her seat,
and stood humbly clutching a leather-bound book to her
bosom as tho' it were her dearest child. "You are the Princess
Tscholikova's maid, I think?"

The words required no translator.

"I was," she said in her guttural way, then muttered a few
hurried French words of farewell to Manon.

"*Restez,*" Manon commanded, and grasped the Russian's
arm. "If it is justice you seek, you must talk to Mademoiselle
Austen. She, too, does not credit the tale of suicide; and for
reasons of her own she has sought the advice of a lawyer, look
you. A powerful man who might discover the truth. Mademoiselle will help you. But you must trust her. I will speak the
words you cannot. It is understood?"

Druschka stiffened, and for an instant I feared she might
bolt as swift as a hare across the open stretch of green, her
precious book hurled to the winds. Then resolve seemed to
break in her, and she sank down once more on the stone
bench.

"Pray ask her, Manon, why her mistress was embarrassed
for funds in the last days before her death."

The question was put, and the answer came in a shrug.
The Princess had never wanted for money before; her in-
come was disbursed each quarter by her bankers, and in
London this was the firm of Coutts. The sum was made over

by her brother; the Princess's husband did not utter her name aloud, tho' he had certainly kept all the wealth she had brought to her marriage.

"Was the Princess a gamester?"

Druschka shook her head emphatically: *No.*

I glanced at Manon, perplexed; perhaps the rumour of indebtedness was unfounded. Yet the Princess had certainly sought my brother's aid, and not her own banker's. That surely bespoke a measure of desperation, or deceit. I attempted another approach.

"Was the Princess's behaviour all that it should be, in the days leading up to her death?"

Manon translated the reply. "My lady was beside herself; she was nearly out of her mind. I have never seen her so. And when I asked her the reason, she would not confide in me. I knew, then, that the trouble was very bad. Hours and hours she spent at her desk, writing her letters—a madness in the paper and ink—and then I would find the ashes of what she had burned. None of them sent."

I could not help but think of Lord Castlereagh, and the salacious correspondence published in the *Morning Post.* Was this the proof of all his lordship would deny?

"Letters to whom?" I demanded.

Druschka lifted up her hands.

"She cannot read," Manon explained.

I glanced down at the leather-bound volume the maid still clutched close to her heart. "Why, then, is this book so precious?"

"It is her mistress's journal," Manon replied. "This, alone, Tscholikova failed to burn. Druschka has been guarding it against the brother—Prince Pirov—for fear he will destroy it. She brought it to me in the hope I might decipher the words—tell her why her mistress died. The Princess wrote in French, *voyez-vous*. Druschka speaks that tongue, but the letters are foreign to her..."

I held Manon's gaze. "And this the Princess did not burn. Good God! What we might find there..."

Manon crouched near the Russian maid, and spoke softly to her in French. Druschka cradled her head in her hands, the book sliding unheeded to the ground. A broken phrase fell from her lips.

"What can women hope," Manon translated, "against all the power of the Tsar?"

"The Tsar!" I cried.

Druschka stared at me in horror, as tho' I had uttered an oath aloud.

"But what has he to do, pray, with the death of Princess Tscholikova?" I pressed.

And so she began her tale.

IT WAS A MEANDERING STORY, FULL OF INCIDENT AND MEM-ory: the Princess as a child, consigned to her English governess from the age of seven and ignored by her bitter father; the Princess's mother, dead in childbirth of a still-born son; the elder brother, Prince Pirov, attached to the St. Petersburg Court, a glittering and distant figure, close to the young Tsar. Evgenia buried in the country, lonely but for her dolls. The wolfhounds by the fire of an evening; the sound of hunting horns in the freezing early dusk. Druschka was her nursemaid, banished by the young woman who journeyed all the way from London to instruct the Princess in French and

Italian, watercolours and the use of the globes; but the Englishwoman was unhappy—she was a cold creature, colder than the steppes—and it was to Druschka the Princess came for stories at bedtime, Druschka who tended Evgenia when she was ill.

I watched as a few tears slid from the aged eyes, Manon's voice a quiet whisper above Druschka's own; the brisk wind of spring toyed with my bonnet strings and I shuddered, as tho' I, too, felt the cold of the steppes in my blood.

When the old Prince died, Evgenia was summoned to St. Petersburg and the English governess was sent packing back home, no companion being necessary for a girl of fifteen on the point of her debut; Evgenia would live with her brother now, in the grand palace on the Neva, and her brother's wife—a haughty woman with vast estates in her dowry, for all she was only a countess—would introduce the child to Society, and find her a husband. Druschka expected her young mistress to leap with joy at the prospect—she did not think the girl could pack her trunks fast enough—but to her dismay, Evgenia was afraid. She bore her brother no love and his wife even less; she feared that she might fail them—too stupid, too ugly, too maladroit.

This last word Manon handed me in its French form, with a sort of flourish; the maid was warming to her tale, I knew, and enjoying the fairy nature of it. But I read the future in the young girl's palpitating bosom—for indeed, she *had* failed them all, she who married well but without love, then slipped into the reckless affairs of youth when once the cage was opened...

I waited until the Russian maid had explained how she came to accompany her mistress, the sole comfort the girl could claim from a past swiftly stripped from her; how Evgenia had been courted for her wealth by the most power-ful men in Russia; how she had fallen in love with an hussar, and seen him killed. When at length Druschka arrived at Prince Tscholikov and his appointment to Vienna—I held up my hand, and said to Manon, "Ask her for whom the Princess abandoned her husband. An Austrian? Another Russian? Who was the cause of her mistress's downfall?"

But Druschka surprised me again.

"The Tsar," she spat. *"C'est lui."*

"The Tsar was her lover?" I blinked in astonishment at Manon. "I have certainly heard that he is a very fine figure of a man—and full young for the lofty estate he claims—but surely . . . was he not in St. Petersburg?"

"Non et non et non," the Russian woman protested in a frenzy of frustration. She then broke into such a torrent of French that I was forced to be patient, and await Manon's translation.

"It would seem," she said at length, "that the Princess was ordered to meet with a foreigner attached to the Viennese Court. The world assumed this man to be her lover—but she met with him only at the behest of her brother, Prince Pirov, who said it was the wish of the Tsar. Druschka does not know why the two met, or what they did together; her mistress would never speak of it. But her husband grew jealous; in the end he accused the Princess of adultery, and banished her from his house. She went first to Paris, and then to London. Now she is dead, and Prince Pirov—the brother—will hear nothing of murder. The Prince does not wish for justice. He wishes for obscurity, and silence, and shame. Druschka be-lieves that this, too, is at the order of the Tsar. And she can-not rest."

My mind was in a whirl; the intelligence was too incredible to apprehend all at once. If Druschka could be believed—if she had not merely formed a tissue of sense from a smattering of facts, interpreted as she chose—then what she described was a woman who had sacrificed her reputation, her honour, her place in society, and eventually her *life*—for reasons of state, and policy.

"Who was this foreigner, Druschka?" I asked. "The one the Princess knew in Vienna?"

"Le français," the maid replied. *"D'Entraigues."*

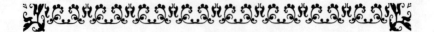

Chapter 18

The Earl's Seal

Saturday, 27 April 1811, cont.

~

AS PRINCESS TSCHOLIKOVA'S JOURNAL WAS WRITTEN IN French, we agreed that Manon would be charged with reading it—my command of the tongue being hardly equal to a native's. I urged the maid to pay particular attention to the last few weeks of the Princess's existence, and to report what she gleaned from the entries with as much despatch as possible. Then Manon and I parted from Druschka with firm promises of support, and adjurations to say nothing of all she had disclosed. Druschka appeared to live in such terror of the long arm of the Tsar, that I felt assured of her silence.

Once returned to Sloane Street, I went in search of Eliza.

She was pirouetting before the mirrors in her dressing room, all thought of the gallows banished. Her cold had very nearly gone off, and her plump countenance was pink with satisfaction at a new gown—a bronze-green silk with a high ruffed collar—which showed off her dark eyes to perfection.

"I might wear topazes with this," she mused, "or perhaps my garnet earrings. What do you think, Jane?"

"Eliza, have you written to your friend the Comtesse?"

My sister pouted at me in disappointment. "I fully apprehend that we are a day closer to the horrors threatened by those Bow Street men—but can we not spend the morning in *pleasure* rather than the pursuit of villains? This is dear Henry's last day for a se'nnight! And if you are gloomy, Jane, he will fear the worst—and believe me in ill-health. He will be such a prey to anxiety that he will never leave for Oxford on the morrow, and we will be forced to go about this havey-cavey business in the most underhanded fashion. It is *vital*, my dear, that we appear gay to the point of dissipation! Fashion must be our subject—millinery and shopping our sole pursuits— so that Henry may trot off to Oxford on his hired mare without a backward look!"

"Are you aware, Eliza, that it was the Comte d'Entraigues who ruined Princess Tscholikova in Vienna—who disgraced her name and caused her husband to break with her forever?"

"No! Was it indeed? Were they lovers, then?"

"Or worse."

Eliza blinked. "What could be worse?"

"Never mind that! You will agree that the association must place your friend's possession of the Princess's jewels in the most sinister light! Recollect the degree of hatred Anne de St.-Huberti exhibited towards the Princess at the theatre, on the very night of Tscholikova's murder—"

Eliza sank onto the silken pouf drawn up near her dressing table. "That *is* unfortunate. I had cherished the hope that the entire business was the result of a misunderstanding...

and how I shall have the courage to look Anne in the face now, I know not."

"You *have* written to her, then?"

"She comes to me today. Four o'clock is the appointed hour—for you know Henry will certainly walk round to his club if Anne is to bear me company, and nothing could be better! I think, Jane, that you should absent yourself as well—for the poor creature is unlikely to admit her sins before the entire world!"

"Impossible, Eliza. I should return to find you lying in a pool of blood!"

"Nonsense," she said briskly, as Manon entered the dressing room with a hot iron, intent upon curling her mistress's hair. "If the Comtesse is not above doing violence to an old friend, who has only ever wished her well—I shall scream for Manon, and she shall send for those odious Runners immediately!"

However unremarkable her degree of sense, Eliza certainly did not lack for courage.

"I shall sit in the housekeeper's room with Madame Bigeon," I relented, "but do not ask me to remove myself further. With so much you must be content."

"Very well, very well," Eliza returned pettishly. "Now take yourself off to Henry! I am determined he shall suspect nothing of our trouble on this day—and if you betray me, Jane, I shall never forgive you!"

I FOUND MY BROTHER IN THE BREAKFAST PARLOUR, CHAIR pushed back from the ruins of bacon, pert head buried in his newspapers.

"There is a letter for you," he offered as I entered the room.

"Cassandra? She will be charging me again with the purchase of green crewels, no doubt, and enquiring after the success of Eliza's party—my letter will have crossed hers in the post."

"Green crewels?" Henry repeated, diverted from his reading.

"She has set her heart on seven yards of the stuff, to make up for a summer gown, and I spent all her money on coloured muslin instead! It will fall to pieces in the first wash, and I shall be forced to endure her reproaches for the remainder of the Season. I must drag you to Grafton House this morning, Henry, to buy what Cassandra prefers.[1] You may carry the parcels for me."

I turned over the post as I spoke, and discovered no letter from my sister—but a heavy packet of hot-pressed paper, addressed to *Miss Austen,* and bearing a crest in black wax on the obverse.

"From whom can this be?" I wondered aloud.

"Moira," Henry said flatly. "You've made a conquest, Jane. Does the Earl wish to take you driving again in the Park, under the guise of spreading Whig rumours?"

I had said nothing to my brother of the substance of my

[1] Grafton House sat on the corner of Grafton and New Bond streets, and was known to provide excellent millinery goods for bargain prices. As a result, hordes of respectable women thronged its counters, and the premises were so crowded that one might wait full half an hour to be served. Jane recounts one such expedition in company with Manon, during which she purchased bugle trimming, and silk stockings at twelve shillings the pair, in a letter to her sister, Cassandra, dated April 18, 1811.—*Editor's note.*

conversation with his lordship. He was as likely to scoff at the idea of treason, as he was to dismiss the value of Lord Harold's papers. With deliberate lightness, therefore, I rejoined, "I must snatch at any chance of an alliance, my dear—even if the swain be dottering, and nearly in his grave! Indeed, I should prefer him to be so, that I might have all the dignity of widowhood, and none of the *longueurs* of marriage."

"As his lordship's heir is but three years of age," Henry retorted with satisfaction, "I believe it is you who should find your grave first. Do not be telling Cassandra of this clandestine correspondence! She will be thinking you quite as abandoned to propriety as poor little Marianne—despatching letter after letter to Willoughby's lodgings!"

And with this fond reference to my novel—which in all the suspense of murder I had very nearly forgot—Henry went to collect his wife.

I broke the Earl's seal without delay.

Brooks's Club
26 April 1811

My dear Miss Austen—
Your interesting communication of several hours past has given me to think, not only of Harry and the blessed days of fellowship that are long gone, but of certain events in His Majesty's government during the years 1808–1809, viz., the conduct of the Peninsular Campaign and certain intrigues of governance surrounding it.
I am, and have always been, devoted to the philosophy and cause of the Whig party, particularly as led and espoused by that great figure of the recent age, Charles

James Fox. The brief fifteen months in which Mr. Fox held
the position of First Minister, during which period I was
also honoured to serve—I speak of what is commonly
known as the Ministry of All Talents—I may frankly state
that he demonstrated to an admiring kingdom that
perspicacity, restraint, and honour that must always
distinguish both the statesman and the gentleman. I say
nothing of his regrettable indiscretions among the female
set, nor of his addiction to gaming. The fact that Mr. Fox
was able to conduct himself with the acuteness and daring
of a born leader, tho' his cabinet united Whigs with men
not of his own chusing but of the Opposition—a union
indeed of the first minds of England—is a credit to his
ability to set aside personal ambition, in the interest of
King and Country, to the very day of his death in harness.

But I digress. In speaking of Mr. Fox, I would merely
illustrate my own degree of experience with those men who
lead the Tory faction. I have not only observed them from
the vantage of my long years in Opposition; I have known
several from the cradle, and others from the ministry in
which we both served. You enquired of me whom I might
adjudge to be enemies of Lord C. In this, I believe you had
my fellow Whigs in view; I believe you expected a recital of
such names as Lords Grenville and Grey, Mr. Sheridan
and Mr. Brougham, Mr. Ponsonby and his ilk—all of them
reasonably opposed to Lord C.'s aims, and certainly to his
conduct of war during the period in which he governed that
ministry. Of Mr. Fox's nephew Lord Holland, whose
dedication to his late uncle's principles has always been
frank and warm, and whose opposition to the endless
campaigns in which we find ourselves has been vociferously

expressed in the House of Lords, I need say little—other than that his contempt for Lord C. is invariably confined to the political realm, and never results in a social breach among their mutual acquaintance.

Your acute understanding, Miss Austen, and the various points you raise in support of your conjectures, have occupied my mind the better part of several hours. The cause at issue—the unfortunate death of that lady to which you referred, and the possibility of her end having been not of her own chusing—is sufficiently grave as to warrant my attention; but the possible consequences of too frank an avowal, and too broad an application of suspicion, must urge me to demand your discretion. Men may be ruined for a whisper; I have seen it done. Therefore, let the intelligence I now offer you be held in the strictest confidence, until such time as you feel you possess sufficient proofs, as to make the employment of your knowledge both necessary and inevitable.

Lord C.'s most determined enemy is undoubtedly not a Whig, but a fellow Tory—Mr. G.C., who suffered at his lordship's hands on the duelling ground. I am sure I need not be more explicit. That gentleman, as he stiles himself, is without scruple or feeling; and tho' his merits are justly regarded as brilliant, and the scope of his ambition no higher than his probable ascent, I cannot regard him as anything but a ruthless and grasping adversary. The claims of party and unity should be as nothing to such a man; and the threat of a rival everything. If you would look for your enemy, find him there.

The two men's names have been much linked of late in the popular press, as objects of the Regent's affection, and as possible candidates for a return to high office in a

*ministry of the Regent's appointing. I will say nothing of
the indignation every Whig must feel, at the defection of the
Prince of Wales from that party which has ever been his
chief support, and among whom he finds the better part of
his friends; that is matter for another day. Suffice it to say,
Miss Austen, that popular report fails in this one instance:
Lord C. is certainly in the Regent's eye, as a lynchpin of
His Majesty's desired ministry; but it is Lord Sidmouth
with whom he shall serve, and the Marquess of Wellesley—
not G.C.* That gentleman *is in bad odour with the
Regent, by dint of his affection for and ties to the Regent's
despised wife—the Princess of Wales.*[2] *Moreover, the
celebrated duel between himself and Lord C. has only
diminished his standing among his fellows, as having been
justified by the underhanded fashion in which G.C.
attempted to oust Lord C. from the cabinet behind his fellow
minister's back. In defending his honour, Lord C. has only
heightened the respect in which he is held, and has gone a
long way towards regaining the admiration and affection
of a populace long inclined to regard him with disfavour.
G.C. knows this; he is aware that his star, already sinking,
may be completely extinguished at the formation of the next
cabinet; and I should not be at all surprised if so ruthless
and ambitious a man should not stop even at violence to
obtain his ends—by throwing scandal on the object of his
jealous hatred.*

You would do well to determine, if you may, whether he

---

[2] The Prince Regent married his German cousin, Caroline of Brunswick,
in 1796, but cordially hated her and maintained a separate household
from his consort for all but three weeks of his married life. Princess
Caroline was tried and acquitted of treason (the basis being adultery) in
Parliament in 1820; she died abroad in 1821.—*Editor's note.*

was acquainted with Princess T——, and what were his movements on the night in question.

I have perhaps assumed and said too much. Acquit me of having a cock in this particular fight; I stand only as observer. In relating so much of a private nature—and indeed, of speculation regarding appointments that remain solely in the Regent's preserve—I have perhaps committed an unpardonable offence; but my esteem for Lord Harold causes me to accept the considerable trust he placed in yourself, as being of unquestioned foundation.

Allow me to express my respect and admiration, and accept my sincere good wishes for your continued health. I remain—

Francis Rawdon Hastings, Earl Moira

Chapter 19

The Shadow of the Law

Saturday, 27 April 1811, cont.

~

THE PREMISES OF GRAFTON HOUSE ARE SO LARGE AS TO permit of an army of occupation's being encamped there—which is indeed the effect of a quantity of Town-bred women, from duchesses to scullery maids, in determined hold of the premises of a Saturday morning. The hour being well advanced when Eliza, Henry, and I made our entrance, we went unacknowledged and disregarded amidst the cackling throng—and Henry had but to eye the several large rooms, letting one into another, with their lofty ceilings and interior casements of paned glass, their bolts of holland and sarcenet draped cunningly over Attic figures, their lengths of trimming depending from brass knobs at every side—to announce, with commendable meekness, that he believed he should much better wait outside.

The few male persons brave enough to confront the crush of bargain-mad women were most of them clerks, arrayed behind the broad counters, heads politely inclined to whichever of their patrons had obtained a place well enough to the fore to command attention. I detected a wall of matrons seven deep before those counters, and resigned myself to an interval of full half an hour before Eliza and I should be attended to; Henry would avail himself of the opportunity to indulge in an interval of cheerful smoking.

Eliza was already in transports over a quantity of satin ball gloves offered at a shockingly cheap price, and I left her to the business of turning over the fingers, and exclaiming at the fineness of seams, and went in search of my sister's green crewel. I had an idea of her heart's desire: a length of Irish linen, worked with embroidered knots or flowers in a deep, mossy green, that should feel like the breath of spring when she wore it—or perhaps a bolt of muslin cloth lately shipped from Madras, with figures of exotic birds or flowers in a similar hue. Cassandra is in general so little inclined to the pursuit of fashion, that I must credit my unexpected fortune in having secured a publisher for my book, and being treated to six weeks in London at the height of the Season, to having inspired her with a vaulting ambition. In her mind she envisioned the sort of delights that had been denied us for the better part of our girlhood—the frivolity of women of means. She had an idea of the Canterbury Races in August, in the company of our elegant brother Edward—Cassandra arrayed in a dashing gown that everyone should admire, and know instantly for the work of a London modiste. I was to be the agent of fulfilling her dream. She asked so little of me in the general way that I felt I could not do otherwise than execute this small commission. My sister and I have reached the age when the pleasures of dress must compensate for the lack of other blessings—such as deep, abiding love—that will not fall in our way again.

I had succeeded in discovering the Irish linen, and was fingering its weave somewhat doubtfully, when a cool voice enquired at my elbow, "Miss...*Austen*, is it not? May I enquire whether your poor ankle is quite recovered?"

It was Julia Radcliffe.

The Barque of Frailty wore a gown of pale blue muslin, arrayed with a quantity of pin tucks drawn up close about the throat—an elegant, modest, and wholly becoming gown for a slip of a girl, as she undoubtedly was. A straw jockey bonnet was perched on her golden curls, and her hands bore gloves of York tan; the whole afforded a picture of perfection that betrayed nothing of her calling. I could well believe what Eliza had told me—that Julia Radcliffe had been reared in one of the first families, and despite the events that had led to her being cast off, she retained an elegance of person that owed everything to breeding and taste. Her maid stood a few yards behind her, quietly supporting a quantity of purchases—Miss Radcliffe was certainly on the point of quitting the linendraper's.

"Thank you," I stammered. "You are very good to enquire—the ankle is perfectly mended. Lord Moira was very chivalrous, was he not, in insisting I should be borne immediately from the gravel? I am sure that I suffered no further indisposition solely because of his care."

"Lord Moira is all politeness," Miss Radcliffe returned, with a gleam of laughter in her looks. "A lady has only to fall at his feet for him to lift her up with pleasure! I am glad you did not incur a lasting injury. And now I am going to test your good will further, and betray that I am well aware that odious man is dogging your footsteps. May I aid you in any way?"

I looked all my surprise. Was it possible she referred to *Henry*? And had he abandoned his position in the street?

"Perhaps you are unaware of it," Miss Radcliffe amended. "He is somewhere behind me, taking great care to appear invisible—and thus must draw excessive attention to himself. Bow Street Runners invariably do."

Bow Street Runners.

My cheeks flaming with colour, I glanced around Miss Radcliffe. There were so few gentlemen dotted among the crowd of women that the Runner's round black hat and scarred visage were instantly perceptible. Bill Skroggs.

He was turning over a set of fashion plates displayed on a gilt stand, as tho' intent upon securing the latest kick of the mode—but as I stared at him, aghast, his gaze rose to meet mine. He must have read my consternation in my looks, for a slow smile o'erspread his countenance, and he raised his hat with savage amiability.

"I shall not press you to disclose why that scoundrel makes you the object of his chivalry," Miss Radcliffe said evenly, "but should you ever require assistance, Miss Austen, you may be assured of mine. He has earned an implacable hatred."

She nodded, and would have passed on without another word—but the suggestion of pride in her carriage, the fear of being rebuffed by an outraged and respectable woman, urged me to call after her, "Miss Radcliffe!"

She turned.

I was tempted to ask *how* Skroggs had made her his

enemy—but found I could not presume so far on acquaintance.

"That is a very fetching hat," I said lamely. "May I know where you obtained it?"

"At Mademoiselle Cocotte's," she replied, a dimple showing, "but you should be shockingly out of place there, I am afraid. You would do better to mention the style at Mirton's. They will have what will suit you, there. Good day, Miss Austen."

Bill Skroggs was not alone in following Miss Radcliffe's passage from Grafton House—she could not fail to command the attention and envy of many wholly unknown to her—but I profited from the Runner's momentary inattention to myself to put as much distance between us as possible.

Eliza had abandoned the gloves for a selection of swansdown trimmings.

"Only look, Jane! Three shillings per ell! I must and will have a quantity. It would do very well to trim a new pelisse—if I could have one made..."

"The counters are too crowded, Eliza, and consider of Henry! We must abandon our errand and return at a better hour."

"Perhaps you are right." She sighed. "I am all too often prey to a kind of madness that overcomes me in this place—and find myself returned home with packets of goods for which I have not the least use! But oh, Jane! Feel the softness of this paisley shawl—and quite reasonably priced too! I saw just such another in Bond Street for nearly fifty guineas, and here they want only ten! *Conceive* of the saving!"

"*Henry*, Eliza," I said firmly, and steered her through the throng to the door. I did not attempt to determine if Bill Skroggs was in pursuit; the mere fact of his presence in

Grafton House informed me that he was spying upon us—
and intended that we should know it. The Runner hoped to
haunt our dreams, and so torment our waking hours that we
must scatter like pheasants before a beater. I had too much
pride to betray to the man that I was, indeed, frightened—
that I met his appearance in this comfortable place with the
deepest dismay. My energy was now bent upon shielding my
brother from all knowledge of how we were pursued. Bill
Skroggs should not cut up Henry's peace—or Eliza's—if I
could help it.

Chapter 20

The Frustrate Heart

~

"SHE IS COME," MADAME BIGEON SAID CALMLY AS SHE CLOSED the kitchen door and returned to her chair by the fire. "Manon has shown her to the saloon. We have now only to wait. The tea, it is hot enough, yes?"

"Quite hot," I returned in a whisper, "but pray, Madame, hush!"

The housekeeper had established me at the oak work table with a pot of tea and a plate of biscuits, the better to fend off anxiety while we endured the Comtesse d'Entraigues's interview. We had barely returned from our expedition to Grafton House—Henry grumbling that it had proved to be a fool's errand—before the hour of the Frenchwoman's visit was upon us; and my brother was very glad to hie himself off to his club immediately, maintaining that he had some letters of business to write, that could only be undertaken in the sanctity of the Members' Room.

The kitchen door was quietly opened, and Manon slipped within, bearing the Princess Tscholikova's journal beneath her arm. "I am to bring them sherry," she observed *sotto voce*, "and then busy myself about the hall, so as to be close at hand if *la comtesse* grows ugly in her manner."

"How does she seem?" I whispered.

Manon shrugged. "Much as usual, that one. She does not betray her fears; she looks always as tho' she has supped on whey. Madame Henri, however, is in high spirits—and will not sit, but has adopted a position in the drawing-room, with her back to the fire. She intends to employ a poker, *voyez-vous*, if her life is at issue."

I took a long draught of tea, and wished that we had admitted Henry to our confidence. From the front of the house the faint shrill of a woman's voice—Anne de St.-Huberti's, by its tone—was audible; she did not sound to be as yet enraged. I prayed that Eliza should have the good sense to betray nothing of her suspicions, and conduct her conversation according to the plan we had determined: no accusations, but a cunning attempt to elicit what intelligence we could.

I feared, however, that the Comtesse d'Entraigues should prove cleverer by far than Eliza.

Madame Bigeon was already setting out the sherry glasses on a silver tray, and was reaching for the decanter. Manon turned over the leaves of Tscholikova's private volume, her brow furrowed. "I find that the Princess was a great one for writing to herself—hours and hours she must have been engaged, *comme d'habitude*, over her pen, *oui*? And much of it *bien mélancolique*. There is a something here," she murmured, "that I particularly wish you to see. It is noted down for the Saturday before she did herself the violence— but the writing is most agitated."

She turned the book so that I might peruse its pages. I am better able to read the French tongue than to speak it— and as the maid lifted up her tray and swept once more into the hall, I attempted to make out the furious hand. Manon was correct: the slim volume was so crossed with writing that it more nearly resembled a letter to an intimate; and I felt a swift stab of pity for the dead Princess. It was as tho' all the outpourings I despatched to my dear sister Cassandra had found no object in the Princess's life—Tscholikova enjoyed no friend of the bosom to whom she might turn—and so the frustrate heart cried aloud to the empty page. I turned back to the beginning, and skimmed the first entries—which had been laid down but six months before. There was little of acute interest to the present investigation—a monotony of visits paid, and rebuffs received; of trips to the milliner's; of plays endured at various houses. Not a word of assignations with Lord Castlereagh—and tho' I looked for the name of d'Entraigues, I could detect it nowhere.

A month before Tscholikova's death, however, was inscribed an entry that must give me pause—if only because of the extreme agitation betrayed by the shaking hand.

> *I saw him today in Hyde Park [she had written in French] and could not approach. The gentleness of his look! And yet the aura of a god that clings to his person! The extraordinary kindness from one who has every reason to despise me—I, who am not worthy to kiss his boot—and yet,*

when I recall the circumstances under which we met—the strange benediction it seemed, to move for even a little while in his orbit, to breathe the same air ... I could not help myself: when he had nodded and passed on, I followed his showy hack and observed the ones he chose to notice, the fortunate few with whom he exchanged greetings! I went veiled, and kept myself at a distance; but he must *have known* me*—must have felt the intensity of my gaze, and the ardour of my spirit. Can so much yearning, from a heart tormented, go unfelt, unrecognised? I will not believe it to be so.*

The tumult of my nerves and reason would not be stilled, tho' I sat quietly once more at home—and thus I am restless and wakeful, long into the night. Where is he now? What is he thinking? Is it possible he has entirely forgotten me? Or is there a hope I may yet be dear to him? I take out his letters from the precious days in Paris—and my own voice will not be silenced. I pour forth my soul again upon the paper, as I have done a hundred times before, and seal it with a kiss. But should the letter be sent? Can it be?

A letter. Could this possibly refer to the disputed correspondence with Lord Castlereagh? But the Princess had mentioned Paris—and his lordship was unlikely to have entered that city since the onset of hostilities with Buonaparte. Did she speak, in her veiled way, of d'Entraigues? But a man less like a god could hardly be described. It was undoubtedly true that beauty was in the eye of the beholder ...

Manon chose this interesting moment to reappear in the kitchen with the decanter and tray. "*La comtesse* is weeping," she said resignedly. "She is wholly distraught. It will require several handkerchiefs, *sans doute*, to stem the flood.

I do not think she poses the least danger to Madame Henri now."

"What has Eliza said to cast her into despair?" I demanded perplexedly. "She was meant to lull the woman into happy security!"

"No doubt they talk of the despicable husband," Madame Bigeon suggested. "His infidelities—her endless sacrifices—the mortification and the scorn of the world—you will know how it is."

Manon disappeared through the doorway again with a feather duster in her hand. I returned to the Princess's diary.

> *I must be careful. I have been too long in the world not to know the way of it—to recognise that the ardent love that animates my being must be an object of ridicule before the ton. I pay my morning calls, and yearn to hear of him; I talk of fashion, and of balls, and yearn to talk of him; I walk in the Park, and yearn to encounter him. He has not answered my letter. I am in a frenzy at every post. Perhaps he has gone out of town—is on a visit to the country—is engaged in the hunt? Or perhaps it is politics that engrosses him—all this talk of government, and appointments... I must consider it likely, however, that he no longer loves me— that the passions which brought me to London, like a dog called to heel, no longer stir in his breast. He no longer loves me. Perhaps he never did.*

This petulant recital was followed by a series of entries describing the Princess's dissatisfaction with her correspondence. These came to an abrupt end a mere week before her murder.

Were I the sort to read newspapers, I might have known long before what the Polite World believes—but if I had known, I might never have set foot outside in daylight again, but stolen from this house at dead of night, and made for Moscow by any road that offers. The shame of it! That I should learn the truth from my modiste—that it should be the girls in the fitting room, slatterns all, giggling over my card as it was sent in to Fanchette—that she should have the impertinence to demand immediate payment, and decline further custom, "the notoriety of the Morning Post *being not what she can like." He has done what he should not—he has betrayed every sacred trust—and my heart is exposed in all the obscenity of print, for the entire world to read! I cannot understand it—I am brought to my knees by his perfidy.* I cannot understand it. *I wander about the prison of this house as tho' dazed from a blow to the head; but anger is as strong as pain. Were I a man, I should demand satisfaction—I should hurl my glove in his face, and look down the barrel of a pistol with rejoicing in my heart, as the blood blossomed in his throat—that perfect, lovely throat I have caressed with my lips so often in memory. I would like to kill him . . .*

I set down the book.

The Princess had discovered the publication of her correspondence, and the imputation the Great had placed upon it. She had never sold her letters; but someone in Castlereagh's household *had*. And with rage stirring in her Russian heart, she had sought his lordship at his very door. To plead with him . . . or to do him the sort of violence that had ended in her own death?

My mind raced at the idea: Tscholikova, bent upon revenge. Castlereagh, unaccountably absent from home and unwilling to admit to the world how he had spent the hours between one o'clock and five in the morning. The lady, calling at his house with a porcelain box in her hands. Had it contained her jewels, as we had supposed? Or the letters she had received from Castlereagh, and intended to hurl back in his face?

Had it contained, even, a *weapon*?

She had not found his lordship at home. She had quitted the house. And four hours later, she lay in a ruined heap upon the flagway, with the lid of her porcelain box in pieces beside her. . . . Where had she hidden herself in the interval? Had she merely lain in wait for Castlereagh's return? Or had they met elsewhere—by chance or appointment—to discuss the furor occasioned by the *Morning Post*?

And then I recalled the carriage described at the inquest, drawn up in the mews behind Berkeley Square: with sounds of passion—or *violence*—emanating from within. For the first time, I could picture the whole in my mind; but how to secure *proofs*?

"*La comtesse* is on the point of departure," Manon hissed from the doorway. "You have seen the oh-so-curious passage I mentioned?"

"They are all of them curious," I retorted.

Manon threw up her hands and withdrew. From the hall came all the bustle of two ladies' *adieux*. I looked for the final entry—that which the Princess had penned on the Saturday prior to her death.

> *I have seen Canning. He has told me all. There is nothing for it—I must take my courage in my hands, and warn the heedless girl. If a man may look like a god and behave*

like the very Devil, then no one is safe in his love. I would
not consign my worst enemy to the Fate I have endured—
and even she, whom the world might consider as having lit-
tle of reputation to lose—even she might be made to suffer. It
will be my last act of kindness before the end. Tomorrow I
will pay a visit to—

"Well, Jane," Eliza said from the doorway, "I must say that
I am pleasantly surprised. Anne was all that was frank with
me—and I flatter myself I learned a good deal more than I
gave away! You will never guess from whom she had the
Princess's jewels! It was not her husband at all. It was that little Bird of Paradise—"

"Julia Radcliffe," I concluded.

Chapter 21

The Opera Singer's Tale

~

"YOU KNOW, JANE, THAT I CAN NEVER ENDURE A FRIEND'S misery, without feeling miserable myself," Eliza said as she drew up a chair to the oak work table—seeming as much at home as tho' she actually comprehended the art of cookery, rather than being the most helpless creature in a kitchen I have ever encountered. "It is so dreadfully affecting to see one's oldest friend quite *undone* by the fear of age, and all the natural affection for her son that one should expect her to feel—particularly when one has lost a child oneself! I declare I was made quite as miserable as Anne, when I had heard the whole, and only the recollection of the esteem in which dear Henry holds me—and the perfect manners he never fails to exhibit, whatever larks he may get up to in my absence—could return me to a sense of happiness again."

"We shall take it as given that you engaged in an orgy of sensibility," I said. "But pray cut line, Eliza! What did the Comtesse say?"

"You were quite in the wrong of it," my sister informed me. "It was *not* Anne who killed the unfortunate Princess and stole her jewels, because she has long since dismissed the Russian as a rival for her husband's affection—Tscholikova was grown too long in the tooth, of late years, and he did not care a fig for her. It is true that the Princess and d'Entraigues were the subject of scandalous rumour during the time they both lived in Vienna—which I believe was something in the year 1801 or '02—but the story of their romance was put about by the French ambassador, who could not like d'Entraigues, owing to his having fled France at the Terror. The Austrians, however, would have it that d'Entraigues was spying for Buonaparte! I ask you, Jane, could anything be the more ridiculous? When he is an émigré nobleman, whom one may meet *everywhere,* and quite in the confidence of the Tory party? Anne very nearly laughed through her tears at the whole, and said the old scandal was inflamed and enlarged by Tscholikova, who must needs fancy herself in love with Emmanuel—their Viennese association being nearly a decade since, when the Comte had still all his teeth. That is why Anne can never bear to hear Tscholikova mentioned, for Anne was excessively fond of the Austrian court, and detested being forced to quit the city for a petty rumour."

"But you said that d'Entraigues had demanded a divorce of his wife," I persisted. "I collect that cannot be laid at Princess Tscholikova's door?"

"Indeed not, for I was in the right when I suspected the Comte is *à coeur perdu* over Julia Radcliffe, and that it is *she* he wishes to offer marriage—but Anne will have it that the girl is merely toying with Emmanuel, being a heartless creature who means to get everything she can. It is not enough that she must have George Canning wrapped around her finger—whom everyone knows will *never* leave his wife and children for a mere Snug Armful, being mindful above all of his political career, and what such a scandal as divorce should do to *that,* I should not like to say—"

"Eliza," I demanded in an awful tone, "if you do not explain how the Princess's jewels came to be in your friend's possession, I shall leave the house for Surrey this instant, and require the truth from the Comtesse myself!"

"I told you she had them of Julia Radcliffe," Eliza returned tartly, "and if you have not sufficient patience to hear the particulars of the story, Jane, I shall not try you further."

I sighed a supplication to Heaven.

"This is how it was." My sister turned a garnet bracelet indolently about her wrist. "When the Comte delivered his ultimatum to Anne—but a day or two before we saw them at their home in Barnes—avowing his passion for the Radcliffe chit, and declaring he should not support Anne further, and insisting that she must take up the instruction of singers—you will know that upon her arrival in London, in 1807, no less a personage than the Duchess of York supported her establishment of an academy of voice, Jane, tho' Anne has *quite* given that up now—"

"The Duchess of York being too great an eccentric to support any new amusement for very long," I supplied.

"Indeed! When I consider the wild beasts Her Grace suffers to wander the grounds at Oatlands, I am only too thankful I have never been distinguished by an invitation! Not that such a connexion would fail to benefit Henry, and I am sure I should suffer *any degree* of trepidation, if it should further his career— But at all events, so great was Anne's fear of destitution and abandonment, that she took her courage in her hands and paid a call upon Julia Radcliffe, to see what pleading might do."

"How reckless of her. That would seem to declare one's weakness to the enemy."

"And only conceive how it must look to any chance observer! As tho' she sought the acquaintance of a Demi-rep! However, Anne veiled herself to the point of obscurity—and went to the unsavoury establishment—which I collect is somewhere near Russell Square. She succeeded in gaining admittance, and abased herself thoroughly by a recitation of her woes—only conceive, Jane, of *Anne de St.-Huberti* doing so, who had ever so many beaux in her youth, and might have outshone Julia Radcliffe before the royalty of several courts—" Eliza pressed her dampened handkerchief once more to her eyes. "I declare, there is nothing so melancholy as advancing age, after all!"

I glanced expressively at Manon, who had adopted a position of watchful interest near the kitchen door; the maid rolled her eyes in exasperation.

"Julia Radcliffe appears to have been not unmoved by Anne's recital. She informed the Comtesse d'Entraigues that if her sole objection to divorce was pecuniary—if, indeed, it was her *purse* and not her *heart* that should be in shreds, from the severing of her ties to the Comte—that Miss Radcliffe would undertake to make all right. She then produced the velvet roll of jewels we now know to have belonged to the Princess Tscholikova, and pressed them upon Anne."

"And your friend *accepted* these jewels?" I cried. "I did not think she was so lacking in honour!"

Eliza shrugged. "One does not arrive at one's fifth decade without certain compromises, Jane—and one never does so in style if one is determined to be improvident! I cannot consider that Anne acted so very ill. She was afforded the means to endure her husband's defection—and was not so foolish as to spurn it!"

"She was paid off," I said grimly, "and with such a treasure as must have landed her on the scaffold, if it does not land us there first. Did Miss Radcliffe disclose the source of her bribe?"

"I cannot make out that Anne even questioned her. Perhaps she believed the jewels to be a courtesan's spoils—the tokens pressed upon Radcliffe by admiring protectors. She certainly had no notion the pieces belonged to Princess Tscholikova—for she bears the Russian such contempt, I doubt that anything could have prevailed upon her to profit by the Princess's wealth."

A faint doubt assailed me. "Eliza, you did not disclose the *truth* about the jewels?"

"When you had charged me expressly *not* to do so?" she returned, scandalised. "Naturally, I breathed not a word of Rundell's despicable setting on of the Runners, nor of our fear that Anne was a murderess. She was so sincerely affected by her troubles, Jane, that I could do little else than encourage her to believe her future was assured—that the jewels should fetch a princely sum—and where I am to find it, I know not! I shall have to apply to Henry for a loan!"

"You will do nothing of the sort," I returned with asperity. "By the time Henry has quitted Oxford, we shall have discovered the whole of this tangled business—or been brought before the Bow Street magistrate. In either case, your friend will learn the unhappy truth. I cannot think the Comtesse d'Entraigues's behaviour or morals merit the reward of security, Eliza—let her suffer all the discomfort of deceit a little longer."

Chapter 22

The Consolations of Religion

~

WITH A HOST OF CLAMOUROUS THOUGHTS DEMANDING MY attention, and no ready resolution presenting itself to my understanding, I found sleep elusive last night. I could not help but canvass the merits of each of the figures that must fall under suspicion, whether as jewel thieves or murderers or both. Was Lord Castlereagh indeed the gentleman whom the Princess had loved—and Druschka's avowals of her innocence but the blind loyalty of a devoted servant? Did the Comtesse d'Entraigues beguile my poor sister with fairy-tales, and disguise a malevolent guilt beneath her crocodile tears? Had her husband cruelly used the dead Princess, or was his indifference as real as his wife claimed? Was Julia Radcliffe *not* the slip of a girl I persisted in regarding with fascination, but a hardhearted jade who deliberately placed the Comtesse in danger of her life?

By half-past six o'clock, I abandoned my bed for the book room and sat in my dressing gown by the ashes of yesterday's fire. I schooled myself to look over the pages of *Sense and Sensibility* most lately delivered from Mr. Egerton's press—he has at last arrived at Chapter Ten, which must be felt to be a triumph—but the gestation of these slim volumes begins to seem like that of an elephant. The effort of concentration, upon a task so generally felt to be enjoyable, proved too much for my strained nerves; by eight o'clock I had abandoned it.

Henry was abroad when I entered the front passage: shaved, put into his neat dark coat by his man, and ready to be thrown up onto his horse.

"I have urged Eliza not to come down," he told me in a voice more suited to the tomb; "we have said our *adieux*. Pray look after her, Jane—I shall send word when I have reached Oxford safely."

"Enjoy the solitary splendour of the Blue Boar," I advised him, "and do not be mourning your undergraduate days. You improve with age, Henry."

I watched him wave from the back of his hired mare and clatter off down the silent streets of Hans Town in a westerly direction; and reflected that there are few sights so gratifying to a female eye, as a handsome man in a well-made coat and hat, astride a horse on a spring morning.

I accepted a cup of coffee from Manon and dressed myself for service in the Belgrave chapel.[1] The day—so nearly

---

[1] According to Austen historian Deirdre Le Faye, this may be Jane's personal name for St. George's, Five Fields, Chelsea. In Austen's day this would have been on the edge of what is now Belgravia, and would have provided a pleasant walk.—*Editor's note.*

May—was fine enough for walking, provided I might persuade Eliza to the exertion; she was prone, however, to suggest a hackney coach bound instead for the Chapel Royal, as being the house of worship most likely to offer an array of Fashionables in Pious Attitudes, for our amusement. Eliza is frank in admitting she is rarely able to keep her mind on higher things, even of a Sunday—but I was determined this morning to be firm. Fanny and James Tilson are often to be found at the Belgrave chapel, in company with their numerous little girls; and I felt such a wholesome display of family devotion must be salutary, after the thoughts of bloodshed, treason, and adultery I had entertained.

"But, Jane," Eliza faltered from amidst the bedclothes, where she was imbibing a cup of chocolate, "should I not stay the sacrament? I cannot think myself worthy to receive it, when a suspicion of lawbreaking hangs over me! And recollect, we are to dine this evening with Mrs. Latouche and her daughter Miss East, in Portman Square. I am sure I should recruit my strength—for they are both of them so voluble as to send one home with a headache!"

I left her propped up on her pillows, reading her French novel in perfect enjoyment; and walked alone through the brightening morning to church. The Tilsons caught me up on my way, all of them handsome and virtuous; and I saw that Fanny wore a decidedly fetching straw hat in the jockey style—not unlike the one I had admired on Julia Radcliffe's bright curls. It seemed the entire world must conspire to remind me of the sordid, when I had trained my thoughts to a more elevated plane.

"Your sister does not accompany you?" Fanny enquired, in a repressive tone. "I should not admit to surprise—I have often found her observance to be wanting, and have imputed it to the irregular nature of her upbringing. One cannot live out one's girlhood in India and France, among such abandoned persons as Nabobs and Bourbons, without receiving quite improper notions of what is due to the spiritual realm."

"I am sorry to say that most of Eliza's notions are improper," I tranquilly agreed, "which is why she is invariably such excellent company! But this morning her cold persists in troubling her; I am charged by my brother with taking the utmost care for her health, and could not permit her to put her foot out of doors. However bright the sunshine, the air is not so warm as one would like."

"And your brother, I collect, has quitted Hans Town for Oxford this morning? You will not reproach me, Miss Austen, for confessing how much I *deplore* Sunday travel; it has not been the habit of my family. But there is a carelessness to Town life that may encourage the lapse of every observance, even among persons one must generally regard as unimpeachable; the business of this world is accorded more weight than the business of the *next;* and in our hurry to pursue a monetary gain, we very nearly lose our eternal souls! James is to join your brother at the Blue Boar tomorrow— but I could not be easy in my mind, should he have travelled *today.*"

I ought not to have found anything objectionable in this speech, which expressed sentiments no different than my sister Cassandra had voiced on numerous occasions—being nearly as grave in her attitudes as Fanny Tilson—but my companion's air of complaisance worked strangely upon me. I desired nothing more than to discompose her this morning, and prick her smug self-regard.

"That is a ravishing hat, Mrs. Tilson! I wonder if you obtained it at Cocotte's?"

"No, indeed!" she exclaimed, staring. "I do not think I have ever ventured within a hundred yards of that establishment—nor do I know of any *respectable* woman who has done so."

We walked on in silence, Fanny's face averted. Then she said, with an air of offering an olive branch: "This straw was made for me by a very competent girl in Hans Town, Miss Austen—and if you should be desirous of examining her wares, I should be happy to accompany you at any hour. I may assure you that her workmanship is good, and her prices not exorbitant. Perhaps Mrs. Henry Austen would care to join us?"

"Thank you," I returned, with a resurgence of humility, and a vow to say nothing further for the remainder of the morning. I am all too prone—particularly under the intoxicating influence of springtime—to allow my wretched tongue to run away with me, and offend the most worthy of persons with my levity. The forbearance of a Fanny Tilson must ever serve as salt in the wounds of one less marked by goodness than she.

VIRTUE WAS REWARDED IN THIS CASE, AS VIRTUE SO RARELY is—with the surprising pleasure of a visit from a gentleman caller. I had returned but an hour to Sloane Street when Mr. Sylvester Chizzlewit's card was sent into the drawing-room.

"Delightful," Eliza murmured. "He looks so well against the scarlet hangings, don't you agree, Jane? One should always have a decorative young man about the room, and well-bred if one may contrive it; it lends so much *tone* to the display. Show him in, Manon! And bring the decanters, if you please. I do not care if it *is* Sunday; I am sure the Good Lord was in spirits, too, on his day of rest."

I said nothing of this deplorable want of respect, acquired no doubt among Bourbons and Nabobs, and rose to greet Mr. Chizzlewit.

While Manon remained in the room, he said everything that was indifferent and proper, in one paying a Sunday call; enquired after Eliza's health; offered a pretty compliment on the style of my gown; and declared that there was nothing, after all, like April in England. When the door had closed behind the maid, however, he turned immediately to business. "I have seen Charles Malverley," he said, "and must congratulate myself on having renewed those ties which a few years' absence on his part, and hard work on mine, had very nearly extinguished!"

"Well done, Mr. Chizzlewit. And how did you find your old friend?"

"Much altered. He was used to be a carefree youth—more concerned with the niceties of dress and appearance than I should like, and an aspirant to Mr. Brummell's mantle, among the Dandy Set—but now he is grown grave and troubled. There is a want of openness which I might have imputed to the difference in our stations, and a disinclination to renew the acquaintance, had he not gladly accepted my invitation to dine this evening, in my rooms; we are to play at picquet afterwards, and I expect my pockets shall be wholly to let by dawn."

"Then you were unable, in your first meeting, to divine any particulars of the Princess's business?" Eliza enquired.

"It was not the place to do so—we met at Jackson's Saloon,

where Malverley was sparring. I knew him to be in the habit of taking lessons from Gentleman Jackson, and contrived to visit the premises at a convenient hour. I may have expressed myself as being sensible of the cares lately placed upon him—and suggested that a bit of diversion among friends might prove beneficial—but beyond that, I could not go."

"Naturally. He did not suspect you encountered him by design?" I asked.

"I should not think so. Charles is not the sort to suspicion an old acquaintance. I shall have more to report on the morrow, to be sure."

"In the course of your dinner, Mr. Chizzlewit," I said, "endeavour to learn whether Mr. Malverley prevaricated, when he claimed never to have seen a letter from Princess Tscholikova at Castlereagh's house. It would be well to sound the fellow on his lordship's habits, too—as both gentlemen are far too closed-mouthed regarding Castlereagh's movements during the hours before the Princess's murder."

"I shall do my utmost," the solicitor replied. "You persist in regarding Lord Castlereagh as the guilty party?"

"There is a simplicity to the notion I find appealing," I agreed. "He possesses, after all, the motive for murder—the opportunity to effect it—and the stubborn persistence in denying all knowledge of the act! When a gentleman will not say where he has been, there is usually good cause for silence!"

"But that cause is rarely murder," Mr. Chizzlewit returned.

"I keep an open mind," I assured him, "and one replete with enough suspicion to tar most of London. I shall not hesitate to act, when the alternative is injustice."

Beside me, Eliza shivered, and reached for her handker-chief.

"I trust you have interviewed your friend, Mrs. Austen?" the solicitor enquired. "The French Countess?"

"Indeed, Mr. Chizzlewit." My sister revived in sudden animation. "And *most* affecting, I found it too! I am sure you will acquit Anne of any wrongdoing when you have heard the whole—"

Anticipating a recital as lengthy as yesterday's, I said abruptly, "The Comtesse claims a member of the Muslin Company gave her the jewels—as recompense for having stolen her husband."

"Indeed!" Sylvester Chizzlewit was hard put not to smile. "And the name of the bit of muslin in question?"

"Julia Radcliffe. Are you at all acquainted with her?"

"Miss Austen!" he cried. "Such a question! I do not know how to answer you!"

"She is a fixture in Harriette Wilson's salon, I believe, or perhaps she rules over one of her own—my intelligence is imperfect on that score, I confess. I merely wondered, Mr. Chizzlewit, if you had found occasion to pay the salon a call."

"Since you put it so unblushingly—then *yes,* Miss Austen, I have," he returned.

Eliza clapped her hands. "Do tell us what it was like!"

He shifted slightly in his chair; the first sign of discomfort he had allowed himself to betray. "Very much of a piece with a gentleman's club—save that the focus of admiration and interest were the ladies present, all of whom conducted themselves with a passable degree of propriety. You will know that those who collect around Harriette Wilson are many of them quite wellborn . . . tho' fallen in their standing due to a variety of youthful indiscretions. Miss Radcliffe is one of these."

"And what is your opinion of her?" I asked.

"She is ravishing—a diamond of the first water," he replied. "The difference in her situation, from what it *ought* to be, must trouble anyone who knows her."

"Except those, apparently, whose first duty it should be to protect her," I observed. "Her family."

"As I am ignorant of the particulars of her folly, I cannot undertake to judge." Mr. Chizzlewit met my gaze squarely. "She is the object of general admiration; a shifting party of gentlemen—many of them among the highest in the land— collect around her, and tho' most bestow expensive tributes, she has allowed no one to become her sole protector. I know for a fact that any number have offered Miss Radcliffe *carte blanche*—and she refuses to take it up.² There are conjectures as to her reasons, of course—some would have it she remains faithful in her heart to a dead lover, others that she is angling for a title willing to offer marriage—but her independence has only increased her desirability." The solicitor frowned. "To figure as the receiver of stolen goods—if indeed she apprehended that they were stolen—and to convey them, with malicious intent, to an innocent victim of her toils—is a piece of villainy I should like to think impossible."

"I agree. There is a dignity in her carriage—a sweetness of expression unmarred by her traffick with the world—that must impress the observer with a belief in her goodness. I

---

² *Carte blanche* was a euphemism for unlimited financial support a man might offer his mistress; it implied an exclusive sexual tie in return for the maintenance of a courtesan's lifestyle.—*Editor's note.*

cannot make it out at all. I believe I shall have to pay Miss Radcliffe a call."

"Pay her a call!" Eliza cried, scandalised. "Jane, you would *never* venture to such a den of iniquity! Only think if you were found out! I should not be able to look your mother in the face—and only conceive how lowering to reflect that in this instance, she would be justified in her poor opinion of me!"

"You speak as tho' you are already acquainted with Miss Radcliffe," Mr. Chizzlewit said.

"We have chanced to meet some once or twice. She was first raised as an object of interest with the Comte d'Entraigues—it is Julia Radcliffe he is said to wish to marry, when once he obtains his divorce."

Mr. Chizzlewit's countenance changed colour. "That old roué! It does not bear thinking of! Why, the girl is young enough to be his daughter—"

He rose, and took an agitated turn about the room.

"I understand she is but seventeen. But recollect what the Comtesse has told us: Miss Radcliffe pressed the jewels upon her as recompense. It would appear that she has made her decision—and means to seek a respectable alliance, even at the price of d'Entraigues."

"Impossible!" Mr. Chizzlewit spat.

I shrugged, as tho' indifferent to his contempt. "Then perhaps she merely intends to use d'Entraigues to secure the interest of another. Miss Radcliffe's name is frequently linked to Mr. George Canning's. But my sister assures me that Canning is unlikely to desert his wife and children—however much amusement he may find in salons of Harriette Wilson's type."

"Canning's eldest son is lame," the solicitor observed, "and Canning and his wife are both devoted to the boy. He would not so wound his family—and there are considerations of public office—"

"Then Miss Radcliffe deludes herself. Her affections, nonetheless, may be ardent and real—and thus could be used to villainous ends, when urged by an unscrupulous man. Mr. Canning has at times been described to me this way."

"Unscrupulous?" Mr. Chizzlewit's brow furrowed. "It is not a word *I* should apply. Bold in his ambitions, yes— implacable in his hatreds—but there is nothing in his career one may point to, as being less than honourable—"

"Even his efforts to unseat Lord Castlereagh, behind that gentleman's back?"

Mr. Chizzlewit laughed. "Oh, well— If you would speak of *politics*!"

"Do not the laws of honour apply, in the House of Commons and Lords? I was assured that was why Lord Castlereagh felt no compunction in challenging his enemy to a duel—and humiliating him before the world. He did but *defend his honour*. It has been suggested to me that Mr. Canning, in fact, was so reduced in his public stature that he has an interest in revenge—and that in Princess Tscholikova he found his tool."

The solicitor was standing near Eliza's fireplace; he thrust his hands in his pockets, and turned his head to stare broodingly into the flames. I said nothing further, allowing him time for thought.

"You would have it that Canning deliberately created an aura of scandal around Castlereagh, through the publication of the Princess's letters, and her subsequent appearance of suicide," he said at length. "For that to be true, the Princess must have been in his power—or intimate to a degree we cannot have understood. How else can he have obtained what was private correspondence?"

"She refers to Canning at least once in her journal, which I have had occasion to read. She also mentions Julia Radcliffe—and is determined, but two days before her death, to *warn* the girl. I use the word because the Princess chose it."

"*Warn* Miss Radcliffe? Against whom? I find the notion fantastic!" Mr. Chizzlewit cried. "Could Canning have both Tscholikova and Miss Radcliffe in keeping? And if the Princess was as deep in love with Castlereagh as her letters suggest—how should she have come to entertain Canning's schemes? She must have known him for his lordship's enemy."

"You go too swiftly, Mr. Chizzlewit, in assuming that Mr. Canning is the sort to show his hand! What if he were to employ an intermediary—a gentleman long known to Princess Tscholikova, one she has reason to trust? A man known equally well to Julia Radcliffe...and a man Canning has often employed before?"

He looked up from his contemplation of the flames. "D'Entraigues?"

"I knew we should return to Emmanuel presently," Eliza said comfortably. "For how else could we come to the jewels? Julia Radcliffe got them somehow!"

"But why should d'Entraigues steal them?" Mr. Chizzlewit argued. "It should be the height of folly to do so!"

"He needed *something* to lay as tribute on the Radcliffe altar," Eliza suggested reasonably. "You told us yourself—the world entire is showering that girl with baubles and frivolities! And poor Emmanuel has not two guineas to rub together! But how diverting that his tribute should come directly back to his *wife*!"

The solicitor shook his head. "D'Entraigues is too old a man of the game to preserve so dangerous a piece of evidence as that treasure. If he stood behind the Princess's death, he must certainly deny all knowledge of her. The jewels alone might hang him."

"Then how came they to Julia Radcliffe?" Eliza demanded.

"Is it not obvious?" I looked from my sister to Mr. Chizzlewit. "Princess Tscholikova *gave* them to her."

Chapter 23

Willoughby's Shade

Monday, 29 April 1811

~

ELIZA'S FRIEND, MRS. LATOUCHE, IS A FAIR-HAIRED AND plump little woman with protuberant blue eyes, who dearly loves to talk a good deal of nonsense about her health, her clothes, and her acquaintance among the *ton*. Born Mary Wilkes in Kingstown, Jamaica, she embarked at seventeen upon a storied career: marrying first Mr. Edward East, a widower with several children, to whom she dutifully presented two more, before his taking off with a fever peculiar to those island parts. In the handsome swell of her twenties, she bestowed her hand, her surviving child Miss Martha East, and her late husband's considerable revenues from the production of sugar, upon Mr. John-James Digges-Latouche, also of Jamaica. Mr. Latouche eventually rose to such distinction as a

Governor-Generalship of that island; when he died, his widow determined to sell her holdings and her slaves, and decamp for England—the better to puff off her daughter in a respectable marriage. But Miss East did not "take," and the hopes that buoyed her first Season in the year 1798, have long since gone off. Like me, she is now firmly upon the shelf, and appears to find that it quite suits her—a spinster lady of some five-and-thirty years, established in all the style and comfort of Portman Square. As she may expect to inherit her mother's fortune when that lady's aches and nerves put a period to her existence, Martha East is hardly to be pitied.

She is decidedly unlike the round little Dresden doll that is Mrs. Latouche, being tall and angular, with what one must presume are her father's sharp features. Moreover, Miss East is of a bookish disposition, quite formidable in her understanding—and has taken to wearing spectacles and a cap. In honour of Sunday dinner among friends, it was a *lace* cap; and Miss East looked very grand last night in her amber-coloured silk. She might almost have been headmistress of a school for girls, and her mother her incorrigible pupil.

I am chiefly useful to Eliza on such evenings in monopolising Miss East's attention, so that my sister might have a comfortable coze with Mrs. Latouche—and canvass all the latest spring fashions. Miss East, I observed, was armed and ready with conversation from the moment of our arrival in Portman Square, for she held in her hands a volume of Mary Brunton's *Self-Controul*.[1]

---

[1] Mary Brunton (1778–1818) published *Self-Controul* in 1810. Austen told Cassandra in a letter written from Sloane Street on Tuesday, April 30, 1811, that she was almost afraid to read the book and find it too clever— and consequently lose confidence in her own work. She finally read Brunton in 1813, and was relieved to be underwhelmed.—*Editor's note.*

"What do you think of this novel, Miss Austen?" she cried as I advanced with words of greeting unspoken on my lips. "It is everywhere praised as a piece of perfection; and tho' I would hope I am more exacting in my tastes than the common run of humanity, I will own there is much to admire in the heroine—for rather than self-control, the author would champion *self-reliance;* and thus in Laura every woman must find a salutary model, do not you agree?"

"I regret to say that I have not yet had the pleasure of reading Mrs. Brunton," I said, "being unable to locate the set of volumes in my last expedition to Lackington's. But how happy for the author that you find much to admire!"

"The *author?*" Miss East repeated, as one amazed; "I confess I never think of the author when reading a book—my mind is wholly given over to the conduct of the characters, to the representation of life as one finds it for better or worse portrayed; I am wholly given up to the situations presented. The *author* never enters my consciousness—except, of course, when I am reading Scott."

"Indeed! I do not think Sir Walter Scott may be barred from *any* woman's consciousness," I returned.

"Only consider what perils to mind and virtue Laura must withstand!" Miss East shook her volume with enthusiasm. "First made the object of a rake's unwelcome attentions—escaping seduction by a hairsbreadth—refusing marriage from that same disreputable (tho' very dashing) gentleman when he sees the error of his ways—she attempts, as so many of us must, to live upon her own resources—and yet finds not a single lover of art willing to sell her paintings in the entire Metropolis! I am only just come to the part where she must escape the savage horrors of America in a canoe; but the whole is of the deepest moral instruction, I assure you. I should not hesitate to press it upon any young girl of my acquaintance, as a warning against the bitterness of the world."

I eyed the book somewhat dubiously, and wondered what best to say; but was happily forestalled by a bustle of arrival in the front passage.

"That will be the Count. How tedious the interruption! But we shall talk more of literature later, I hope."

"The Count?"

"Young Julien. He was supposed to bring his mother—but in the event, she is lying down with a sick headache." My companion made a moue of distaste. "These elderly women and their disorders! I refuse to countenance Mamma's continual appeals for attention, on the score of some megrim or another; but naturally she was inclined to sympathise with the Comtesse d'Entraigues, and accepted her refusal—tho' Watkins had already laid the places—with her usual grace."

I glanced towards the door, and there he was: slim, elegant, dark-haired, and roguish of eye, with an exquisite air of fashion. He was bowed low over Eliza's hand, his lips grazing it; then with a swift, laughing look he muttered something in French that caused her to giggle, and rap him with her furled fan.

"Naughty boy! And my poor husband not twelve hours absent from London!" she cried. "Jane—come and say hello to Julien!"

I approached the young Comte with a strange sensation of trepidation. Could this scion of a scheming roué and an opera singer be other than venal in his habits and intercourse? He was present only briefly in the drawing-room at Barnes when we descended upon Surrey a week ago, playing an air upon the pianoforte before quitting the house; Eliza had explained carelessly that a young man of nineteen could not be expected to spend his evenings with a parcel of dowds. I understood Comte Julien had set up his own establishment in the Albany, where any number of single gentlemen take rooms; but how he lived, when his parents' pockets were entirely to let, must be cause for conjecture.

"Miss Austen," he said with a bow. "I am honoured to renew the acquaintance of one whom la Comtesse de Feuillide must always speak of with esteem and affection."

"The pleasure must be mine, monsieur," I returned. "I hope your mother is not decidedly unwell?"

"A trifling indisposition—the return of an old complaint."

"And your father, Julien?" Eliza put in with unusual acid. "Does he sit by her bedside, bathing her temples with lavender water?"

The gentleman smiled as tho' she had offered him a jest, and turned to greet Martha East.

"Is he not a buck of the first stare?" Eliza murmured. "And but nineteen!"

"He bears himself with the possession of a man twice that age."

"Your Frenchmen usually do. They are not suffered to run about with guns and dogs as our English boys will; their sport is of a deadlier kind, involving swords and hearts, and their apprenticeship is from infancy. I wonder where the old Comte has gone this evening?"

"To sit at the feet of Miss Radcliffe."

"Let us hope she kicks him, then," Eliza said, and went off to coze with Mrs. Latouche.

"YOU HAVE QUITE THE LOOK OF YOUR EXCELLENT BROTHER," Count Julien observed, as the first covers were removed from the table. "He is from home, I collect?"

"Yes—called away to Oxford, on a matter of banking business."

"And you are not uneasy? Forgive me—but the violence of the neighbourhood of Hans Town—the suicide of the Russian Princess—and your house now unprotected by a man—"

"My brother left his valet in Sloane Street," I answered evenly, "and the Princess died in Berkeley Square."

"Indeed. I was forgetting. My family was a little acquainted with the lady, you understand, and all I have heard in recent days is *Hans Place.*"

"I suppose it is only natural for émigrés to know one another," I observed.

His smile twisted. "Our very un-Englishness makes us cling to one another? There is some truth in that, *tant pis.*"

"I am sorry—I did not mean to offend—but her death must have come as a shock to all your family. I believe your mother felt it so."

"They were not on the best of terms," he said, fixing his eyes on my countenance, "but I esteemed the lady, and pitied her loneliness. Yes, I felt her death to be a horror. I had seen her alive that very evening."

"At the Theatre Royal? I had not known you were one of your parents' party."

"I sat in the pit, among my acquaintance," he said simply. "But I do not think I noticed the Princess then. I saw her later in the courtyard of the Albany, where I have my rooms."

A frisson of interest swept up my spine, but I schooled my voice to indifference. "I wonder what she can have found to take her there?"

He shrugged. "*Un amant, n'est-ce pas?* It is an abode for

single gentlemen, after all; and at such an hour—it was all of two o'clock in the morning. *Pauvre enfant.* She was an unhappy woman."

This was the first hint of information I had been certain must elude us—a suggestion of the Princess's tragic course, in the hours between her first visit to Castlereagh's house, and her death four hours later.

"She was alone, I collect?"

"Always—that night, and every night, no matter how many persons she gathered about her. La Tscholikova had a genius for solitude; she carried it, like the Russian winter, within her."

"What very extraordinary behaviour! I wonder whom she might chuse to visit in the Albany? Nothing of a friendship in that quarter was mentioned at the inquest."

His expression sharpened. "You attended the coroner's panel?"

"My brother was required to give evidence," I said primly, "and I merely accompanied him, my sister being indisposed."

"I see." He hesitated an instant, as tho' weighing my words; then said, "Whomever she sought, she did not find him. She would not otherwise have been standing like a lost child in the courtyard."

"Did you speak to her?"

"I did not. I was already in my rooms, *vous comprenez*, and observed her from the window. And as I watched, she turned and quitted the courtyard for the street. I assume she had a carriage waiting there—for she was still in evening dress."

It was remarkable how neatly he offered this intelligence, pat as a rehearsed recital, and I must be forgiven for meeting it with as much suspicion as interest. I studied Count Julien's profile as he bent over his dinner, and noted once more the maturity behind the youthful façade—the look of a young man too well-acquainted with the world.

"You are an admirable son to devote your evening to a parcel of dowds, Count. What is the meaning of such charity?"

I had used the phrase deliberately, as reflecting Eliza's careless remark, but in truth the insipid conversation of several women in their fifties, two spinsters nearly twice his age, and a clutch of gentlemen whose long association with Mrs. Latouche's husbands recommended them to her society, must have proved unbearably tedious to the boy. I was certain some other interest compelled his attendance; and my evil genius whispered that he was come in the guise of spy—at his mother's behest. Was it possible that the Comtesse d'Entraigues had learned to fear her oldest friend—Eliza?

"Dowds!" the Count returned, with an easing of his expression; "you move me to utter a compliment on your beauty, Miss Austen—for certainly no one treated to the vision you present, could proclaim you a dowd!"

"I hope I am not such a gudgeon as to credit such stuff," I said calmly. "Do admit that you are bored to desperation—and accept our thanks for enlivening the party. What are the usual pursuits for a gentleman of nineteen? I enquire as the aunt of several young men, who shall be on the Town in a few years."

Count Julian allowed me to turn the conversation from the Princess with good grace. "For those of means as well as birth, the possibilities are legion! There are the clubs, where one might play at cards or dice; the wagers on horseflesh; the carriage-driving in the Park; cockfights and mills—these are the prize-fights, you understand—and of course, the pleasures of Society, such as assemblies at Almack's, or the private parties of the *ton*."

"Decidedly, you mortify your flesh in enduring this evening! I am even more in your debt, sir. Do gentlemen such as yourself patronise the Muslin Company? Or is that reserved for an elder set?"

If I had expected to jar his complacency—excite his consciousness of his father's affairs—I was to be disappointed.

"I spoke of those who possess *means*," he reminded me, "not merely birth. The High Flyers scorn those of us whose hearts are ampler than our purses; and if I may be so coarse as to declare it, Miss Austen, your genteel ladies are much the same. I have a title—a certain breeding—but I am heir to a *château* presently in ruins somewhere in the Auvergne, and the doors of the *ton* are not always open to me, you understand. When the gift of friendship is offered—as Mrs. Latouche offers it—I should be a fool to do other than honour her. Presently she will beg me to play the pianoforte—that is my gift—and after a little show of modest unwillingness, I shall oblige. It is possible I may have to earn my bread in such a way, with time."

"Surely not! Even in England there are any number of expensive young men, whose fortunes are unequal to their births," I persisted. "Second sons, for instance—or *seventh* sons. Surely they shift and contrive?"

"You think me suited to the Church?" said he, with a sardonic lift of the brow. "My father's cleverness and my mother's art are my sole inheritances, Miss Austen; neither is given to a pious turn. I had much better marry my fortune—if any schoolroom chit possessed of means will entertain my suit. *That* is the solution so many of your second sons employ. But which heiress? Perhaps Miss East will have me, if I can but acquire a taste for reading."

The cynicism of the speech should have been an effrontery, had it not been uttered with a boy's painful bitterness; and for an instant, I glimpsed the raw youth full-blown behind the polished manners, and pitied Count Julien. He reminded me a little of my Willoughby—born to a station he could not maintain, but for a desperate gaming—the courting of aged relatives—and finally, the sale of his soul in pursuit of an heiress. Society is reckless, in teaching its youth to despise honest labour.

"If not the Church, then consider the Law," I suggested. "Or, my dear Count—! You might be endlessly useful as a secretary, particularly among such men as require translations from the French! Consider the realm of politics. Surely with your father's connexions... I know of an Earl's son, Charles Malverley, who finds no shame in such a situation...."

Count Julien rose abruptly from his chair, tho' the second course was hardly begun. "I can well believe that Malverley is insensible to shame," he said, in a voice tense and low. "He has no feelings to offend. You must forgive me, Miss Austen— I find I cannot support this party after all."

He would have quitted the room on these words, but that Mrs. Latouche clapped her hands, and said with obvious delight, "*Julien!* Do you mean to play? His performance on the pianoforte is *most superior,* I assure you."

With effort, and an enchanting smile, the impoverished nobleman bowed. "Of course, *chère madame,*" he said. "You have only to call the tune."

IT WAS, WITHOUT QUESTION, THE MOST EXQUISITE MUSIC I have ever been privileged to hear. His fingers moved with a delicacy and precision that lacked nothing in skill; but the emotions they conjured forth owed everything to passion. I had only to listen once to Count Julien d'Entraigues, to know that in him I had met a young man of complex forces; a man whose obvious charm hid a subtler, more potent self; a man who might be capable of anything.

I quitted the house on Portman Square not long after his hands had stilled, and the sweetness of the final notes died away in the air. There seemed nothing more to keep us in that over-furnished drawing-room.

"Beethoven, I think," Eliza murmured as our hackney pulled up in Sloane Street; and I was still sufficiently bemused—canvassing every detail, every word of my conversation with the Frenchman that evening—that I failed to pay sufficient attention to her words, or even to Eliza herself. I was already mounting the stairs as she paid off the jarvey; I had opened the door—it had been left on the latch—and had stepped into the front passage as the hackney pulled away. It was only as I turned to pull off my gloves and remove my bonnet, that I caught Eliza's sharp cry.

Chapter 24

The Gentleman in His Cups

~

SHE LAY IN A CRUMPLED HEAP OF FEATHERS AND SILK ON the flagway, but a yard from the door.

"Eliza!" I cried in horror. "Manon—*Manon,* come quickly! Your mistress has swooned!"

I hastened back across the threshold and knelt over the limp form. Eliza's arms were flung above her head, and her reticule had slipped from her hand; in the glow of the street-lamp her pallor was dreadful.

"Good God, what can have happened?" I placed my arm behind her shoulders to support her, and raised her from the stones. She groaned pitiably.

"*Sacre dieu!*" Manon muttered beside me. She wore her nightdress and cap; the faint scent of lavender rose from the fresh linen on the chill night air. The maid's fingers, where they touched my arm, were icy; and I saw that she had not stayed even to don a dressing gown. "Let us take her inside."

I grasped Eliza's torso, and Manon supported her knees; and so we half-carried, half-dragged my sister's lifeless form inside the house. Madame Bigeon was standing in the front passage, her candle raised, her aged face piteously crumpled.

"*Pauvre madame!* She fainted?"

"I must suppose it to be so—and then struck her head, perhaps, on the flagway. She is certainly insensible."

"With that little indisposition, and her delicate constitution—she ought not to have gone out. I told Monsieur Henri how it should be, if he left her—how she would be gay to the point of dissipation, at the very risk of her life—"

"Lay her on the sopha, Manon, and Madame Bigeon— some hartshorn, please, or feathers we might burn beneath her nose—"

"Brandy is what she requires," Madame Bigeon said bluntly, and turned towards the kitchen.

We settled Eliza on the sopha, and I bent to untie her bonnet strings. Manon threw a log on the drawing-room fire, which had been allowed to go out, and began to work the bellows.

"Never mind that! Chafe her wrists," I commanded, and removed the bonnet.

Eliza groaned more violently than before, and her eyelids fluttered open. Then, with an expression of acute agony, she murmured, "Oh, Lord! My *head*," and fell back once more into a swoon.

"I shall step next door to Mr. Haden's," I said hurriedly, and ran for the surgeon.

"SHE WAS STRUCK A FEARSOME BLOW FROM BEHIND," I told Mr. Chizzlewit when he called in Sloane Street this morning, in answer to the summons I had penned in the wee hours and despatched at first light in the hands of Henry's manservant. "The instrument was a cobblestone, Mr. Haden believes—and but for the cushioning effect of her bonnet, the force might well have cracked her skull. We may thank God that my sister lives; and other than a tenderness in the region, a lump the size of a potato, and a good deal of indignation at the way in which she has been served, she suffers no severe effects. Indeed, she will not even allow me to inform my brother of the event—which shows her to remain unaffectedly silly, despite her sufferings."

"I am shocked," he said with unwonted gravity—"indeed, I am grieved. That so lovely a creature as Mrs. Henry should be assaulted with such violence— But is there no one who can describe her assailant?"

"Sloane Street—all of Hans Town—is a rural vicinity," I reminded him, "and its denizens are not much in the habit of such dissipation as *dining out late* on a Sunday night. It must have been all of eleven o'clock when our hackney arrived at the door; and by then, nearly every candle was extinguished. We have not your expensive gas-lighting in these parts; the oil lamps are dim at best; and even I, who was but three yards from her position, heard and saw nothing—until it was too late. Can you have an idea how I blame myself?"

I broke off, and shielded my eyes with my hand. "Forgive me. I passed an uneasy night."

"Not at all," he murmured. "And the surgeon—Haden? Has he given you cause for concern?"

"He believes she will recover fully—and when I hear how she orders all of us about, and how thoroughly she enjoys the attention, as she reigns like a queen among her bed-clothes, supplied with draughts, and panadas, and sur-rounded by the latest numbers of the *Ladies Monthly Museum* and *La Belle Assemblée,* I should laugh to think she gives me the smallest moment of anxiety![1] If it were not that my brother charged me expressly with taking the utmost care of her in his absence—"

"She saw nothing, heard nothing, of her attacker?"

I shook my head. "The wheels of the departing hackney obscured every sound; and in the darkness—"

"Of course." Mr. Chizzlewit turned the brim of his curly beaver between his hands; it was a handsome article, as was everything about his neat and elegant form. "But what I must demand is *why?* Why should anyone chuse to strike down Mrs. Austen? Her reticule was not stolen, I collect?"

"Nor anything else she carried on her person. The sole object of violence was Eliza herself. And so we must conclude that the attack found its motivation in this dreadful business of the Princess's murder." I held the solicitor's gaze. "For my part, I can think of only one person who has reason to fear my sister—and that is the Comtesse d'Entraigues, who may now believe she divulged too much of a private nature, in her

---

[1] A panada was a dish made of bread or crackers, boiled to a pulp and fla-vored, and generally served to invalids.—*Editor's note.*

various interviews. Perhaps she has learned somehow of the jewels' discovery, and restoration to Prince Pirov—perhaps her entire story was a fabrication, intended to obscure a far more malevolent history—I do not know. I may only say that the Comtesse was promised to dine with us last evening, then sent her son as proxy, complaining of a sick headache."

"—So that she might lurk in wait for your carriage in Sloane Street, and murder her friend?" Sylvester Chizzlewit's brows soared. "I should call the idea fantastic—were the whole business not already so!"

I raised my hands in supplication. "One has only to consider of her story as a farrago of lies from beginning to end, to admit that she is ideally positioned to have murdered the Princess—and thus to fear my sister's knowledge of her affairs. A woman who has killed once, should not hesitate to kill again."

"But happily, she failed to do so. I think perhaps I should consult my grandfather—and enquire whether he knows of a likely personage in Barnes, Surrey, who might be set upon the d'Entraigues household. We ought to be informed of their movements—provided the informer acts with discretion."

A bell sounded somewhere above—from Eliza's room, no doubt—and Mr. Chizzlewit said, "I have trespassed too long. I stay only to enquire if there is any way I may serve you, Miss Austen? —Any want of Mrs. Henry's I might supply?"

"You are very good! For of course you must apprehend that I called you hither only to presume upon your generosity. I should like the hackney driver questioned, if possible. He may, indeed, have seen something as he drove off that he failed to put to the proper account."

"Of course! The jarvey! You engaged him in Portman Square?"

"There is a stand of such men, waiting on the custom of the inhabitants. It is possible that our driver makes a habit of loitering there—"

"—and thus might be readily found. I am happy to oblige you—and shall search for him instantly."

"Not *so* swiftly, I hope." I raised a hand as tho' to hold him back. "There is one other who might well have observed Eliza's attacker—tho' if he should have done so, I am all amazement that he did not come forward."

"Indeed? You observed someone in the street—or a neighbour, perhaps, whose lamp was yet lit?"

I shook my head. "Nothing so comforting. For the past several days, I have been aware that the Bow Street Runner, William Skroggs, has dogged our movements—following us when we leave the house, much as you desire someone to watch the d'Entraigueses. I have said nothing of this to Eliza, not wishing to alarm her. But it is possible Skroggs witnessed the whole of last evening's episode."

"The scoundrel!" Mr. Chizzlewit cried. "And if he did so, he should better have sounded a hue and cry! I shall certainly seek Mr. Skroggs in his lair—for I have been desiring to inform him of my interest in your affairs. The shadow of a reputable solicitor may well be enough to dim a Runner's ardour for the hunt. We have a nasty tendency to make them *prove* their allegations."

Mr. Chizzlewit bowed, and would have set his beaver upon his head, and departed without another word; but not even the press of events could entirely quell my curiosity.

"Sir, before you go—"

He halted, and looked his enquiry.

"May I know whether your dinner engagement with Mr. Charles Malverley proved of interest?"

"Malverley!" he repeated, as tho' recalling an old acquaintance long since laid to rest. "To be sure, it was a delightful evening, full of reminiscence and interest! Particularly as pertains to our present enquiries. But have you the time—the energy—to devote to a recital?"

"I should like nothing better," I told him. "From something that was said last evening, I have a burning desire to know more of the gentleman. Pray—sit down."

Mr. Chizzlewit obliged me, and commenced his tale.

"I keep a suite of rooms in Ryder Street, near St. James, and it was there I had engaged to dine with Malverley. He arrived at half-past six o'clock, and at seven we sat down to the meal my man had prepared; beefsteaks and Yorkshire pudding, with a couple of roasted fowls. I took care to see Malverley amply supplied with claret—which you must know my grandfather himself laid down years since, when our family's intercourse with France was customary, and not subject to the Monster's embargoes. I intended that he should be pretty *well to live* by the conclusion of dinner, when the decanters of port and brandy were set out; and he did not disappoint me. He set aside the air of reserve acquired so lately in Berkeley Square, and talked with a freedom more characteristic of the Malverley I recalled from Oxford days."

"So you thought him altered, then, from when you last knew him?"

"Much altered. The Malverley of memory was a rackety fellow enough, full of high living and dash; the sighing object of every maiden's heart; not the sort to set up as a statesman's clerk, bowing and scraping to a man whose bloodlines he may best by a full five centuries. I confess I was astonished to learn of his accepting such a position of Lord Castlereagh—I should rather have expected him to follow a rake's progress, dicing in the clubs and embarrassing his father the Earl with his obligations; wagering on horses that always fail to place; pursuing an heiress when nothing else served to tow him from the River Tick.[2] But I collect that in his final year at Oxford he overstepped the line too rashly—and committed a sin so unpardonable he was banished for a time to the Continent—or that part of it unfettered by the Monster's chains. I do not know the whole, but must conclude that he returned a reformed character, ready to earn his bread by honourable means, in the service of his country. His father the Earl of Tanborough being a notable Tory in Lords, the position of secretary to Lord Castlereagh was readily obtained—my friend's return to England coinciding with Lord Castlereagh's resignation from office, some eighteen months since."

"How convenient. And has Malverley enjoyed his honest labour?"

Sylvester Chizzlewit hesitated. His gaze turned inward, as tho' in consideration of the evening's talk. "I should not describe his feelings in those terms," he concluded. "The reserve descends once more, in speaking of his lordship. Perhaps the events of recent months—the publication of the letters—the estimation of the Regent—the possibility of high office—the Princess Tscholikova's death—"

"Perhaps he does not like his employer."

---

[2] This was a cant term for indebtedness, as the wellborn who lacked means tended to live "on tick"—or credit.—*Editor's note.*

"I have thought that too," the solicitor admitted. "I noticed that Malverley could not meet my gaze when he spoke of Castlereagh, tho' his words were entirely correct—such phrases of admiration as one might expect to fall from the lips of a grateful follower."

"Could *Lady* Castlereagh be the cause? The idea of an improper liaison was pregnant in the air at the inquest."

"Lady Castlereagh!" Mr. Chizzlewit's countenance broke in amusement. "I wish you might hear the way Malverley speaks of her! If it were not so callous, I should repeat his endearments in this room—but that my good manners forbid it! She is a creature of caprice, and malice, and self-consequence, to hear him tell it—a lady who dearly loves to sway Society, and influence politics, but whose use for her husband ended at the altar!"

"I see. And her use for Malverley—?"

"From the bitterness with which he refers to her ladyship, I should judge that she treats him as a lackey—attractive in company, and caressingly addressed before the Great, in tribute to his style and beauty and breeding; but sent about his business as soon as they are shut into the carriage together."

"Deplorable! And is his heart bestowed on another?"

Again, Mr. Chizzlewit hesitated. "I cannot undertake to say. I collect that he is in the habit of patronising the Muslin Company—but has resisted the respectable lures thrown out to him by enterprising mammas. In truth, I should wonder that any such lures *are* thrown—for he is but a third son, after all, with limited expectations. If Castlereagh's star should rise again, he may go far in politics—"

"—But if scandal and suicide dim the star to the point of

extinction, friend Malverley shall be forced to desert the ship," I concluded, with a lamentable mixing of metaphors.

"Exactly. Hence the restraint I detect when he speaks of his lordship. He does not wish to commit his loyalties too far. In fact, at one point—" He broke off, biting his lip. "Malverley was in his cups. He burst out, as tho' in the grip of passion, *By God, there are* some *things no gentleman will do, even for hire.*"

"And you took this to refer to Castlereagh?"

"I did. I collect the demand his lordship made was of a personal nature, and repugnant to Malverley."

"How intriguing. And what of your friend's loyalties on the night in question? Were you able to divine anything of Malverley's real movements during the early hours of Tuesday morning?"

"If I failed, it was not for lack of trying." Mr. Chizzlewit smiled. "We are now come to the latter part of the evening I spent, in trespassing on the trust of an old friend—when we sat down, rather more foxed than not, to play at picquet.[3] Malverley was bosky enough to throw caution to the winds, and suggest pound points; but I had not so far shot the cat as to render me agreeable to such folly, and insisted upon shillings. It was after the third hand that he began to talk of the horror of that night."

My interest quickened. "He felt it to be so?"

"Horrible? It was the very word he used. I cannot tell you what he found to do in Castlereagh's office for so many hours before dawn—I cannot believe that a man whose pres-

---

[3] *Foxed, well to live, shot the cat,* and *bosky* are all cant terms for inebriation.—*Editor's note.*

ent pursuit is the raising of merino sheep on his country estate, may be deluged with letters requiring immediate reply—but in any case, Malverley's dismay at finding the Princess's body at the door was real enough. He broke down when he spoke of it, choking with sobs over his hand of cards—and every attempt at play had to be abandoned."

"What exactly did he say?"

"*God, her throat!* is what I chiefly recall; and, *the poor creature, to use herself so vilely!* He shuddered like a child in the grip of nightmare—and seemed deeply affected by the memory. It was all I could do to calm him."

"Then I collect, in such a fit of hysteria, you could get little more of sense from him?"

Mr. Chizzlewit grimaced. "Very little. But I would swear to it that Malverley was astonished to discover the corpse in Berkeley Square. His aspect last evening was not that of guilt, but of misery and regret. The death was perhaps more deeply felt, for having burst upon him like a shell."

"I see. You explain it very well. What did you then?"

"I called for ale and coffee, a judicious mixture of which will invariably set the brandy-drinker to rights; and a little after three o'clock, he toddled home towards the Albany. He would have walked, but that I insisted on putting him into a hackney."

"The Albany?" I repeated, much struck.

"Yes. Any number of single gentlemen lodge there—you must know it: the old Duke of Albany's pile, converted to some seventy apartments, just off Piccadilly."

"Indeed I do! My brother Henry kept a branch of his bank there some years ago, before moving to Henrietta Street. It is possible Malverley referred to his rooms at the inquest. But the *Albany*! It is just—" I stopped short, considering.

"Go on," he said.

"I, too, dined out last evening—and one of the party was the young Comte d'Entraigues, Monsieur Julien. He professes to have seen the Princess Tscholikova some hours before her death, standing alone in the middle of the Albany's courtyard. He lodges there himself, and says he witnessed the lady's arrival from an upper storey window."

"Good God! Then you think she went in search of Malverley? But *why*?"

"To plead his intercession with Lord Castlereagh, perhaps? Malverley admitted to a glancing social acquaintance with the lady." I paused. "But we are too previous. As you say, some seventy gentlemen lodge in the Albany—including young d'Entraigues. We cannot assume it was Malverley she sought."

"Not without we know more—whether there was indeed a connexion between my friend and the Princess."

"That alone might account for his sense of horror at finding her dead..." I raised my eyes and met Sylvester Chizzlewit's. "Of one connexion, however, I would know a good deal more. A *something* exists between Julien d'Entraigues and Charles Malverley; I am certain of it."

Mr. Chizzlewit frowned. "What would you imply?"

"The young Count spoke of your friend in such terms, last night, that I should judge he hated him," I said.

Chapter 25

A Call in Russell Square

~

WE SPENT A QUIET MORNING AFTER MR. CHIZZLEWIT DE-parted on his various errands of intrigue and mercy. I com-pleted the work of proofing Egerton's pages; practised for an hour upon Eliza's pianoforte; and embroidered a set of handkerchiefs I have been working for Henry, while sitting at Eliza's bedside. By one o'clock she was quite bored with her novel, had run through her frivolous periodicals; con-sumed a bowl of Madame Bigeon's sustaining broth, and was sleepy enough to close her eyes for an hour. I drew the silk draperies and saw her comfortably disposed with a pillow be-hind her back.

"Do not be doing anything I should not like," she warned as I crept to the door. "And do not, I beg of you, embark on any adventure so exciting that I should mourn to have missed it! I will be on my feet tomorrow, Jane."

She was an endearing, if slightly comic figure, with her head wrapped in Haden's neat bandage, and a lace confection perched rakishly over the whole.

"May I write to Henry, and assure him of your safety?"

"On no account are you to send him the *least word* of what has occurred," she forbid sharply. "He would post back from Oxford on the instant—and then where should we be?"

"—Forced to divulge the whole, which I may say I cannot think an unalloyed evil."

"That is because you have had the good sense to remain unmarried! I should never hear the end of Henry's reproaches, should he learn of my folly in brokering Anne's jewels. He should believe me a creature sunk in deceit, Jane—one who must always prowl on the sly, behind his back—and that I cannot bear; for if one is to be judged very nearly a criminal, it ought to be for indiscretions of one's *own*. One therefore may claim all the pleasure, as well as the pain, of a misdeed. But to figure as reprehensible in Henry's eyes on account of that...that *French opera dancer*...I can't and won't do it!"

"Eliza! —When Henry is the kindest man alive? And loves you so entirely? How can you utter such falsehoods?"

She drew a square of linen from the sleeve of her nightdress, and mopped lugubriously at her eyes. "It is his very kindness that makes everything worse! *Go away,* dear Jane, before you cut up all my peace!"

RUSSELL SQUARE IS A SECTION OF NEW-BUILT HOUSES, north of the genteel part of Town, thrown up by the archi-

tect Mr. Burton on the ruins of the Duke of Bedford's pile—
which was pulled down some ten years since, to make way for
a great clearing of the land, and the raising of a row of
houses adorned by Ionic columns, which Mr. Burton dearly
loves. Indeed, construction yet continues on a section of the
square, and is not likely to be concluded for several years; the
whole vicinity is so raw and fresh as to fairly squeak with pain.
Bedford Square is to the west, and the Foundling Hospital to
the east; and in general, Eliza should declare the situation in-
eligible, without one is a mushroom or a cit.[1]

In this marginal locale, the beautiful Julia Radcliffe
leased a house: an *entire house,* for the enjoyment and display
of a daring seventeen-year-old; furnished up and decorated
in the latest style, full of green and gold satin and rosewood
tables. I was moved to wonder at the largesse which had established the whole, and discount the rumour that would
have Miss Radcliffe refusing *carte blanche* from a host of suit-
ors; *someone* had certainly put down a good deal of blunt to
trick the Barque of Frailty out in stile. If Sylvester Chizzlewit
had not furnished me with the address, I should have believed myself mistook when I was shown by the housekeeper
into the small anteroom reserved for callers on the ground
floor. I had not troubled to veil myself, as Eliza would have
urged; both anteroom and square were respectable in the
extreme, with the sort of emphatic rectitude common to
families in trade. Miss Radcliffe, I must suppose, was merely a

---

[1] *Cit* was an abbreviation of *citizen* and designated a person engaged in
trade in the City, or square mile of merchant London east of the genteel
neighborhoods bordering Hyde Park. *Mushroom* designated a cit who as-
pired to the upper classes, either through conspicuous consumption or
marriage with the gentry; like mushrooms, such people were viewed as
unattractive social growths who sprang up overnight.—*Editor's note.*

merchant of another order; her charms being synonymous with her wares.

A good fire burned in the grate, with a settee drawn up to it; I warmed my hands an instant, for spring had forgot its carefree airs of Sunday, and turned chill once more. A gilt pier glass in the Adam style held reign over a marquetry console; I studied my reflection in the glass, and thought how hagged I looked, now that I have twice Miss Radcliffe's years in my dish. The sound of a woman's laughter, and a man's low voice, drifted from the drawing-room above. I deserted the fire and glanced instead in the porcelain bowl that held pride of place in the middle of the console. It held calling cards.

The housekeeper had gone to report my name to her mistress, and request the favour of an interview—but from the sound of conversation above, I could not doubt Miss Radcliffe would deny herself. I turned over the cards in the bowl idly, awaiting the housekeeper's return. *The Honourable George Ponsonby*, one said; *Horace Beckford*, another; Lord Luttrell's card was there, and Frederick Bentinck's. All men of fashion—including George Brummell. And at the bottom, as tho' left a few days previous, a card that must stop me cold.

Julien, it read in delicate black lettering, *Comte d'Entraigues*.

Did the son worship at Miss Radcliffe's altar, no less than the father? Or had Julien come on some errand of his *père*'s?

"Miss Austen," Julia Radcliffe said.

She regarded me from the doorway, as elegant in her appearance as ever; her dress being straw-coloured silk, with a worked bodice—hardly morning wear, but I must suppose that Miss Radcliffe's mornings were vastly different than my own.

I made her a courtesy. "I do not disturb you?"

"Only a little," she returned with frankness. "I have a sur-feit of visitors today—several are even now upstairs. But I have ordered refreshment to be sent in to them, and may spare you a few moments. Pray, let us sit down. Has that odi-ous Bill Skroggs been haunting you again?"

She was studiously free of artifice or reserve; and for so much I ought to be thankful. No time would be wasted in meaningless pleasantries.

"I believe it was his colleague, Mr. Black, who shadowed my movements this morning," I answered calmly, "but I did not come to speak to you of that. Miss Radcliffe, am I correct in believing that Princess Tscholikova called at this house a few days before her death?"

"She did." The girl's countenance did not change. "Were you at all acquainted with her?"

"I was not—but Bill Skroggs chuses to believe I am re-sponsible for her death. A great quantity of precious stones belonging to the Princess were placed in my keeping; and by a series of circumstances, were revealed to the Magistracy in Bow Street as having been stolen. I am now suspected of their theft—and worse."

Miss Radcliffe rose abruptly from the settee and moved to the hearth. Her composure was absolute, but for this sud-den shift; she stood immobile, as tho' desirous only of warm-ing herself at the flame.

"Does my communication surprise you at all?"

She smiled faintly. "No, indeed. I have been waiting for some further intelligence of what I may only describe as a mys-tery, Miss Austen—but hardly looked for enlightenment from this quarter. How did the jewels come into your keeping?"

I was sensible that the girl was entirely mistress of herself, and governed by a profound caution. She intended to learn more than she revealed; and for all her frankness of manner, it must be my lot to fence with her, as two potentates might navigate a treaty.

"Before I tell you—may I know the substance of the Princess's errand in this household?"

"She wished to pay a call." Julia Radcliffe sank back onto the settee, her posture upright and watchful. "I must observe that you have done the same, and on as slight an acquaintance."

"You were known to one another, however?"

"By name only. I had never spoken to Tscholikova before in my life, tho' I had often noticed her at the opera, and similar places. Tell me, Miss Austen—why are you come?"

"Because the threat of the gallows hangs over me."

"And what have I to do with that?"

The coldness of the remark gave me pause. "Much, I must imagine. I have been told the jewels were in your keeping, before they passed into ... *mine.*"

"Have you, indeed?" A look of incredulity lit her perfect features. "Then I have been betrayed by one whose discretion I believed to be infallible."

"The Comtesse d'Entraigues?"

The expression of shock drained from her countenance; composure was once more regained. "Ah. The *Comtesse...* and what did she tell you?"

"Surely you may surmise!"

"I hardly know of what that creature is capable. I should like to have the recital whole, from your lips."

I shrugged, aware that in giving way to her request, I accorded her the ascendancy in our battle. "You must forgive me if I offend your sensibilities—if I tread too closely on matters of an intensely private nature—but the pressure of events, and Mr. Skroggs's attention, are very great, and must urge me to be explicit."

"I prefer plain dealing."

"Very well. Anne de St.-Huberti informed me that she had come to Russell Square to beg you to renounce her husband; that she feared the loss of her household and security, under the threat of divorce; and that by way of recompense for your conquest of the Comte, you pressed upon her Tscholikova's jewels."

"*I* pressed them upon her?" Julia Radcliffe's delicate brows rose. "I see. Then there is very little point in my denying it."

The swiftness of the admission convinced me, as outcry or argument would not have done, that she lied. Julia Radcliffe had accepted the Comtesse's claims as a matter of policy—a tactical choice, rather than an admission of guilt.

"Miss Radcliffe," I demanded, "did Princess Tscholikova place her jewels in your keeping when she called here, several days before her death?"

"She must have done so. The Comtesse d'Entraigues would have it I gave the jewels to *her*—and for that to be true, I must have received them from the *Princess*..."

Her tone was almost one of amusement. I studied her visage searchingly.

"If I am to escape the threat of hanging," I said slowly, "it will be chiefly through the implication of guilt in *others*—Bill Skroggs will have his prey. I should not like to think it is *you*, Miss Radcliffe, I am coursing into his jaws."

A silence fell between us.

"I must consider all you have said." She rose gracefully, her countenance betraying nothing. "I cannot possibly know what may be told—what I may...in short, I must consult with another. If you would be so good as to give me your direction—"

"I am staying with my brother, Mr. Henry Austen, of No. 64 Sloane Street, Hans Town."

"Very well. I shall call upon you at the earliest possible moment, Miss Austen. At present, however, I am sadly neglecting my guests."

She bobbed a curtsey; I returned it; and then Julia Radcliffe was gone.

I HAD THE LENGTH OF MY JOURNEY HOME TO REFLECT upon all that had passed. I was not, in the event, entirely downcast: I had learned that Miss Radcliffe had indeed seen the Princess before her death; that she was aware of the existence of the jewels—for she had betrayed no surprise or curiosity when they were mentioned—and that there was *some other* she would shield, consult, and protect. For all that she had revealed so little, I felt I must be nearer my object. I had played my trump card: the threat of pursuit from Bill Skroggs—a man whom at Grafton House she had owned she hated. I had merely to wait for Miss Radcliffe to return my call—and such a well-behaved, gently-reared girl was unlikely to neglect the exertion.

Chapter 26

Tales to Frighten Children

Tuesday, 30 April 1811

~

SHE CAME TO ME TODAY, FAR SOONER THAN I HAD EX-
pected, and such a show of breeding must be imputed to her
Radcliffe rearing.

I woke early to the muffled hallooing that invariably con-
notes a London fog, and the magnified clatter of horses'
hooves, carriage wheels, carters' drays and peddlers'
screeching; the chill of yesterday had brought with it rain,
which gurgled in the gutters. So dim was the light—or so
great my exhaustion from the previous night's broken
rest—that I had overslept myself, and discovered by the bells
that it was full nine o'clock. Manon had crept in on cat's
paws and made up the fire; but I should have to ring for my
morning tea. I rose, and reached for my dressing gown—

when the sound of a horse's terrified neigh brought me to the window.

In the swirling wisps of fog and rain below, a black carriage had misjudged its pace and run full-tilt into a cart; the team of horses—also black as pitch—had broken the traces, and the leader was plunging wildly in the shafts; the driver was struggling to rein in the beast, while a groom reached for its tossing head; and the carter abused all within hearing for the quantity of sacks that had spilled into the carriageway, several of which had split open, and strewn grain onto the rain-wet paving.

This might have been enough to engage my interest and arrest my sight, had such incidents not proved wearisomely familiar after six weeks' habitation in the Metropolis; but my quickened senses detected another reason to linger by the casement: the jet-black coach and its midnight horses were clearly agents of mourning. I glanced the length of Sloane Street, and understood from the procession of sombre carriages and dusky teams that what I witnessed, on this day of fog and rain, was a funeral procession. It must—it could only be—Princess Evgenia Tscholikova's.

The weather alone—the sulphurous glow of side-lamps— the plunging leader snorting with terror—rendered the aspect positively spectral, as tho' the equipages and all their occupants should be swallowed up in a cloud of hellish vapour. I shuddered, and drew the drapes against the scene—and wondered into what ground the poor creature's body should be laid. The wretched woman had been adjudged a suicide, and might rightly have been refused consecrated ground—buried instead at a crossroads without even a marker, so that her blasted soul might wander the earth in endless lamentation—but I hoped that Prince

Pirov had found the proper palms to cross with silver. I did not like to think of a woman I believed to have been cruelly murdered, left in a pauper's grave. To be scorned even in death—!

I dressed hurriedly and went in search of Manon.

"Druschka tells me the Duke of Norfolk—who is a Papist, *vous savez*—has offered to take the Princess's remains in his family's burial ground." The maid glanced over her shoulder, and despite years of habitation in England, crossed herself hurriedly against the Evil Eye. "Not the ancestral vault, of course, but a plot near the home chapel. Prince Pirov was most grateful."

"The Prince is capable of amiable feelings, then?"

"Towards men of standing, who show him favour—but of course! To Druschka he is a monster. He has ordered her to be ready to quit London on the morrow; they are all to be off for Paris, and then by degrees to Moscow, and I think she will break her heart with crying, me. She does not believe she will survive the journey."

"Could she not secure a suitable position here, in London?" I enquired.

Manon shook her head. "The Prince will not allow it. That woman is almost a slave, mademoiselle—it is the nature of things in Russia. She does not command her own life, she has no power to determine her future; she must wait upon the will of her master. The Prince finds it imperative that Druschka leave the country."

"I wonder," I mused as Manon set a tea cup by my place, "what exactly is he afraid of?"

"The Tsar, no doubt."

"Manon—I wish you will put a question to Druschka before she is whisked away."

"Certainly. I shall walk in Cadogan Place at three o'clock. What would you know?"

"—Which gentleman Princess Tscholikova was in the habit of visiting, at the Albany," I said.

I FILLED THE NEXT HOUR IN ANSWERING A LETTER FROM Cassandra I had received that morning—two pages of sun and spring air and Kentish nonsense, for she is in the midst of a visit to my brother Edward at Godmersham. She is full of enthusiasm for our musical evening, and requires further particulars of my dress: *How had I done my hair? Did I mean to trim my old pelisse fresh?* The cleric, Mr. Wyndham Knatchbull, had sent a report of the evening round his Kentish relations, and thus by degrees his judgement arrived at Godmersham: Miss Jane Austen is "a pleasing looking young woman." I must be satisfied with such tepid praise—at five-and-thirty, one cannot pretend to anything better. I have not yet sunk, it seems, to looking *ill;* and in truth, the notice of a man who may talk only theosophy at one of Eliza's evenings should never be necessary to my happiness.

"There is a lady who wishes to see you, mademoiselle," Manon said from the book room doorway.

I set aside my correspondence—it was rather tedious in any case, as so many topics of interest are embargoed, being too perilous to communicate. "It will be Mrs. Tilson, I suppose. We are to dine with her this evening."

"No, mademoiselle—a Miss Radcliffe. She has sent in her card."

I rose hastily from the writing table and smoothed my gown. "Pray, Manon—show her directly into this room. We may be assured of privacy here."

The careful control of expression Miss Radcliffe had maintained, while I fenced with her in the anteroom in Russell Square, was less perfect this morning. Her face, framed by a dashing bonnet with a short and upswept poke, was paler than ever; the delicate bloom of peach and rose had fled her cheek. I imputed the cause to an unhappy night, and guessed that a period of uneasiness had been capped with a failure to eat during the interval. "Miss Austen," she said as she curtseyed, "I am thankful to find you at home."

"The pleasure must be entirely mine. Won't you sit down? Manon—be so good as to bring some refreshment for Miss Radcliffe."

The Barque of Frailty glided towards one of Eliza's French chairs, and sank onto it—ramrod straight, as I remembered. Did the child never allow herself to unbend? The picture of perfection she presented was surely purchased at the cost of rigid self-control—and I found a phrase of my acquaintance, Miss East's, lingering in the mind. Not self-control, she had said, but *self-reliance* ought to be the theme of Mrs. Brunton's novel. *Self-reliance.* Julia Radcliffe could presume upon no one's disinterested support—and thus had made of her slender frame a column of steel.

Manon appeared with wine and cakes upon a silver tray. Miss Radcliffe refused a macaroon, but accepted a glass of ratafia, and sipped a little before she spoke.

"I have been thinking almost continuously of what you said," she began after an interval, "and I believe I ought to help you ward off that terrible man, Bill Skroggs, to the utmost extent of my power. As you so rightly observed, Skroggs will be satisfied only with a victim—and if you are determined it shall not be *yourself,* I am equally determined he shall not settle upon *me.*"

"So far, our interests are allied."

"I cannot answer all the questions you might pose—indeed, for many of them I have no answer—and in some cases, I freely state that I *will not* supply the solution to your puzzle, for not only I am encompassed in it. Others there may be whose well-being must be injured by any communication of mine. But one matter at least I might illuminate—Princess Tscholikova's visit to me, on the Sunday morning prior to her unfortunate death." Miss Radcliffe's blue eyes rose to meet mine. "I am right, I think, in apprehending that she did *not* die by her own hand—as has been reported in the newspapers?"

"The coroner's panel returned a verdict of self-murder, but I cannot credit it."

"Why not? She was certainly miserable."

"You felt as much, on your sole meeting?"

"I did." Miss Radcliffe swayed a little in her seat, as tho' she would dearly love to lean against the back of the chair, and let down her guard a little; then she recovered, and went on.

"She appeared in Russell Square at half-past two o'clock that Sunday, in a state bordering on strong hystericks, and would have it that she came on an errand of mercy. She had heard somewhere, I must suppose, that I am so fortunate as to have any number of gentlemen dancing attendance upon me, Miss Austen—you will apprehend, no doubt, that I am in no position to discourage any one of them..."

"I *have heard,* Miss Radcliffe, that neither have you succumbed to the charms of a particular suitor—but prefer to maintain an interesting independence."

She flushed. "If, by that remark, you would suggest that I deliberately play off one man against another, in order to enflame the ardour of each, it is a gross misrepresentation of my life and circumstances."

"I did not mean to imply a calculation I am persuaded you should never employ," I returned gently. "I would merely point out that rather than seeking the protection of *one,* you have found a kind of safety in the numbers that flock to your door."

Miss Radcliffe studied her gloved hands. "The Princess believed me on the point of contracting just such a tie of obligation with a man whom she had reason to fear herself, and whom she believed should certainly be the ruin of me. His name is Emmanuel, Comte d'Entraigues."

"I am a little acquainted with the Comte."

"She related a part of her private history, as pertained to the Count, that must convince any woman of sense that he is not a man to be trusted. Her motivation, as she claimed, was to prevent my life from being blasted as hers had been."

"The episode in Vienna, I collect?"

Miss Radcliffe inclined her head. "I apprehend that a liaison of passion, on the Princess's side, was perverted on the Comte's to one of political utility."

"I see. Pray go on."

"I assured *La Tscholikova* that others had succeeded in determining the sordid nature of my fate before ever I knew the Comte d'Entraigues, and that her energy—as well as her presumption—were wasted."

The blandness of this statement must send a chill through my soul. "In short, the rumour of divorce—which so acted upon the Comtesse d'Entraigues—had come to Princess Tscholikova's ears as well?"

"I must suppose it to be so. I have never intended to

marry the Comte d'Entraigues—the respectability of the institution and the position such a tie might convey, being insufficient recompense for the gentleman's age, manners, and vicious habits. But the Princess felt it necessary to urge me from the prospect, and despite my assurances, would not be satisfied. She said she had endeavoured to borrow a remarkable sum—several thousands of pounds—from a banker of her acquaintance, so that she might secure my safety and her own departure from London at a single stroke; but in the event, her banker had failed her. Therefore, she proposed to press upon me a considerable treasure, in the form of her jewels, to *preserve me against want*—as she said—and thus against the Comte's appeal. When I consider how little fortune d'Entraigues may command, I own I find her earnestness risible. I refused the contents of her velvet roll—"

"It was the roll she would have given you—not a porcelain box?" I interrupted.

A veil of incomprehension moved across Miss Radcliffe's brow. "I saw no porcelain box."

"Very well. Pray continue."

"I refused the gift, and assured her I had no need of such charity." Miss Radcliffe's chin rose. "Tho' my family chuses to cut all connexion, Miss Austen, and does not deign to recognise that I share the name of Radcliffe, you will know that I possess a little competence—a small but adequate income—through my mother's family. It came to me upon her death. My father and brothers cannot strip me of that sum, however much they should wish to do so; indeed, it represents the foundation of that independence you profess to admire."

"Then why—?"

"Why do I pursue a career as reckless as it is reprehensible?" The perfect composure broke a little. "Perhaps I possess a vaulting ambition. Perhaps I am a creature of greed. Perhaps I merely wish to throw that craving for respectability, which my family sets beyond all other feelings, in the face of those who wish me to submit to it. But in any case—I did not accept the Princess's jewels. When she had left me, however, I discovered the velvet roll thrust down among the seat cushions of my drawing-room sopha."

"Ah." I sighed. "I begin to understand."

"I was promised at Harriette Wilson's that evening—she collects a certain party of gentlemen and ladies around her most Sundays—and so I caught up the roll as I quitted the house, intending to return it to Hans Place at the first opportunity. But while at Miss Wilson's, I encountered the Comte d'Entraigues—and a spirit of mischief provoked me to entrust my errand to him." The blue eyes began to dance. "I thought that if the Princess were to receive her jewels from the hand of the very man she had intended to thwart, she might be discouraged in that spirit of interference which sent her headlong to my door—"

I studied the youthful face poised before me, and wondered at the truths its serenity of expression concealed. "And so you would have me believe it was the Comte who miscarried his charge—and gave the jewels to his wife?"

Julia Radcliffe shrugged. "I cannot say how it was. I may only tell you how the velvet roll entered my hands—and how it left them again. What occurred after, others must supply. The jewels certainly were never returned to Hans Place."

"No. They came instead, by degrees, to me."

Miss Radcliffe had owned there were *others* she refused to

expose; *others* whose well-being must be injured by any communication of hers. The memory of a certain calling card, engraved with the name of Julien d'Entraigues, rose in my mind. What if she preferred the beautiful young man to his father? There was but two years' difference in the young people's ages; how natural that the dazzling Bird of Paradise, well-bred but forever fallen in reputation, should be drawn to the impoverished young Count—with his passion for music, his ruined estates, his air of suppressed desperation? What if the Princess Tscholikova's jewels had meant freedom from want forever, for Julien d'Entraigues? And the possibility of a different life, for Miss Radcliffe? The two might have made their futures anywhere. I could imagine the Barque meeting *Julien* at Harriette Wilson's, and pressing upon him the key to his fortune—but how, then, had the *Comtesse* brought them to Eliza's door, with her raddled tale of divorce and recompense?

"I have trespassed on your goodness too long," Miss Radcliffe said, rising.

"Not at all."

There was a frailty to her figure that must burn the sight of any who regarded her; I wished that she had partaken of the macaroons. Impulsively, I said, "Before you go—I have no right to enquire of you—save the interested concern of one who must sincerely wish you well—can you not endeavour, with time, to heal the breach between yourself and your family? Surely, if you possess independence of means, there can be no loss of face in extending an olive branch. Is not a quiet retreat in solitude, preferable to the risks you undoubtedly invite, in your present mode of life?"

She stared at me, her impassive countenance a shade of remotest marble.

"When I was but fourteen years old, Miss Austen," she said in a voice low with passion, "I was forced to intimacy with a cousin some eight years my senior. I resisted, for I had always regarded him with terror and revulsion; but I was as a fly beneath his hand—crushed. When I went to my father in pain and shame—my mother being then dead some years— he regarded me with horror. I do not think he was able to look me in the face from that day forward; some flaw in me had invited my rape. My father and *his* cousin—whose son my attacker was—agreed that at all costs the affair should be suppressed; I must and should be married to my predator. Can you have an idea of it? To be *chained*, my whole life long, to one I regarded with *loathing*? I should rather have died—"

She paused, and pressed her hand to her mouth.

"So great was my parent's insistence, that I required only a little time to know my cousin better, that I was powerless to withstand him. I agreed to see my cousin again. He chose to regard my pliancy as invitation to a second rape. I found myself, a few months past my fourteenth birthday, pregnant and unwed—the object of my father's cordial hatred. My obdurate refusal to accept my cousin in marriage, he called undutiful; and gave my cousin orders to beat me with his hunting whip."

"Good God," I whispered.

"I fled at night to the home of my old nurse—who had removed some thirty miles distant from my family—and from thence I refused to be moved, until the child was brought to bear." Her fingers clenched on her reticule. "My implacable dread of this man, my cousin, led to a breach between our families. He was sent away; and I, too, was denied all further admittance to my childhood home. In short, my name was struck from the Radcliffe rolls. I determined, at the age of fifteen, to fulfill the very worst assumptions of my life—to pursue a course so glittering, so heady, that no man should ever again have the power to disturb my peace or command my heart. I am certain of the evils attached to my situation, Miss Austen—but I am equally sure they will never approach those I suffered in the bosom of my family; and for this, I must be thankful."

"Forgive me," I said, and held out my hand.

She took it in her gloved one, and pressed it an instant. "Why? What sin have you committed?"

"—That of vulgar curiosity. I encroached on ground that must forever be private."

"Not at all," she returned. "You enquired because you care—and for that, I must always honour you, Miss Austen."

I SAW JULIA RADCLIFFE INTO HER PHAETON—THE GROOM had been walking the horses some time—and watched her drive smartly away; and observed, with misgiving, the black-clad figure of Bill Skroggs loitering near the lamps of Cadogan Place.

Chapter 27

The Jarvey's Tale

Wednesday, 1 May 1811

~

"THERE IS NOTHING LIKE THE EXERTION OF DINING IN HANS Place," Eliza observed as we closed the door last night on Mr. James Tilson, who had escorted us from his home to ours, "to make me feel truly *good*, Jane—for if I were not, how should I possibly support the *tedium* of Fanny Tilson's conversation?"

The engagement was less onerous than it might have been, had Fanny presided over her table alone; but Mr. Tilson being prevented from joining Henry in Oxford, due to an indisposition of three of the little girls, which tied him to London, the circle had gained in liveliness and interest. Eliza, however, could not be brought to own it; she had been placed at Fanny Tilson's right hand.

"I confess I was very proud of you," I said as I helped Eliza remove her hat. "You never once permitted yourself to gape, when she spoke so earnestly of her charitable works among the females held in Newgate prison. Indeed, I believe you posed your questions quite prettily. One might almost have believed your whole dependence hung upon the improvement of those unfortunate souls."

"And I never betrayed the slightest *hint* that I might end in Newgate myself! I *do* think I carried it off tolerably well, Jane—even when she would discourse on the subject of ablutions, and the best methods of treating lice. You may say what you will of Mrs. Latouche and her Bluestocking daughter, but do admit they never bore one to tears! And Jane—" Eliza stared at me tragically. "Fanny is increasing *again*! As tho' seven daughters were not more than enough to dispose of! And the last one as yet a babe in arms!"

"Perhaps her condition will keep her quietly at home for a period."

"Then she will be less likely to detect us in our cells," Eliza said decidedly, "when once we have been handed over to the warders. Tuesday is already gone! And we have but two days left before that *dreadful* man is to return on Friday!"

"I have the matter in hand, Eliza," I told her gently. "Do not be troubling your head about it."

"It is my *head* that is troubling *me*. It aches frightfully. I believe I shall go up to my room—if you will send Madame Bigeon with a glass of Henry's brandy..."

The Tilsons are abstemious folk; they do not regard claret or burgundy as contributing to the elegance of their table—particularly as such luxuries must still be got from

France, through the intermediary of a Free Trader.[1] Ladies are to be served with ratafia, or perhaps a small amount of Madeira; and Mr. Tilson was left in solitary state to nurse his decanter of port. I quite sympathised with Eliza's desire for a snifter in the bedchamber.

I went towards the kitchen, and discovered Manon loitering in a passageway.

"Madame Henri requires a little brandy," I told her.

"*Oui, mademoiselle.* On the instant. And you should know," she added as she turned away, "that I spoke to Druschka this morning. The gentleman whom her mistress found occasion to visit at the Albany was the Earl of Tanborough's son . . . one Charles Malverley—"

IT WAS OF MALVERLEY I WAS THINKING THIS MORNING, AS I alighted from my hackney in Lincoln's Inn Fields. Sylvester Chizzlewit had summoned me to his door with a missive delivered by courier—an apology and an invitation at once, which I perused in silence over breakfast.

> *Mr. Chizzlewit could not undertake to bring his interlocutor to Sloane Street, in deference to Mrs. Austen's delicate health; but if Miss Austen would deign to step round to Mr. Chizzlewit's chambers, she might learn such intelligence as would shed light on the problem presently under*

---

[1] *Free trader* was a euphemism for a smuggler who brought cargoes from France under cover of darkness, thus avoiding importation duties. At this time, Napoleon's Continental System—which forbade all trade with England on the part of France or its imperial satellites—still inhibited direct importation of a host of goods.—*Editor's note.*

consideration, and every accommodation would be made for her comfort . . .

On this occasion there was no confusion on the part of the clerks as to my merits or precedence among Mr. Chizzlewit's clients. I was met in the doorway, relieved of my wrap, and escorted immediately to the private parlour where I had previously gone through Lord Harold's papers. A fire burned brightly in the grate, tho' the first of May had banished yesterday's rain and the weather was fine. I stood near the warmth, and saw in memory Charles Malverley's face as it had appeared in the publick room of the Brown Bear, Covent Garden.

The classic purity of his features—the beauty of his form—the impression he generally gave, of being one whom the gods favoured . . . could not the Earl's son be the very object of Princess Tscholikova's ardent passion? But he had denied her utterly in death. *One might meet her often in certain circles, and perhaps exchange a few pleasantries,* he had assured the coroner. *I should never say that we were* well *acquainted.*

Malverley had lied—or he had told the truth, and the Princess's visits to the Albany were a blind for interests she held in another quarter. If the Earl's son had deliberately uttered a falsehood, however . . . the construction to be placed upon such reserve could only be a guilty one.

I had remarked the pallor of his looks that morning, but also his extraordinary self-possession before the coroner's panel. Little could dismay that well-bred gentleman; but then again, Mr. Whitpeace had not troubled to press Malverley too closely on his movements during the hours between one and five o'clock in the morning of Tuesday last. He claimed to have been at his desk during the small hours, diligently pursuing his employer's interests; but what if he had gone home to the Albany—and found Princess Tscholikova waiting for him in the courtyard? Julien d'Entraigues had seen her there, and remarked upon the desolation of her countenance.

But if Malverley were the Princess's lover—how, then, to account for the correspondence published in the *Morning Post? My limbs burn with the desire to lie once more entangled in your own... There is nothing I would not sacrifice, would not risk... I can hardly write for anguish...* It was unlikely the lady should have addressed such phrases to *two* gentlemen. I must be mistaken. Perhaps the private secretary had seen—and copied—and sold—Lord Castlereagh's intimate letters for personal gain! Sylvester Chizzlewit had said Malverley was fond of deep play; and thus the young man might have considerable debts of honour that must be satisfied. Had the Princess, shamed before the eyes of the *ton*, confronted her enemy at his lodgings in the Albany that fateful night—and had Malverley cut her throat?

Why, then, should he have left the body on Castlereagh's doorstep?

"I cannot make it out at all," I murmured vexedly. "I require more information."

"And you shall have it," Sylvester Chizzlewit said behind me.

I turned, and surveyed the individual he ushered into the room: A man of indeterminate age and weather-beaten appearance, who might have served as Ordinary Seaman on one of my brother's ships. His stooped shoulders were clad in a patched and faded coat of kerseymere; his trousers were black; and his boots were worn. He nodded deferentially as my eyes swept over him, and turned a round felt hat in heavily-knuckled hands.

"This is Clayton," Mr. Chizzlewit informed me, "who drives a hackney coach, and is desirous of telling you his story, Miss Austen."

"Are you the fellow who carried two ladies from Portman Square on Sunday evening?" I enquired eagerly.

Clayton shook his head. "I don't work Portman Square, miss. That'd be a covey o' mine named Davy. It was Davy as took you off that night, and when the gentleman come asking his questions, Davy thought o' me—my story being just as odd, seemingly, as his."

I looked enquiringly at Mr. Chizzlewit, who gestured towards a chair set at a comfortable distance from the hearth; I sank into it.

"The man Davy did, indeed, convey you and Mrs. Austen from Portman Square to Sloane Street, but he failed to observe anything subsequently but the coins Mrs. Henry pressed into his palm, the night being one without moon, and the vicinity imperfectly lit. He can tell us nothing of the misfortune that befell your sister. In the course of my enquiries among the jarveys, however, I thought to ask whether any man had taken up a fare in Berkeley Place, on the evening of Monday last. I was interested, Miss Austen, in the interval between Princess Tscholikova's leaving her card at the Castlereaghs', and the hour in which her corpse was discovered in front of No. 45—a period of some four hours. I had an idea that the lady might have engaged a hackney."

"Naturally," I agreed, "it being unlikely she should have walked the streets of London in her evening dress for so long a time."

"The locale being somewhat infamous, due to the unfortunate death of Princess Tscholikova, I did not have to put my questions very long. Davy—your jarvey—had heard a story of his friend, Clayton, here; and Clayton was very soon introduced to my acquaintance. Pray tell the lady what you saw and heard, Clayton."

"It did ought to have been brought before the crowner," Clayton said belligerently, "but that I couldn't get a place inside the Brown Bear; the house was that full of gentry, an honest man couldn't set foot over the jamb. I'd have spoke to crowner himself, if I'd found the time—but what with one thing and another, and me not knowing how to find the gentleman, and the press of work—and the panel saying it were self-murder . . ."

"You took up a lady in Berkeley Square last Monday night?" I asked.

"Took her up in Covent Garden," he corrected, "when the play was done at the Royal. Half-past twelve o'clock that would have been, near enough as makes no difference—and her walking the length of Bow Street alone, in search of a hackney. Most of those as goes to the Royal has their own carriages, you see, and the street was that full of them. But I lit on *her* quick enough—a dimber mort if ever I seen one, and full of juice I reckon."

By this, I concluded that Clayton regarded the late Princess as attractive enough, and wealthy in appearance; a likely prospect for a fare. "You saw her into the hackney," I suggested, "and took her . . . where?"

"Lord Castlereagh's," Clayton replied glibly. "She told me to wait. I walk my horse if the party's longer than ten minutes, naturally. But she weren't long inside, and the porter handing her back up in my coach, and telling me as I was to take the party to the Albany, Piccadilly."

"—Where she went in search of Charles Malverley," I murmured. "Perhaps it was always Malverley who brought her to Berkeley Square in the first place, and not Castlereagh, as we had thought."

"Eh?" Sylvester Chizzlewit enquired, with a startled air. "Malverley was acquainted with the Princess?"

"Her maid says she was in the habit of visiting him at his lodgings. It was Malverley, no doubt, who was the object of her earnest and steadfast gaze at Castlereagh's box, during the interval of *Macbeth;* and the Fashionable World read in her regard a confirmation of scandal—the letters published in the *Morning Post.* I begin to believe they were always letters written to Malverley—which he sold, and passed off, as his employer's. Why should he run so high a risk of dismissal, in serving Lord Castlereagh such a brutal trick?"

"Because he bears him no love," Mr. Chizzlewit answered abruptly. "You will recall that I apprehended as much, when he spoke of his lordship over dinner in my rooms. Malverley's reserve *then* was uncharacteristic; and the heat with which he later referred to insults—that he had been asked to do what no man should, even for hire—may suggest a repugnance, a disgust of his employer, that might well have led him to mischief. Did Malverley wish to be rid of Princess Tscholikova, and revenged upon Castlereagh, he found in the lady's correspondence ample scope for both."

"Very well," I said. "We shall accept, for the moment, that he did as you say; and leave aside the motivation for his actions. It is possible, I suppose, that a desire for revenge might lead to murder. But how did the two encounter one another that night? Malverley would have it he remained at Castlereagh's the whole of the morning."

"He maintains it without witnesses, however; the coroner's panel merely relied on his word."

"True." I glanced at the jarvey, who stood in respectful silence, comprehending perhaps one word in five of our conversation. "Clayton, what did you then at the Albany?"

"Stood to, as before, while the lady spoke to the porter. I reckon she got no satisfaction from the lad, for she waited in the courtyard a deal o' time, looking up at the darkened windows. It don't do for a lady alone to enter the Albany; the porters won't have it. She gave up after a bit, and mounted into my hackney. That was when we drove to Russell Square."

"Russell Square!" I cried, astounded. Whatever I had been expecting, it was hardly this. "And the number to which you were sent...?"

"The lady didn't seem rightly to know. She told me to drive right round the square—alongside of the parts of it that are finished, where people are living—and stop in front of one that had carriages waiting, and torches burning at the entry. All lit up it was, something lovely."

"Having heard Clayton's story already, I required him to drive me to Russell Square," Mr. Chizzlewit put in quietly, "and point out the residence Princess Tscholikova visited. I shall not surprise you, I think, Miss Austen, when I say that it is the house presently leased by Miss Julia Radcliffe."

"But Miss Radcliffe would have it that Tscholikova called upon her the day before her death," I said in puzzlement. "Why should she then have been ignorant of the house's direction?"

"Perhaps we are mistaken," Mr. Chizzlewit returned, "in crediting Miss Radcliffe's account."

A faint chill stirred along my spine; I had accepted much

of what the Barque of Frailty told me, and held in reserve only the knowledge that she had not told me *all*. But if duplicity there was—must it not have been in the service of a great deceit?

"The lady quitted your hackney before the door with the flaming torches?" I persisted.

"And told me to wait," Clayton averred. "I waited a deal of time. Walked the horse, I did, and had a word or two with the grooms and coachmen standing in the square. Some were that affable; Mr. Ponsonby's man, and Lord Wildthorn's. Others were too good to pass the time o' day with the likes of me—I knew Lord Alvanley's coach by the crest on the door, but the livery stuck up their noses. One by one, they all took their masters in charge and toddled off home. The torches were doused, but a light still burned in the first-floor window. I began to grow uneasy—thinking as maybe the mort never would come out, and I'd be short my fare for a double trip, first to Berkeley Square and then to Russell. The horse was tired and I'd missed a deal of custom, waiting on the lady."

"Malverley must have been there. He must be acquainted with Julia Radcliffe!" I said. "Can you have an idea of it, Mr. Chizzlewit? The discarded lover confronting her rival for your friend's affections?"

"Just after the bells went three o'clock," the jarvey continued, "the door opened and out she come."

"Under her own power?" I enquired.

The man Clayton frowned. "Not rightly. She was in a dead swoon. Had to be nearly dragged down the flagway with her head on the fellow's shoulder. *Drunk as a wheelbarrow*, I thought."

"The fellow," I repeated. "A tall, handsome young man

with golden curls? Could you see his countenance? Should you recognise him?"

"I might be able to tell his voice," Clayton returned, "but he weren't no young man, and no golden curls, neither. This fellow was a Frenchie, by the sound of him, in a fine dark coat and a grey beaver."

"Good Lord!" I stared at Sylvester Chizzlewit, aware that our thoughts must be fastening upon the same figure: grey-haired, rakish, and elegant in a degree that must always be foreign.

The Comte d'Entraigues, who had made Russell Square—and Julia Radcliffe—his private hunting ground.

"The lady's weight would have been a sad trial to him. When he got to the cab, he gave it up and lifted her in his arms. 'Open the door, you fool,' he says. 'She's took ill. I must see her home.' "

"Home?"

"Aye. 'Berkeley Square,' he ordered—'Pull up in the mews, behind No. 43.' "

Chapter 28

The Evidence of One's Eyes

Wednesday, 1 May 1811, cont.

~

FAR FROM HAVING ILLUMINED THE TANGLE UNDER CON-
sideration, the jarvey's interview had merely increased my
confusion. Would Julia Radcliffe shield the *Comte d'Entraigues*
with her carefully-chosen confession? What, then, was I to
make of her contemptuous tone in speaking of him? Had
the Princess's jewels ever been given over to the Barque of
Frailty, as she claimed, or had d'Entraigues seized them outright? And why had the Princess gone to Russell Square on
the night of her death?

One question at least must be satisfied: Whether the lady
had met her end in Julia Radcliffe's house—or had come to
it later, in the chill of Berkeley Square.

"Did you drive here this morning in your own hackney,
Clayton?" I asked the jarvey.

"O' course." He glanced at Sylvester Chizzlewit doubt-fully; the solicitor nodded encouragement.

"I suppose it is pulled up in the courtyard?" I persisted. "May I view the interior? You might tell me, as we proceed thence, what you did in the mews behind No. 43."

I rose; Mr. Chizzlewit threw open the door. As I passed him I detected a faint smile upon his lips; he would be silently applauding so much decision, and the strength of mind that animated it. If I must detect blood-stains and a knife thrust down among the seat cushions, and know the Comte to be guilty, I should not flinch from the task.

"Ought we not to summon William Skroggs to taste of these delights?" Mr. Chizzlewit whispered as I passed him.

"He is certain to believe them fabricated, if they come without a neck for his noose. Let us wait a little, if you please."

The hackney was of the usual run of such vehicles—an outmoded town chariot originally designed for the accom-modation of only two persons abreast, with a facing seat and a coachman's box upon the top; a single horse was required to draw this vehicle, and the poor beast looked as tho' it had descended by degrees from a gentleman's stable, much as the carriage itself had.

"When we come to Berkeley Square," Clayton said, "I turned in at the mews and pulled up before No. 43. The side-lamps were burning, naturally, and the party asked as if I'd douse 'em—the lady being yet ill, and him being wishful to rest her a bit, before attempting to escort her to the house."

"I see. You did so?"

"Aye. We sat there in the dark maybe half an hour, maybe more, until the bells rang four; and him talking low to the lady all the time, in that soft foreign voice of his, as tho' he were talking to a child."

"You heard him speak from within the carriage?" Surprised, I studied the jarvey's countenance. "Did the lady reply?"

"She might have groaned, like. Being foxed out of all reason."

"And what did you then?"

"The Frenchie asked me to stand lookout, as he was worried for the lady's reputation—didn't want her seen, while he got her to the door. I climbed down from the box, and went right out into the square, but there weren't nobody about—not even the charley."

"Old Bends, on his quest for ale and bread," I murmured. "That would be the moment to effect it."

"When I got back to the cab, they were gone."

"Gone?"

"Aye. The Frenchie left a guinea on the box for my trouble. He took her the back way, I reckon—but how she ended on the street with her throat slit, I cannot say, and that's the truth. I never saw no murder done, miss—nor self-murder, neither, as God is my witness."

It was possible that what the jarvey saw as inebriation, had been nothing less than the nervelessness of death; the Princess might well have been extinct from the moment she was carried from Russell Square. D'Entraigues would have chosen the mews behind No. 43 for its proximity to Castlereagh's residence—the scandal of the published correspondence, perhaps, providing him with inspiration. But I said nothing of my speculation to Clayton. "May I glance within your hackney?"

Upon his throwing open the door, I observed the springs to be negligible, and the squabs dirty; but the jarvey had taken pains to provide a lap-robe for his passengers' use. This was folded neatly on the facing seat.

"You have employed this equipage for your trade in the week since Princess Tscholikova's death?" I enquired.

"All but Sunday—the horse and I always have our bit o' rest, tho' there's some as work even on the Lord's day."

"You carry how many fares each day, Clayton?"

"Upwards of thirty, miss. London's a rackety enough place."

"And have you found occasion to clean the interior in recent days?"

"*Clean?*" he repeated, staring.

We were unlikely to discover anything of value, but I leaned within and sniffed expectantly. The odour of old leather, dust, and mould from yesterday's rain met my nostrils—but no lingering note of an animal nature, the curdling smell of blood.

"Mr. Chizzlewit, have you a lantern?"

While he went in search of one, I unfolded the lap-robe and surveyed it narrowly. The faded wool exhibited a quantity of brownish stains, but these I adjudged to be dried mud—hardly capable of exciting interest.

"Here you are, Miss Austen," Mr. Chizzlewit said behind me, and handed over a square-paned lantern. "Allow me to help you inside."

I took his proffered hand and mounted the single step. The light shone brightly on the smudged and raddled interior, illuminating a score of years' adventures in traversing the streets of London—with bandboxes, giggling girls, foxed gentlemen and women of the streets all packed within—but I could not discern a blood-stain anywhere.

It must be impossible that a throat so torn as the Princess's—which the watchman, old Bends, had declared to be still wet with blood when discovered at five o'clock—should fail to daub everything it encountered. I was forced to conclude that Princess Tscholikova had entered the hackney *alive*.

"What do you make of it, Miss Austen?" Mr. Chizzlewit enquired.

"Very little," I admitted. I set down the lantern on the floor of the chariot, drew off my gloves, and felt with bare hands between the cushions of the seat.

My fingertips encountered a scrap of paper. I snatched at it eagerly, and drew it forth.

"A fragment of correspondence," I said. "The sheet has been torn in pieces."

"Princess Tscholikova's?" Mr. Chizzlewit thrust his head into the coach.

"No," I admitted. "This hand is strange to me. I have read the Princess's words before, you know, in the private journal I spoke of—"

"Stay," Sylvester Chizzlewit ordered, his voice taut with excitement. "I may name the author. I saw his hand almost daily, during my years at Oxford."

"Charles Malverley," I concluded. "It was, I suppose, to be expected. But I confess, Mr. Chizzlewit, that having spoken with your jarvey, I understand this affair even less than before. Why should this scrap, alone among its fellows, be thrust down into the seat cushions? Why should d'Entraigues have carried the Princess to Berkeley Square? And most puzzling of all—why did she exit the coach alive, only to be found dead by the watchman?"

"Because d'Entraigues chose to do murder?"

I shook my head in perplexity. "We shall have to confront the gentleman."

"Which gentleman? D'Entraigues—or Malverley?"

"I cannot tell. The former was in possession of the Princess's jewels, and her person; the latter, merely of her heart."

"Perhaps it is Miss Radcliffe we should interrogate." He spoke the words unhappily; I recollected too late that there was an interest there—Mr. Chizzlewit was susceptible, as I own myself to have been, to the Barque's charm.

"Are you willing to play escort?" I enquired. "I should feel less of a traitor to the poor child, did I have *you* to bear me company."

"I should be most happy." He reached into his smart coat, and drew forth a purse of coins. Handing the jarvey a guinea, he said, "Thank you, Clayton. That will be all for now. I may find you, I suppose, in Portman Square?"

"At any hour, any day but Sunday," the hackney driver said cheerfully, and bobbing his head in my direction, took himself off.

"We shall have need of that fellow, to give evidence," Mr. Chizzlewit said thoughtfully. "I ought, perhaps, to have invited Bill Skroggs to listen to the man—but that I was desirous you should be before him, Miss Austen. I wished to learn the construction you should place upon his information; tho' Skroggs is cunning, he lacks your subtlety of mind."

"You have spoken with him?"

"Indeed. I sought him where one must always seek the Bow Street Runners—in his cups, at the Brown Bear." Mr. Chizzlewit smiled, and I reflected that despite his youth, he had a remarkable gift for inspiring trust.

"Mr. Skroggs admitted that he was, indeed, in Hans Town observing No. 64 when Mrs. Henry Austen was struck from behind with a cobblestone. Her attacker fled, with Skroggs in pursuit; but the Runner was at a distance, and the lady escaped his clutches, by hastening down Cadogan Street and mounting into a carriage kept waiting there for the purpose. He never saw her face."

"A lady," I mused. "That might be anyone—but at a guess, I should call her Anne de St.-Huberti, Comtesse d'Entraigues. Julia Radcliffe should have attempted to murder *me*, not my sister."

"I am happy to hear it. That is one less painful episode we must address in Russell Square."

"Shall we go there immediately? We ought to have retained Clayton—and had the jarvey drive us to the door!"

Mr. Chizzlewit hesitated. "I should not advise it. The hour is already advanced—nearly two o'clock—and the day is hardly auspicious for paying calls."

I stared at him. "Whatever can you mean?"

The solicitor's smile deepened becomingly. "I collect that for all your worldliness, you are yet in ignorance of the significance of the First of May, my dear Miss Austen. Among certain circles, it is most notable for being the annual date of a glittering event never patronised by the most elegant ladies of the *ton,* but to which every male member of Society is sure to be invited. We refer to it as the anti-Almack's."

"Anti-Almack's?" I repeated, bewildered. "But Almack's is the most exclusive private assembly in London! Would you mean that this is a publick rout?"

"Hardly. But just as Almack's is called, by the knowledgeable, *The Marriage Mart,* so the Cyprians Ball must be acknowledged as Almack's opposite—the very death of respectability, in fact!"

"The Cyprians Ball...An assembly presided over by..."

"...The Muslin Company," he returned cordially. "They will have engaged the publick rooms of Limmer's; it is the dirtiest hotel in London, to be sure, but also the most sporting—and the Demi-reps shall feel entirely at home there. Among the members of White's and Watier's, Brooks's and Boodle's, no other event is anticipated with such enjoyment as the Cyprians Ball. Miss Wilson and her sisters, Mrs. Johnstone and Moll Raffles, Julia Radcliffe and Desirée Moore—all shall be in attendance. I must believe Julia Radcliffe to be recruiting her strength, before such an evening—she will certainly not be at home to visitors. We must endeavour to call upon her *tomorrow*, Miss Austen—well after one o'clock."

"The Cyprians Ball," I murmured. "The Comte d'Entraigues shall certainly be at Limmer's this evening."

"—And firmly under my eye. I hold a card of invitation, and shall certainly dance."

"Will Charles Malverley be there?"

"I should be greatly surprised, were he not. Castlereagh must certainly be in attendance, and George Canning—there is not a gentleman who would risk offending the Patronesses, any more than they should snub Lady Jersey at Almack's."

"But *Malverley*, Mr. Chizzlewit—that buck of the first stare, who is up to every rig, the greatest go in the *ton*— Have you ever chanced to meet *him* in Russell Square?"

"Never," he replied.

"And yet... *and yet*...we presume Princess Tscholikova to have sought him at Julia Radcliffe's on the night of her death. *Why*, Mr. Chizzlewit?"

"He was undoubtedly absent. The Princess certainly did not meet him there, no matter how long she waited."

"And if Malverley alone, of all his set, neglects to pay court to Julia Radcliffe," I said slowly, "that fact in itself must be considered significant. I shall take my leave of you, sir— and must thank you for putting me in the way of considering this tangled business in an entirely *new* light."

I RETURNED TO SLOANE STREET, AND FOUND ELIZA GONE out—our Chawton neighbour, Miss Maria Beckford, having called with her Middleton niece to take my sister for an airing in the Park. I had an idea of the petulant Miss Middleton, forced to sit opposite two elderly ladies, in a hired barouche that must be accounted insufferably dowdy; and sighed for the lost ambitions of girlhood.

I whiled away an hour in perusing a guide to the peerage I discovered among Henry's books, paying especial attention to those lateral branches and degrees of cousinage obtaining among the most elevated families in the land; and then I penned a firm note of my intentions to Sylvester Chizzlewit. Manon was so good as to carry it to Lincoln's Inn Fields—but my second letter, to William Skroggs, she refused to accept. She regarded Bow Street and all its kind as the worst of London's evils; and so, in the end, I was forced to run *that* errand myself.

Chapter 29

At Limmer's Hotel

Wednesday, 1 May 1811, cont.

~

As it happens, I was forced to place all my confidence in Eliza—as is so often the case. Who else should know better how a Fashionable Impure must look, in order to gain admittance to the Cyprians Ball?

"Ring for Manon," my sister instructed briskly, "and Madame Bigeon as well. We shall have to alter one of my gowns on the instant! I am not so tall as you, Jane, but I daresay we may contrive a lace flounce to make up the difference—and it will do very well if your ankles *are* exposed, and your stays rather tighter than not, as display must be the order of the evening."

"Must it, indeed?" I faltered. "But Julia Radcliffe always appears so elegant!"

"Be assured that rather *more* of her elegance will be

visible tonight. A ball-dress, off the shoulder, with considerable décolleté—and your hair dressed with diamonds!"

"But I have no diamonds!"

"Then let them be paste! I am sure quite *half* the Snug Armfuls will be wearing nothing but such trumpery—and will be clad in the most shocking peacock colours! I can do nothing about *that,* I am afraid; you will have to go in straw-coloured silk, for it is just the gown to suit the purpose—and quite eighteen months old, so I shall not mind a bit if we must cut it to shreds."

Manon and her mother appeared in the doorway of Eliza's boudoir. Manon, as should not be surprising, had begun to look a trifle weary.

"Mademoiselle is attending a fancy dress party this evening," my sister said, in a voice that brooked no argument, "and will require a little contrivance in her gown. Manon, have you time to step round to the Pantheon Bazaar?"

"Naturally, if madame wishes it."

"We require quantities of false diamonds for the dressing of our hair, and loo masks—as we shall have to go disguised."

"*We?*" I repeated, thunderstruck.

"I *adore* masquerades," she said comfortably, as she lifted the straw-coloured silk over my head. "It puts me quite in mind of the old days, at Versailles. I should not submit to being left behind for anything, Jane—and I daresay I shall give some of those Demi-reps a run for their money."

She stepped back to survey my appearance; I felt both naked and foolish, and could not meet her scrutiny.

"Sandals, I think—and we shall paint your toenails with gold leaf, as it is considered *very fast.* Madame Bigeon, a quantity of wadding, if you please—we must endeavour to provide mademoiselle with a *bit* more décolleté . . ."

IF IT *was* THE DIRTIEST HOTEL IN LONDON, THE QUAN-tity of candles, and the magnificence of the scene within the assembly rooms, contrived to dazzle the eye so thoroughly that every hint of grime was obscured. Eliza and I alighted from our carriage a few minutes past ten o'clock, and were admitted without much more than a cursory perusal of our figures and dress; two such bold pieces as we presented, the better part of our faces obscured by black loo masks and our hair dressed with gems, should never be turned from the Cyprians Ball.

I am not sure what I feared more: to have my bottom slapped in a familiar way as I attempted with dignity to nego-tiate the stairs; to find that my arm had been pinched, or my skirts snapped above my heels; but the attitudes of the horde of gentlemen lounging along the banisters were refreshingly circumspect. If their eyes roved over the frank presentation of my charms, they kept their opinions to themselves; all but one foxed fellow, who studied Eliza with protuberant eyes and snorted, "Damme! If it ain't mutton dressed as lamb!"

I grasped my sister by the wrist, the better to prevent an unseemly fracas as she rounded on the jackanapes indig-nantly, and whispered, "Never mind! You are not here to make a conquest, recollect—but to preserve your innocence and reputation!"

"Then I fear we are the only ladies likely to do so," my sis-ter returned grimly.

The assembly rooms were in fact two dining parlours

thrown together, by the elimination of certain doors, and the contiguity of a passage, with a small anteroom at its far end— Limmer's being not the sort of place to run to dancing, in the ordinary way, and thus failing to possess a ballroom. Indeed, I had heard my brother Henry refer to the place as akin to Tattersall's, where gentlemen of the turf laid bets of an evening in the smoke-filled coffee room. But the Patronesses, as Mr. Chizzlewit had called them in unconscious mimicry of Almack's, had worked their magic in transforming the dingy place, with yards of striped silk suspended from the ceiling to suggest an Oriental tent, and quantities of blooming lilies in tubs, grouped round a dais, on which the musicians played.

"Well, my dear, if the quality of the refreshments is any indication," Eliza observed, as she sipped at a glass of champagne, "this is most *certainly* the anti-Almack's. All one ever receives there is tepid lemonade. I do believe the Demi-reps have hired Gunter's! Only observe the lobster patties!"[1]

"Pray pardon the intrusion," said a gravelly voice behind us, "but I could not help noticing how ravishing you appear this evening, my sprite! Such a bewitching colour! So entirely suited to one of mature years, and experience...."

I turned, and found to my astonishment that no less a personage than Francis Rawdon, Earl Moira, hovered on the fringe of our charmed circle. The core of my being was seized with apprehension, as tho' with a vise; I could no more speak than I could trust myself to glance at Eliza. She

---

[1] Gunter's was the foremost confectioner of Regency London and was frequently hired to cater the refreshments at private debutante balls.— *Editor's note.*

had been acquainted with Lord Moira these ten years at least; and her husband was the man's banker! Had the Earl detected us in our scandalous subterfuge? Should we be disgraced, and exposed?

He bowed to both of us, but extended his hand to my sister—who might certainly be declared ravishing, by one several years her senior, as she stood ample-bosomed in her claret-coloured gown. Moira, it appeared, followed the Prince Regent in his tastes—that Royal personage being known to favour well-endowed ladies of a certain age.

Eliza uttered an hysterickal giggle that could not be suppressed—put her champagne glass into my hand with trembling fingers—and dropped the curtsey that had graced Versailles itself. As I watched her sweep into the waltz on Lord Moira's arm, I reflected that so game a pullet as the Comtesse de Feuillide should never betray my schemes.

By eleven o'clock, the rooms had filled to such an extent that the Cyprians Ball should certainly be declared a frightful squeeze, and thus, an unqualified success. Everywhere one looked, the bright plumage of the Birds of Paradise—who ranged in age from fifteen to fifty—twirled about the floor, or dangled indolently from the shoulders of various gentlemen, or held pride of place at a supper table. I will confess that I witnessed scenes that should be adjudged a *trifle warm*—the habits of some of the ladies, and the inebriation of some of the gentlemen, passing the bounds of what must be acceptable. I will also say, however, that the chief difference between the venue in which I found myself, and those which fell within the realm of the *ton,* is that such incidents were allowed to occur within *full view* of all assembled—for certainly as many proceed behind the cover of shrubbery, when such balls are sponsored by the Quality. I applauded the Cyprians for their lack of hypocrisy, and accepted the offer of a quadrille, and a country dance, from a dashing man in his thirties whom Eliza later assured me was no less than Freddy Ponsonby.

He is acquitted one of the rakes of the age, and I shall always regard his anonymous, and quite unconscious, gallantry towards myself with affection; but at his attempting to steer me into the passage, in an effort to run his hands the length of my overlaced body, I told him tartly that I required a better sort of introduction before I should permit such freedoms. He then produced a fifty-pound note from his breast pocket—*fifty pounds!* Which is no less than I contrive to live on, for the space of a year!—and I was so overpowered I could do nothing but stutter out my apologies, and back away in shame from his laughing good looks. The experience forced me to contemplate seriously the attractions that must have weighed with one such as Julia Radcliffe— disgraced, unwed, cut off from her family, and entirely dependent upon the good offices of rakes.

Julia herself was in high bloom. She appeared at Limmer's at half-past eleven o'clock, unmasked and queenly, her white dress deliberately innocent—and the last word in daring exposure. I am sure she had dampened her undergown, for it clung to her limbs as she moved in a shocking degree, outlining the curves of her body, which emerged like the torso of Venus from her tightly-laced bodice; and the jewels that she wore were hardly paste. This was the ideal that such dashing, tho' respectable, ladies as Caroline Lamb meant

to emulate, in snubbing their noses at the *ton;* but Julia was
the embodiment of the raffish dream. At her appearance,
she was instantly surrounded by the highest names in the
land; I could not have approached her, had I dared. Even
Harriette Wilson, the dark foil to Miss Radcliffe's white and
gold beauty, was left to command a lesser court—those who
discovered Miss Radcliffe's card to be already filled, her
dances already bespoke.

Eliza, who had sustained full *three dances* with Earl Moira,
was cooling her overheated cheeks on a balcony, well
supplied with champagne and dexterously employed in
foiling her old friend's unwitting sallies. I left her to her
amusements—saw Freddy Ponsonby exerting himself to
charm a girl scarcely escaped from the schoolroom—and observed instead those whom Miss Radcliffe favoured.

One was the heir to a dukedom; the other, a marquis. A
third lucky fellow was George Canning, who was permitted
to stand up with the Barque; and included among them all,
as tho' by special favour or afterthought, was an impoverished French count... young Julien, Comte d'Entraigues.

I had observed the father long before, purring French ob-
scenities into the ear of a tittering child; but Julien must have
come in Radcliffe's train, for I had not encountered him yet
this evening. He looked, as a Pink of the *Ton* must, *exquisite:* His
linen snowy, his satin breeches unimpeachable, his dark coat-
ing cut within a hairsbreadth of his shoulders. He had adopted
Mr. Brummell's maxim, which dictated that if a common man
of the street turned to stare after one, one was certainly over-
dressed. Julien's rule was to render himself inconspicuous by
the sheer exactitude of his raiment; and allow his dark good
looks—his refined countenance—his complete mastery of

self—to speak for themselves. Such qualities must always distinguish the gentleman of breeding, no matter how impoverished.

Any number of illustrious men might be everywhere seen, but I had eyes only for two of them: George Canning, who danced with an energy and enjoyment that must testify to his love of the fair sex—for the most part with Harriette Wilson, once Radcliffe released him; and Robert, Lord Castlereagh. The latter held himself aloof, his hands clasped behind his back, and a faint expression of distaste upon his lips. He had dressed with his usual style and care; he looked every inch the distinguished gentleman; but was equally so far above his company, as to support the long wall of the principal room to the exclusion of every other amiable activity. On one occasion when Lord Sidmouth chanced to speak to him, Lord Castlereagh deigned to answer; but in general, the Great Man preserved the air of an Eton schoolmaster, forced to administer an exam. I believe he presently entered the card room, and sat down to whist, from which he did not emerge until well near dawn.

Of Sylvester Chizzlewit there was no sign, until a few minutes before twelve o'clock. I was engaged in going down a country dance—having been solicited by a portly fellow whose wet mouth must give me a disgust of him, but whose awkward embarrassment at the whole situation in which he found himself, suggested the country cousin being shown the delights of the Metropolis—when I observed my solicitor standing a little apart from the general throng, with his friend Malverley by his side.

I still went masked, and must thank Heaven for my obscurity. Despite all his regard for my pluck and daring,

Chizzlewit should be shocked to discover my presence in this place—I had suppressed the full intelligence of my plan, from a fear that he should hasten to discourage me from attempting it. In the note I had sent round to his chambers, I had urged him only to bring Charles Malverley up to scratch: At all costs, the Earl's son *must* put in an appearance at the Cyprians Ball. But my plans must not miscarry—Malverley could not be allowed to take fright, and leave Limmer's Hotel before my object was achieved—

I stumbled on my modish sandals, and let out a faint cry of pain.

The country cousin was immediately all solicitude; nothing could exceed his concern and anxiety; I was escorted, limping, from the crowded floor and established in a vacant chair, not far from where Chizzlewit stood. I sent my puffing swain in search of a claret cup, saw him disappear into the frenzy of the refreshment tables—and moved immediately towards my solicitor.

He had separated a little from Malverley, who was encircled—much as Julia Radcliffe had been—by a host of admiring acquaintance.

"Mr. Chizzlewit," I hissed.

He turned, and bowed. "Fair lady. May I be of *service?* No improper pun intended, I assure you—"

"Good God," I said, nonplussed. "Can it be you do not know me?"

I lifted the mask a fraction from my face, and had the satisfaction of hearing his sudden indrawn breath. I grasped his arm, and led him from the floor.

"Miss Austen—I beg your pardon—I should never have expected—I should not have presumed—"

"Yes, indeed, but there is no time for that now. Has Malverley seen her?"

"Miss Radcliffe? I do not think she has yet fallen in his way."

"Then bring him to the little anteroom at the end of the passage," I said, "in ten minutes' time."

I left Chizzlewit, and recruited Eliza—who parted from Lord Moira with what seemed like regret.

"My dear," I consoled her, "only reflect how you shall be in whoops, when next you encounter the Earl in the Park! Nothing else may possibly have come of it, you know."

"I *do* realise the truth of what you say, Jane, but only conceive how delicious it is to be engaged in flirtation again! I felt myself quite twenty years younger! I do believe he was on the point of offering me *carte blanche*! And not the *slightest* chance that I should be discovered by dear Henry!"

"Eliza, only succeed in bringing your old friend the Comte d'Entraigues to the little anteroom at the end of the hall—in twenty minutes' time—and you may return to the Earl with my blessing," I promised.

I FOUND JULIA RADCLIFFE ESTABLISHED ON A STIFF-BACKED chair in the supper room, surrounded by her acquaintance. She was nearly impossible to approach. Julien d'Entraigues stood behind her chair, and at a motion of her finger, bent low; something she said, sent him immediately from her side. I saw my chance, and contrived to put myself in the young Count's way.

"*Pardon,*" he murmured, and would have stepped around me, but that I returned his word with a hurried phrase.

"Julien! Are you not to play this evening? Have I only to call the tune?"

He stopped short, and stared at me, frowning.

"I do not apprehend..." he said; then, "Miss *Austen?*"

"The same. Do not ask what I cannot answer, I implore you—but bring Miss Radcliffe to the anteroom at the end of the passage as swiftly as may be contrived. My life—and *hers*—depend upon it, *monsieur le comte!*"

Chapter 30

Crimes of the Heart

Wednesday, 1 May 1811, cont.

~

THE DIM FIGURE OF A COUPLE, ENTWINED ON THE SETTEE
against the wall of the anteroom, brought me up short when
I would have entered—but I perceived at a glance the pair
were unknown to me. It was essential that they should be
forced from the room, and so, on the spur of imagination, I
reeled a little as tho' drunk, and muttered, "Lord! My head!
If I do not get a little air soon, I am sure I shall be sick!"

I had only to press my hand against my mouth, and
choke a little, for the two to beat a hasty retreat—at which
point I swiftly closed the double doors.

The room was such as any respectable inn might offer, as
private accommodation for a member of the Quality: the
sort of parlour that should be hired for dining, by a gentle-

man in Town on a matter of business. It offered a round deal table and the aforementioned settee by way of furnishing; but there was also a hearth in which a fire was burning, and a window, draped in tarnished silk. I went to this window, and lifted the drapery from its place, to reveal—as I had expected—one William Skroggs, Bow Street Runner.

"Miss Austen." He saluted me with a leer.

"You encountered no difficulty in entering the premises?" I enquired.

"None." The contempt of his tone must suggest that no Runner should be barred from as respectable an amusement as the Cyprians Ball. "But if you mean for me to stand all hours behind a smoky curtain, while light o' loves plies their trades under my very nose—"

"Do be quiet," I said crossly. "I have done the better part of your work for you. Someone is coming."

I hid myself behind the opposite drapery, the far edge drawn sufficiently back for me to observe the centre of the room, and waited for the door to open.

As I had suspected, Charles Malverley was first to enter the room, followed by Sylvester Chizzlewit, who took up a position by the doors.

"—for the same reason, I collect, that you would bring me here," Malverley was saying carelessly as he entered. He held a wine glass in his hand, and the beauty of his countenance was flushed. "I must thank you for your solicitude—my tortured heart is warmed by your amiable concerns—and there is at least this to applaud: You have thrown *women* my way, rather than the boys old Castlereagh is partial to. The man studied too much of the Greeks, during his time at Eton."

"Some of these girls are devilish pretty," Chizzlewit observed mildly, "and High Flyers too. I wonder you aren't susceptible. Has no lady ever touched your heart?"

"Lady?" Malverley returned contemptuously. "There is not a *lady* among the lot, thank Heaven! I have had my fill of your *ladies.* Give me a Barque any day, and I'll sail her straight into harbour! The Muslin Company! Long may they prosper, and empty men's purses!" He raised his glass in a mocking toast.

I wondered whether Chizzlewit had divined what he must do—whether my terse missive of the morning had been explicit enough. But I should not have doubted him; he was ever his grandfather's heir. "Not all of these women are low-born," he said reasonably. "Miss Radcliffe, for example. Family's devilish high in the instep. Some sort of relation of yours, is she not?"

For an instant, I feared Malverley might strike his friend. He stood rigid, his hands clenching about his wine glass so that the frail crystal stem snapped.

"I ought to draw your cork," he said evenly as he tossed the shards of glass into the fire, "or demand satisfaction for such an insult, Sylvester—but we'll agree that you're foxed, and have no idea what you're saying. Don't ever mention that jade's name in my presence, damn you."

Chizzlewit reached behind him, and thrust open the door into the passage. Julia Radcliffe was outlined in candle-light, divinely fair and effortlessly tempting.

"Why should he not mention my name, Charles?" she enquired, her voice low. "Why should it be *my name* that distresses you so, when it was you who sullied it?"

"I!" he retorted, his countenance flaming. "Look at yourself, Julia! Always desperate to excite admiration—

tormenting decent men with your looks, your bearing, *your refusal to submit*—but now the whole world knows you for what you are—what you always were: a whore. You may cut me direct in the middle of Hyde Park—you may refuse me admittance to Russell Square—you may flaunt your wares before every rogue in London—but the world should never reproach me for serving you a lesson. The world knows me to be right—for *disciplining you,* for teaching you conduct—for *breaking you to bridle*—"

The nastiness of the words was like a lash. I found that I had closed my eyes tight, so as to avoid the spectre of Malverley's face, unmanned by passion, violent with hatred. But a sound brought my eyes flying open again. Julien, Comte d'Entraigues, stood between Julia Radcliffe and Charles Malverley with his hereditary sword unsheathed— and the point was at Malverley's throat.

"Put it away, my son," said a lazy voice behind him.

Chizzlewit moved to one side of the door, and Emmanuel d'Entraigues entered the room. Eliza was with him, her mask discarded.

"*Mon dieu,*" Julien whispered. "These Austens!"

"I have nothing more to say to you," Julia Radcliffe told Malverley. "You have insulted me in every possible way, from the first moment of our acquaintance. I say nothing of the outrage you visited upon my person; of the deplorable want of feeling and all decency you *then* exhibited, and forever after. In my infancy I knew you for a man to be feared—one whose honour is as hollow as his title. The world shall soon know you for a blackguard."

"Fine words, Julia," Malverley said, "but *my* world does not regard the calumnies of a doxy! You can do nothing to me!"

"I might accuse you of murder," she returned quietly.

Malverley threw back his head and laughed.

"When that poor creature came to me last Monday night, and begged me to listen to her, I could not turn her away," the Barque continued. "I knew your violence of old. She told me how you had made love to her—charming her in Paris, squiring and cajoling her—from a belief that her husband might be persuaded to pay you off. When you returned to England and discovered your mistake, you cut her utterly from your life."

"A moving story," Malverley said. "Would that I knew to whom you referred!"

"Princess Tscholikova. She showed me your letters." Julia moved towards her cousin, her eyes fixed unflinchingly on his face, and Julien d'Entraigues let his sword fall to his side.

"She begged me to have nothing to do with you. She claimed that I was first in your heart—that you had abandoned her love for pursuit of me—and I laughed in her face. I knew, as Tscholikova could not, *why* you were in Paris—where no proper Englishman should be in these days, paying court to Buonaparte. I knew why you were banished from Oxford in your final year—why your father the Earl nearly cut you off without a cent. Because you had tampered with *me*. Because you had got me with child."

"I was sent off in disgrace, my cunning jade, because *you* refused to marry as your father bid," Malverley shot back through bitten lips.

"I should sooner have died—and very nearly did die, rather than accept Tanborough charity. Thank God I may still command my own fortune; it is a preservative against torture."

Malverley moved, swift as an adder, and struck her a vicious blow across the cheek. Her head snapped sideways with such violence I thought her neck must have been broken, but she did not utter a sound.

"Is that how you served your mistress?" she asked steadily, her palm nursing her cheek. "Is that how you killed Tscholikova?"

"*Julia,*" said the old Comte d'Entraigues warningly.

"I will not be silenced—and never by *you,*" she exclaimed, rounding on the Frenchman. "You promised to escort her, drunk with sorrow and self-pity as she was, back to Hans Town—and you carried her instead to Berkeley Square!"

D'Entraigues smiled faintly. "That was a matter of politics," he said. "I have never loved Lord Castlereagh—he would see me ruined if he could—and my loyalties are wholly Mr. Canning's. Somewhere between Russell Square and Hans Town I saw my way clear to rendering George Canning a service—a way to ensure Castlereagh should never enter the Regent's Cabinet. And so, *yes,* I gave way to politics. I left her on his doorstep, with her precious box of letters by her side. I thought it might amuse the oh-so-respectable Viscount to learn that he was betrayed to the *Post* by his own secretary—by that godlike young man for whom Lord Castlereagh has conceived, shall we say, *a less than decent passion*—"

"That is a lie," Malverley choked. "By God, sir, if I could get near you—"

"But my son has a sword, *voyez-vous,*" d'Entraigues observed, "and this is not yet the night when my throat shall be slit. As no doubt you slit the poor Princess's."

Malverley's eyes widened. "Upon my honour, I did not!"

D'Entraigues shrugged. "Your honour is not worth a sou in this room, monsieur. The Princess yet breathed when I left her at your door. She was found, perhaps a quarter-hour later, her ragged throat wet with blood. You alone were awake, of all the household. What is one to think, *mon vieux?* That she killed *herself?*"

Malverley looked wildly around the room. "Sylvester!" he cried. "*You* know I should never—that I am innocent! For the love of Christ, man—tell them how it was!"

Sylvester Chizzlewit did not reply, but put his back to the doors.

Quite near me, behind the protective shield of the drape, Bill Skroggs shifted restlessly in hiding, on the point, as I guessed, of springing his trap—and taking Malverley in bonds.

I thrust aside the drapery, and looked out at the astonished faces before me.

Charles Malverley stared at me uncomprehendingly. "Who the Devil are you?"

"Consider me a friend of the Princess," I said gently. "I think it is time, Mr. Malverley, that you told us all about the box."

"The box?" he repeated, as tho' stunned.

"The porcelain box, which the Comte d'Entraigues left by the Princess's side, and which *La Tscholikova* had filled with your letters—the box that was *not* retrieved by the charley, or mentioned as evidence at the inquest. The Princess gave it into your keeping, did she not?"

"Yes," he muttered, running a hand through his hair. "I have it still. I suppose I must explain how it was."

"SHE RANG THE BELL OF LORD CASTLEREAGH'S RESIDENCE a little before five o'clock," Malverley told us, sitting like one beaten in battle on the settee before the fire, "and I answered the summons. I thought it was his lordship, returned from a debauch without his key, and I did not wish the porter to find him thus—I had become accustomed to waiting up for his lordship, long after the household was gone to bed, in order to preserve his reputation as much as possible. There was no saying in what state Castlereagh might return—not even his valet should be allowed to see him, on such occasions.

"I went to the door, and discovered—when the bolts were thrown back—that I had erred, and my own indiscretion awaited me."

"Princess Tscholikova."

Malverley nodded. "She was thoroughly foxed—swaying as she stood—and she looked as tho' she had traversed most of London in the interval between the Theatre Royal, where I had previously observed her, and this moment in Berkeley Square. 'I loved you,' she said. '*I loved you*. I would have died for you. And you regard me no more than a bit of refuse beneath a carriage wheel.'

"I feared she might set up a screeching in the street—that she would rouse the household, if not the entire square—and so I urged her to hush, and said I should be happy to discuss our acquaintance in my rooms at the Albany, if she would but call there in a few hours' time—but she refused. She was quite resolute, quite calm; but she told me she had been to Russell Square—that she had learned everything of my sordid past I had not told her, and from the very one I should have wished none of my friends to know—Miss Radcliffe."

Malverley's eyes lifted malevolently. "Was it d'Entraigues who told the Princess your name, Julia? He bears the distinction of having enjoyed you both, I believe."

"I shall worship the Fair Julia to my grave," the French-man said simply. "But it is my son who has won the lady's heart. Wisdom and experience, *vous savez*, must always give place to youth and beauty."

Malverley smirked unpleasantly. "I fear that most of us must give way, where Julia is concerned; she has a habit of displacing one man for another—don't you, my pet?"

Julien surged violently towards the Earl's son, but Sylvester Chizzlewit seized his arm, and held him back.

"The porcelain box," I reminded Malverley.

"She was clutching it," Malverley went on. "When I told her I would see her that very day, at a proper hour, at the Albany or anywhere else she could name, she said—and I shall never forget the sound of her voice—*It is too late. You have broken my heart before the world. You published my letters— sold them for a lie. Why, Charles? Why?*"

"You could not explain, I imagine, that you hated Lord Castlereagh," I observed in a matter-of-fact tone, "as much for his treatment of you—his lascivious nature—as for his policy. Was it in Paris you became a Buonapartist?"

Malverley regarded me steadily. "What kind of witch are you? How have you divined so much of my life, when I do not even know your name?"

"What did the Princess do then?"

"She threw the porcelain box at my feet. It shattered, of course. I was terrified of the noise—that she might rouse the household—and so I gathered up the wretched letters and slammed the door."

"We discovered a fragment of one of them in the hackney that carried d'Entraigues and the Princess to Berkeley Square. But I wonder, Mr. Malverley, why you did not simply quit the Castlereagh household immediately, and escort Princess Tscholikova home? That should certainly have been one way of silencing her."

The godlike countenance flushed. Malverley's eyes darted towards the old Comte d'Entraigues, then to Sylvester Chizzlewit, but he did not answer. It was Eliza, oddly enough, who tumbled to the truth.

"Of course!" she said brightly, as tho' a clever child at a parlour game on a winter's evening. "The business that kept you in his lordship's study for so many hours of the morning! Were you copying his private papers, perhaps? Perusing his memoranda—his letters—his despatches from the Regent? I must imagine he is a gentleman often consulted on government policy, for all that he is not yet returned to Cabinet. An excellent patron for a spy...such as yourself."

Malverley rose, his eyes glittering. "I fear we are unacquainted, madam, and I will not even deign to answer you. Your insinuations are as false as they are impertinent; but happily, they do not bear on the matter at hand. I returned to pack up the necessary papers I had employed in answering his lordship's correspondence, and threw my own—which Tscholikova had returned to me—on the study fire. It was then I heard the charley, old Bends, shouting murder from the street—and went to see what was amiss. I found her dead, as I have already told the coroner's panel; and so I shall maintain to my final breath."

There was a silence, as all those collected in the anteroom weighed Malverley's words. It was possible that the wretched creature, disabused of every cherished notion of her lover's worth and fidelity—the door slammed in her face—had indeed done herself a violence. I had an idea of her shivering in the cold of an April dawn, and of the desertion and essential bleakness of the square in that hour; the sharp fragments of porcelain gleaming whitely at her feet. Such a little thing, to reach down and seize the agent of her death—the agent of her peace, at last...

The remaining drapery was thrust aside, and William Skroggs stepped forward. "Mr. Charles Malverley, it is my duty to carry you before Sir Nathaniel Conant, of the Bow Street Magistracy, on suspicion of the murder of Princess Evgenia Tscholikova..."

Chapter 31

End of the Season

Wednesday, 29 May 1811

~

AND SO I AM ESTABLISHED COMFORTABLY ONCE MORE IN the sitting room at Chawton, where I may write my nonsense in peace at the Pembroke table, alerted to every advancing busybody by the squeak of the door-hinges. The countryside is in full bloom, the air is sweet, the considerations of each person in this village of so modest a nature, as to prevent the Kingdom's survival from hanging upon them—tho' equally consuming to the principals, as the Regent's latest flirt must be to Him. I cannot regret anything I have left behind in London but the excellent society of Henry and Eliza, and the book room at Sloane Street, where I enjoyed so many hours in perusing Mr. Egerton's typeset pages; even Mr. Chizzlewit is not entirely absent from my days, having adopted the habit of correspondence—in the guise of a respectful solicitor, regarding the affairs of a Lady Authoress. It was necessary to let him into the secret of *Sense and Sensibility*, as I foresee a time when I might require a smart young fellow's offices in the matters of copyright, and payment.

I have received a missive from Mr. Chizzlewit's chambers only this morning, in a packet of letters from London and Kent; Cassandra, who remains in the bosom of Edward's family, having sent the news of that country—and Eliza offering a full two pages, crossed, of gossip concerning our mutual acquaintance in Hans Town. The Tilsons have determined to become advocates of the Evangelical reform of our Church of England, and have left off serving even ratafia at their suppers; Lord Moira is deeper than ever in debt, but betrays not the slightest knowledge of having mistaken Eliza for a Woman of the Town; Miss East has decided to write a novel of her own; and the d'Entraigueses are, for the moment at least, reconciled—the Comtesse having lost a fortune in jewels she might have sold, and the Comte his Julia Radcliffe.

That lady, contrary to expectation, did not capitalise on the ardent feelings of Julien d'Entraigues, by accepting his hand in marriage. She has chosen instead to continue much in the way she had begun: with independence, and strength of mind, and the lease of a cottage in Gloucestershire, where she might supervise the rearing and education of her son. The ruin of Charles Malverley having been achieved through no exertion of her own, she wisely determined that she need no longer make a display of her name and person— and has retired to a pleasant and comfortable obscurity. The comet of Julia Radcliffe, tho' it blazed across London's firmament for only a season, shall linger long in the memory of most of the *ton;* and such fame has been enough for her.

Of Charles Malverley himself there is little enough to

say. He maintained his innocence in the death of Princess Tscholikova to the last; but it being represented to him, by so pointed an intelligencer as Bill Skroggs, that his perfidy towards Lord Castlereagh, and the suspicion of his having betrayed his government to the French Monster, were so thoroughly and generally understood in government circles, that he could never hope to be noticed by the *ton* again— that the unfortunate young man shot himself while yet awaiting the Assizes. It is thought that his father conveyed the pistol to Malverley in his gaol—the Earl of Tanborough being concerned, first and foremost, with the *appearance* of a gentleman in all respects.

Malverley's death served to confirm the suspicions generally held, of his conduct towards the Princess—and cleared Lord Castlereagh of all scandal, without a word of denial having to be spoken by that gentleman. Lord Castlereagh's name is still broached as a possible member of government— and Lord Moira's with him; but of George Canning, I hear nothing.

Henry tells me that Egerton hopes to produce my darling child—*Sense and Sensibility*—by the end of October at the latest, and that I am to submit *Pride and Prejudice* for his consideration. I am resolved to commence work, therefore, on an entirely new novel—a story of innocence enshrined in the heart of dissipation and debauchery; of a heroine invested with sound Evangelical principles, that shall put shame to the Fanny Tilsons of this world; of a charming young man thoroughly given over to vice, and the frivolous world of the *ton* that smiles upon him. I should call it *A History of Julia Radcliffe, as Told by a Lady*—but must settle for something less particular. Perhaps... *Mansfield Park*?

Editor's Afterword

SENSE AND SENSIBILITY WAS FIRST ADVERTISED BY ITS PUB-
lisher on October 31, 1811, and similar advertisements appeared for several weeks following. It was a modest success
that was capped by general admiration and clamor for *Pride
and Prejudice,* when that novel appeared in 1813; and although Jane Austen was not then revealed as the author,
subsequent novels were promoted as having been "by the author of *Sense and Sensibility,* and *Pride and Prejudice.*" Jane's career and reputation were in a fair way to being made—and
have endured for all time.

   Readers of this detective amusement may be interested
to learn the fates of some of its characters. Emmanuel,
Comte d'Entraigues, and his wife, Anne de St.-Huberti, were
murdered at their home in Barnes, Surrey, on July 22, 1812.
They were discovered in bed with their throats slit; and a
household servant was charged with the crime. When the
news of this horror reached Jane, she must have experienced a certain sense of what we would call closure.
D'Entraigues's biographer suggests that during his lifetime
he was employed as a spy against England by several

governments, Russia and France being among them; but he was also certainly employed by George Canning, to provide intelligence to England of those nations' intentions. The confusion of motives, policy, and fact that Lord Harold Trowbridge described in his 1808 journal, while analyzing the turf battles between Castlereagh and Canning, probably resulted from the deliberate design of Canning's chief spy— Comte d'Entraigues. Which of the governments and patrons d'Entraigues regarded as meriting his true allegiance—if he was capable of any—is difficult to know; but he certainly promoted distrust between Russia and Great Britain. Those who wish to know more of his life may consult Léonce Pingaud, *Un agent secret sous la Révolution et l'Empire: Le Comte d'Antraigues* (sic) (Paris, 1894).

Julien, Comte d'Entraigues, lived out his life in London in a home in Montague Place, Russell Square, dying in 1861.

Spencer Perceval, who led the government during Jane's visit to London, was assassinated in Parliament May 11, 1812. The Regent asked the Tory Lord Liverpool to form a new cabinet, and Lord Castlereagh to serve as foreign secretary—a post he held until his death. George Canning, who had wished to be named to that portfolio, was given nothing in 1812; Lord Moira was named governor-general of Bengal, where he lived for nine years. In 1817 he was made Marquis of Hastings.

Lord Castlereagh's later career was not untouched by scandal. In 1822, having acceded to his father's estates and title as Marquis of Londonderry, he began to receive blackmailing letters accusing him of homosexuality. Apparently, as Castlereagh told the story, he had been seen entering a brothel with a prostitute he later learned was a transvestite male. Whatever the truth of the situation, by mid-August of that year, Castlereagh was subject to a severe mental collapse and depression; he confessed his "crimes" to both the Prince Regent and the Duke of Wellington—two of his closest friends—and despite being under the watchful guard of his medical doctor, slit his throat with a razor.

The chief biographer of both Canning and Castlereagh is Wendy Hinde, whose workmanlike studies of the celebrated Regency statesmen, *George Canning* (London: William Collins Sons, 1973) and *Castlereagh* (London: William Collins Sons, 1981) are well worth reading.

> Stephanie Barron
> Golden, Colorado
> September 2005